TAKE TWO

A GIA, SAN FRANCISCO ROMANCE

STEPHANIE SHEA

Copyright © 2022 by STEPHANIE SHEA

All rights reserved. No part of this publication may be reproduced, distributed, or transmitted in any form or by any means, or stored in a database or retrieval system, without written permission from the author, except in the case of brief quotations embodied in critical articles and reviews. To request permission and for all other inquiries, contact stephaniesheawrites@gmail.com.

This is a work of fiction. Names, characters, businesses, places, events and incidents are either the products of the author's imagination or used in a fictitious manner. Any resemblance to actual persons, living or dead, business establishments, events, or locales is purely coincidental.

Edited by Jessica Hatch

ACKNOWLEDGMENTS

Say, thank you for lighting up all my gloomy days, and for being my alpha and my best friend.

Lauren, thank you for the beta notes and the talks that come almost too easily, even when stuff gets heavy. You're officially my favorite Brit.

Laura, thank you for your friendship and being the best hype woman, even when I don't deserve it.

Noel, thank you for trusting my words and sharing your thoughts with me. We have some book club catch up to do.

L, thank you for being my beta, writing buddy and friend. Let's do writing hour soon.

To my editor, Jess, thanks for diving in and making this collaboration so easy. I'm working on those sentence fragments, I swear.

To my readers, none of this would be possible without you. Your support is everything. Thank you, thank you, thank you.

PROLOGUE

Fuck Valentine's Day.

Whitney winced, adjusting her grip on Wes's lead as she shifted the bouquet of red roses to the same hand. A thin streak of blood trickled toward her empty palm, and her thumb throbbed from the microscopic thorn still lodged in her flesh. Figures something this tiny would hurt like a mother—

Wes tugged on his leash, abandoning his sniff inspection of a sweet bay tree to continue his cruise down the rain-dampened sidewalk. She rolled her eyes, sucking on the tip of her injured thumb as she stumbled after him. He *did* walk himself, after all. Whitney was merely an obliging chaperone who'd taken up this routine of leaving work midafternoon to accommodate her temperamental terrier. She'd learned the hard way that leaving him alone for more than eight uninterrupted hours would lead to some well-thought-out act of rebellion. Twice now, he'd peed on the couch, only to cower under the dining table the minute she got home—all gleaming, dark eyes through his shiny, black coat and *just* the right measure of demure to still weasel his way into a nighttime treat.

She retrieved the thorn from her thumb and flicked it toward a patch of soil, then shifted the bouquet to her free hand again. Two dozen red roses. What the fuck was she going to do with two dozen roses on Valentine's Day? Ten minutes ago, when she'd been cajoled into the florist's shop, the rational part of her had wondered the same thing. But the older man who'd been artfully standing outside, flowers already in hand, skin bronze and wizened by the years, had the kindest smile and a voice bordering on frail when he asked, "Roses, hermosa?" Whitney didn't need the roses. She didn't have anyone to give roses to, but how could she say no to that? Especially when there'd been a woman of a similar age—his wife, probably—beaming at her from beyond the counter.

The idea of giving them to Isabelle lurched to the forefront of Whitney's mind, but they'd both agreed that with only three dates between them—two cut short by Isabelle being needed back at the hospital—maybe it was a bit early to hang too much on...

How had Isabelle framed it?

A commercialized occasion for supposed lovers.

Whitney hadn't bothered to mention that she didn't think of it that way at all, that she enjoyed this celebration of love, even if it was cheesy.

Would it be presumptuous for her to approach any of the limitless pairs of people strolling hand in hand, giggling and whispering into each other's ears, and offer the bouquet? Surely someone would appreciate not having to spend the money. Or was paying it forward only a thing at drive-throughs? Now that she thought about it, $130 was an obscene amount of money to spend on something that was hell-bent on stabbing her every three seconds and would die in less than a week.

Forget flowers, chocolate, and jewelry. Valentine's Day was violence.

Wes paused at another tree, his tiny paws prodding at its much sturdier trunk, and Whitney dropped her head back, huffing as she glanced skyward. Perpetual singledom was turning her into a cynic. She *loved* love. She was the type of person who found something new to fall in love with every day. Something in her once grim and industrial, now revolutionized district. South of Market Street. Home to luxury condos *and* quaint Victorians, where, even after a morning of heavy clouds rumbling across gray skies and pounding the pavement with rain, the sun now gleamed brighter than ever, and lovers of every race and orientation flocked the streets in fleece jackets, umbrellas at the ready.

Didn't she used to *be* one of these people?

Her chest clenched at the thought—the answer too swift, too present in her mind even after six years. What did it say that she recalled the exact moment she'd last been so hopelessly captivated by another person that strangers on the street could tell?

Wes took off at a sprint, yanking her out of her thoughts. She flailed for a tighter grip on his leash, but the leather slipped from her fingers, and he disappeared farther down the sidewalk in a blur of black fur.

"Jesus fuck—Wes!" She darted after him, mumbling a thanks to the well-meaning passerby who had doubled over trying to catch Wes, only for him to whiz right through their legs. "Wes, come on, buddy! I thought we agreed last time was the last time!"

Whether moved by the desperation in her voice or because he'd gotten to the end of the street, he paused at the edge of the curb and glanced back at her before nuzzling the legs of the woman standing next to him. Whitney braced herself for a startle and a yelp, punctuated by a lecture about her dog being off his leash. Though, technically, he was very much still wearing it. Instead, the woman, back still turned, bent to scratch the top of his head.

Whitney furrowed her brows, slowing to a jog. There were many things wrong with this picture. Or maybe just one. Wes never let strangers pet him. He'd almost taken Landon's fingers clean off his hand the first time he'd tried, and he was her brother.

In her perplexity, Whitney scrutinized the woman—the polished, black curls atop her tapered pixie cut, leather jacket stretched across her shoulders down to the exposed small of her back. Close to her spine, edges of a deep brown mark stood out against her tawny complexion, and Whitney's gaze latched onto the shape with paralyzing interest, the way the mark crested and curved at the base with a bizarre likeness to the Floridian peninsula.

She halted her steps, heart rattling in her chest, one hand numb from her grip on the stupid fucking roses. "I'm so sorry..." The words died on her tongue almost as if her brain had decided against the impulse to spit them out.

"No worries. He's adorable." The woman stood, turning. "Whitney?"

Whitney blinked, swallowing the lump in her throat as she took a step back. "Andy." She didn't mean to sound quite as shell-shocked as she felt. Hadn't her brain made sense of it before Andy had even turned around? It's not like she'd ever met another person with a birthmark shaped like *that*. It's not like she didn't know it in intimate detail, hadn't traced it with the tips of her fingers and kiss-swollen lips.

Her mind blanked. She retreated another step, gaze

shifting from Andy's hazel eyes and arched brows to the cupid's bow of her full lips and the cut of her jaw accentuated by her pixie cut. Beautiful. Jarringly beautiful. Although, the Andy Whitney knew would never have cut her hair this short, even if the leather jacket and pair of Doc Martens on her feet held traces of the same grunge-intrigued teenager Whitney had met in high school.

A beckoning bark and light pressure against her knees drew her attention to Wes, paws in an insistent tap against her thighs as if to verify she hadn't slipped into a full-on coma. She couldn't blame him, standing as she was, motionless on Market Street with roses that suddenly weighed a ton, no one to gift them to, and no words for someone she used to tell everything.

"Um..." Andy licked her lips, extending the hand that held Wes's leash toward Whitney.

Whitney willed herself to snap out of it, take Wes, mumble a thank-you, and get on her way. Instead, she found herself fixated on all the tiny details. The delicate but precise way in which Andy offered the lead, leaving no way for their hands to touch when Whitney accepted. The way the air hinted of petrichor, roses, and *her*. The glint of the left tragus piercing she hadn't had six years ago. The fact that she was here. Not in London. Not in New York or even LA.

"Happy Valentine's Day."

Whitney frowned, tilting her head. "What?"

"Sorry." Andy's brows twitched, the motion reminiscent of a quiet show of irritation Whitney used to undo with a single brush of her thumb. "I don't know why I said that like it's Christmas or something. It's just... your flowers."

"Oh. This isn't—" Whitney shook her head, then cut herself off. She wasn't about to reveal the ridiculous tale of how she'd come by flowers she didn't need. Because maybe there was a dormant, niggling part of her that was perfectly okay with Andy's mind running wild with assumptions right that second. Maybe there was a part of Whitney that was okay with some version of her existing, even if only in Andy's imagination, who wasn't merely on an hour-long break to walk her dog, then spend the rest of the night combing through reports back at the gym. A version who had someone to make February 14 feel a little less like torture. Besides, Whitney *did* have someone. Maybe. Sort of.

"I should get going. Thank you"—she held up the lead in an awkward exhibit—"for catching this guy."

Andy's shoulder lifted in a shrug. "I didn't do anything. He kind of just wiggled his little body against my leg."

"Right. Okay then." Whitney turned on her heels, heading in the direction she'd come instead of subjecting herself to the clumsiness of standing at the crosswalk next to Andy and waiting for the light to change. She even made it three whole steps before spinning again. "Andy—"

"Whit—" A breathy laugh slipped from Andy's lips, and she shoved both hands into the pockets of her light blue jeans in a gesture so gut-wrenchingly familiar.

Their gazes held, twisting Whitney's stomach into knots she still hadn't figured out how to unravel. But maybe it was supposed to feel like this, seeing someone she used to love for the first time in years, today of all days—nostalgia and hurt chasing each other around her brain so fast she was fucking dizzy.

"You first." Andy's voice barely carried over the rush of traffic and chitchat all around them.

Whitney shook her head, already retreating again. "It was nothing. Take care, Andy." She jangled Wes's leash as he dawdled, reluctant to follow. "Come on, boy."

1

*R*ain hammered against the balcony floor as Andy stared out the windows of her rental condo. The relentless downpour of a passing storm had always been one of her favorite sounds. All she wanted was to curl up on her sofa, chin rested on one hand, glass of red in the other, listening to the rumble, then crack of thunder as she watched water droplets chase each other along the clear floor-to-ceiling windows.

Coming back to San Francisco—coming *home*—hadn't been as simple as she'd hoped. Her mind had been bleeding thoughts the shade of red roses for four days. The air still reeked of rain-dampened soil, petitgrain, and jasmine. The sound of her own name in Whitney's sure yet breathless cadence looped in her mind. Should she have mentioned that she'd be in town? Mentioned that—No. After six years, it would be presumptuous to assume Whitney even cared. And why should she after—

"Andy."

Andy blinked at her laptop screen as her film producer,

Riva, came back into sharp focus, their violet hair coiffed to perfection, one brow arched at her in impatience.

"I know rainy afternoons are essential to your whole brooding artist aesthetic, but I think this takes precedence," said Riva.

"No. I know." Andy pressed a thumb and forefinger to her eyes. *Focus.* She needed to focus, and thoughts of Whitney had never been helpful for that.

"Our deadline's looming, and all our emails and calls have gone unanswered. We need a meeting with Jenn Coleman."

"I know, Riv. That's why I'm here."

"For all the good that's done us," Riva mumbled.

Andy leveled a glare at the screen, though she couldn't blame them. It had been near a week since she'd driven up from LA to San Francisco, and she had nothing close to a plan for getting a sit-down with Jenn.

Riva held up a hand in contrition. "I'm just saying. Why haven't you used your *in* yet? You've never been one to squander a contact."

"Because she's not a contact, Riva." Andy rolled her chair back toward the leaning bookcase behind her and stood. Stacks of nonfiction titles occupied four shelves in an alternating pattern. Another housed a potted plant Andy sincerely hoped was low maintenance. Then there was the ceramic urn the host had promised was decorative. A contemporary condo on the twentieth floor of The Alexander didn't exactly radiate haunted vibes, but since when were urns categorized as fucking decorative? She shook away the thought, pacing.

Jenn Coleman.

All Andy's energy needed to be focused on getting a notoriously misanthropic, Michelin-starred chef to commit to being followed around by a camera crew for a week. Not only that, she needed to do it without Whitney's help. Despite having stumbled onto a photo of Whitney, Jenn, and another woman who'd featured heavily on Whitney's socials lately, waltzing back into town and asking Whitney for an introduction was the one thing Andy refused to do. No matter how much she needed Jenn to be a part of her docuseries.

It still haunted her, though—images of Whitney in that honey-colored dress, skin radiant and eyes alight, beaming that heart-stopping smile that made Andy's breath catch. It still haunted her, creeping through her thoughts and clinging to her consciousness at the most unexpected moments, like while she waited for her coffee on a random Tuesday afternoon or passed a little kid in an *Encanto* costume on the street. The other pictures from that day— peppered with shades of white, flowers, and a pair of euphoric grooms—gave away that they'd been at a wedding. Andy liked to tell herself that was why, sometimes, when the memory came in those seconds before she drifted off to sleep, Whitney had been wearing a white gown instead.

"She's not a contact," Andy repeated. She stopped in front of her laptop, bracing both hands against the edge of her desk as she locked eyes with Riva. "She's someone I used to know, someone who apparently knows Jenn."

"Which is, by definition, a contact." Riva frowned, reclining against their velvet wingback chair. "Gatica won't commit to funding without her."

"I know, Riv."

Andy had lost track of how many times she'd said those words over their call, and it had only been ten minutes. Did Riva somehow believe reiterating details they were both aware of would make this situation less frustrating? This was the docuseries Andy had been dreaming of making since she was seventeen years old. She was the one who hadn't slept for weeks, who'd slaved over seven-page proposals, who'd sat through the meetings with agents and publicists and sometimes the candidates themselves, never mind the fucking investors. She was the one who'd had to learn the painstaking art of *schmoozing*. Maybe Riva was better versed in being social, but they'd joined Vahn Productions after Andy had already won four IDA Awards.

"I know that you know, which is why this is so baffling, Andy," said Riva. "It's also why I'm asking, is there something else going on here?"

For all of Riva's careful phrasing, the question hit like a wave—cresting and crashing into Andy, washing away her annoyance in its retreat. "What do you mean?"

"I mean, we've worked together for three years. Three years of work-first-no-bullshit Andy Vahn, and I've never seen you this... I'm not even sure what to call it. But you don't really seem *yourself*. So, I'm asking, is everything okay?"

Distracted. Maybe that was the word Riva had been looking for. Except it was like they'd said—Andy didn't get distracted. She swallowed the lump in her throat and closed her eyes on a resolved exhale before looking at them again. "Everything is fine. Jenn Coleman won't answer our emails, but she also hasn't explicitly said she's not interested. Maybe she hasn't been getting them?"

"Maybe. Unlikely, though."

"Right."

Riva sat up straighter in their seat, eyes gleaming with unwavering confidence. "What if I drive up there and we try to get a meeting together?"

"Don't worry," said Andy. Riva meant well, but

suggestions like those reeked of the kind of forfeit and failure that made Andy's skin prickle beneath the collar of her overpriced Nirvana crewneck. "I'll get it done. Let's regroup and pick up next week."

Riva dropped their chin, glancing down at something out of view. "Sounds good."

"Did we get the contract back from Senator Cortez?"

"Signed and sealed."

"Perfect." Andy's lips split in a grin that was instantly tempered by Riva's reserved response. She sighed, settling back into her chair. "Listen, I know delegation isn't my strength."

"I'm not asking you to delegate, Andy. I'm offering to come help. Maybe I know someone who knows someone who can get us in the door."

"Okay, then work that angle, but I need you running point in LA right now. There's no one else I trust to do it."

Riva released a long exhale. "Okay. I get it."

"Thank you. And you'll let me know if anything comes up over the weekend?"

"You know I will," they said, a singsong note to their tone.

"Thanks, Riv. Have a good one."

"You too, Andy."

As the call disconnected, Andy fell back against her chair, huffing a breath through puffed cheeks. She really needed to get her head in the game. Still, she couldn't deny that running into Whitney earlier that week had rattled her. It wasn't like she hadn't planned on seeing Whitney while she was here. She just wanted to prepare, just like she wanted to prepare before seeing her best friend, Kasey. Not that they were even friends anymore, thanks to time, distance, and a bout of self-sabotage on Andy's part.

Surprises were not her friend. They left her feeling off-kilter and flustered and so much less herself. But maybe this was one of those rare rip-off-the-Band-Aid moments she'd worked so meticulously to avoid all her life. If she had any hope of reconnecting with Whitney and Kasey, her temporary return home would be speckled with a lot of tough conversations. Assuming they even wanted to see her.

With a resolute sigh, she reached for her phone and swiped to Kasey's contact card, hoping for two things: first, that Kasey had maintained the same number all these years; and second, that maybe, just maybe, she hated Andy a little less than Whitney did.

An electropop hit streamed from concealed speakers as Whitney exited the short hallway into the lobby of W. She dropped the hand holding her tablet to her side, exchanging smiles with a pair of women headed in the opposite direction, gym bags clutched to their shoulders. A slim-framed man with thinning, dark hair loitered by the counter as the fitness center's receptionist, Robbie, tapped away at the keyboard behind the front desk.

"And that would be the year-long membership?" Robbie asked the man.

Whitney tuned out the conversation, scanning the otherwise empty lobby in search of Jaxon. A minute ago, when she'd left her office, the cameras had offered a clear view of him standing by this very counter. Now he was nowhere to be seen.

"Something I can help you with, boss?"

Whitney winced at the nickname, turning to find Robbie's interest piqued at her presence despite his fingers working at the keyboard. She'd all but given up on getting him to stop calling her "boss" about a week into his start as a front desk clerk at the gym. Somehow, six months later, her supporting his journey to becoming a certified trainer had exacerbated his use of that specific moniker.

She flashed him a smile. "Point me toward Jax?"

"Juice bar." He hooked a thumb to his right, not missing a beat as he launched into an explanation of the terms of membership for the man in front of him.

Whitney nodded her thanks, crossing the pristine hardwood floors toward the juice bar. Impulse led her gaze to the lounge area—a quick assessment of how many chairs were occupied and the length of the line. The tally totaled less than a dozen people, with two captivated by their laptop screens, a table of four chatting over smoothies, and another set of individuals reading or swiping through their phones.

Most people came to W with only enough time to complete their workouts before scurrying back to their jobs or homes, but Whitney found quiet satisfaction in knowing Jax's idea for a small lounge area that offered fresh juices and smoothies had been another successful channel to increase revenue for the gym.

She stopped by the less trafficked side of the counter as Jax popped out of the adjacent storeroom with two boxes of almond milk in his grasp.

He lowered the boxes to the floor, his lopsided grin gleaming against umber skin as he stood to his full six feet, two inches. "I'm late. I know. Daph was drowning over here."

Daphne, the smoothie barista, spared him a glance while pouring milk onto what looked to be a mixture of nuts, dates, and bananas. "Oh. Thanks, Jax," she deadpanned. "Don't throw me under the bus or anything."

Their collective laughter rang out above the low whir of the blender.

Jax gave a good-natured shrug, brushing his palms against his gray, gym-branded track pants, never one to shy away from getting his hands dirty or grabbing an apron and blending smoothies whenever the juice bar was swamped, even if he was Whitney's right-hand man at the gym and in life. He gave the prep counter one last swipe with a dishcloth before falling into step next to her in an unspoken agreement to head back to her office.

"Can you give me the really, really good reason you still haven't put your paternity leave in the system?" she asked.

Jax rubbed the back of his neck with one hand, though it seemed more from strain than agitation. "See, I was going to, but then I thought it might be better to just keep going as long as I can. That way, when the baby comes, I'll have more time at home with Michelle."

It was sound enough reasoning, especially considering he and Michelle already had a five-year-old daughter. "We still need to at least have that meeting so you can get me up to date on your desk."

"Whit..." Jax chuckled. "We have a meeting every week. You *are* up to date. Plus, Michelle's not due for another three weeks."

"In my complete lack of experience, babies come whenever they're ready, and as much as I hope that sweet, tiny human stays put until the absolute healthiest point for delivery, there's no way of knowing he will. Besides, knowing what you have on your agenda this week and having to put them on mine are completely different things."

"Okay. We'll sit down and go over it, but I could also chip in from home while I'm out."

"Jaxon, with respect to those Vin Diesel guns of yours, you are not superhuman. You can't support your wife, care for a newborn and toddler, *and* work from home." Whitney held up a hand, index finger raised as he opened his mouth to object. "You're my best friend, and I will miss your stupid-cute face every day of those twelve weeks, but no. You can't be everything for everyone all the time. That includes me. *I will manage*, but we need to prepare," she finished with a laugh.

Whitney had never been a huge fan of overplanning either, and she loved how awesome Jax was at balancing everything the world threw at him, but what he'd proposed would only result in him being overwhelmed and swamped the second he returned to work. Besides, there were aspects of his job—daily sales and labor reports, payroll, review of inventory levels and ordering for the juice bar—that simply could not be left to the chance of him being available between diaper changes and peewee soccer pickups. Someday, Whitney wanted all the beauty and chaos of having children too. She hoped whenever she tried to be equally stubborn about this gym—her second dream turned second home—Jax would tell her to focus on her family. At least in those ever crucial months before she learned to balance it all.

"You're right," said Jax. "I'll get Daphne up to speed with some of the management duties for the bar. She's our best smoothie barista. Reliable, efficient, and the clients love her. Must be all that dry humor."

Whitney nodded. "I can get on board with that."

"Think Kasey would be up to supporting you with admin on the gym side?"

"Maybe."

Whitney's thoughts drifted to their marketing manager.

After becoming friends in the last few years and watching Kasey fumble through an entry-level job a year, it had been a simple decision to take her on at W. She had an underused marketing degree and graphic design skills to boot. If Whitney hadn't thought it might seem condescending, she would've offered to hire her sooner. Kasey only came in once a week, and she would be compensated for slotting in while Jax was out, but after Wes's little runaway stunt had led Whitney straight to Andy earlier that week, Whitney couldn't think about Kasey without wondering if she'd known Andy was back. As far as Whitney knew, Kasey and Andy had stopped talking years ago, but the Andy Whitney used to know would've never set foot in San Francisco without so much as a hello to her best friend. Then again, that Andy wouldn't have come without telling Whitney either, and after six years, it was safe to assume Whitney didn't know Andy anymore.

Whitney gave a clarifying shake of her head. Her brain's inconvenient tangent had nothing to do with ensuring Jax's duties were covered when he was on leave. She peered up at him, clutching her tablet in both hands as if to keep herself grounded in the present. "I'll talk to Kasey and let you know."

2
———

Andy slipped both hands into the pockets of her jeans, rocking back on the heels of her boots. Scuffed cream walls, a single window and door guarded by black screens, and a worn-down intercom of fading apartment listings stared back at her. The numbers fixed atop the front door tugged at something buried not so deep in her memory. It had been six years, but twice as long couldn't erase the memory of home to someone she used to call her best friend—the one person she probably should've told everything she couldn't tell Whitney.

Andy's stomach lurched as the front door rattled and swung open to reveal Kasey standing in the archway, one hand shielding her eyes against the last rays of daylight. Her black T-shirt rode up, drawing Andy's gaze to "The Cranberries" printed across its torso, spiraling her thoughts into memories of how obsessed Kasey had been with the song "Zombie" when they were teenagers. She tried to not think about where her own Cranberries T-shirt must be now, but Kasey standing on her doorstep like she was seconds from bursting into flames had Andy smiling in seconds.

"Don't tell me you finally found a Damon Salvatore to make all your fantasies of becoming a vampire come true," she said.

"Regrettably no." Kasey tucked a strand of her deep chestnut hair behind one ear, then crossed both arms over her chest. "Did you plan on actually coming in, or should I leave you to the staring and brooding?"

"I wasn't"—Andy grimaced—"*brooding*."

"Sure you weren't." Kasey sighed, dramatizing an eye roll as she extended one hand in a beckoning motion. "Just get in here already. We've barely talked in years. It's going to be a little weird. Five more minutes out here and neighbors are going to think you're casing the place."

Andy jolted forward but glanced over her shoulder. A few pedestrians occupied the sidewalks as a steady stream of traffic rushed by, but she didn't even want to imagine what the elderly pair sitting on the first-floor balcony across the street, whispering to each other, had surmised from her near ten-minute delay outside Kasey's apartment. Still, if she was going to plan a burglary of homes in the Financial District, a studio apartment on Joice Street at five in the afternoon didn't fit the bill. Unless Kasey's extensive teen drama DVD collection was her target—assuming she even had them anymore.

"Home sweet home. I'd give you a tour, but it's exactly the same as the last time you were here." Kasey passed the kitchenette into the open space doubling as a living room, with a smaller bedroom area behind the sofa.

The idea of further scrutinizing the space stirred a tightness in Andy's chest, so she didn't. Instead, she plopped down on the couch next to Kasey and clutched a throw pillow to her abdomen as she faced her. "Rafa still at work?"

Kasey squinted, smiling, though there was something in

the gesture that telegraphed she was anything but amused. "Andy, Rafael and I broke up. Two years ago."

"Shit. Kase, I'm sorry. I don't know what I was thinking."

"You were probably thinking we'd just pick up where we left off." She shrugged as if it was the most obvious thing.

Andy wasn't sure what she'd been expecting when she'd messaged Kasey asking if she could come over. She wasn't expecting it to be easy—going easy on people, even someone who used to be her best friend, wasn't really in Kasey Santiago's DNA—but Andy hadn't expected anger either. Was that the undercurrent in Kasey's response? The hint of a snap, a callout? Or was it purely matter-of-fact?

"Kase..."

"I'm just going to say it, because I really fucking missed you and all I want to do is gush about how gorgeous this new"—she gestured, haphazard and frenzied and so *herself*, toward Andy's pixie cut before motioning in the general direction of her boots—"well, everything about you is. And I want to know how you've been, and how it feels to be an award-winning documentarian, but—" She cut herself off, her excitement dissipating with a drop of her hand against her lap. "You left, Andy."

"I didn't leave. I went to school."

"Yes, you went to school. In London. But it's not about that. You disappeared. You disappeared on me, and you disappeared on..." Her jaw clenched as she trailed off. She didn't have to say it, though.

Whitney.

"That's not fair. We'd already broken up. There was nothing left to say."

Kasey scoffed. "Nothing left to say to someone you'd been in love with since you were fifteen? Come on, Andy. Was that what you thought about me too?"

Andy huffed, standing. She needed to pace. "You and I *did* talk while I was there." Not as often as they used to, not often enough, then barely at all. But Andy hadn't disappeared. At least, she hadn't meant to. It was just hard. She'd loved every second of school in London, but it was fucking hard. Two years of hands-on, practical experience—shooting, directing, losing days in the editing suites for a master's program that produced *sixty* films a term. Even when she hadn't been busy with her own projects, she was constantly in demand by her colleagues. Then there was the time difference, and the never acknowledged fact that perhaps Andy had always been a little too good at emotional detachment in the face of physical distance.

Maybe absence didn't always make the heart grow fonder. Not that she didn't miss Kasey; not that she didn't miss Whitney with every beat of her heart. But maybe, sometimes, absence just removed the pressure of constantly having to be present. Maybe that made her the worst friend in the world, or maybe she'd learned from the best. Attachment hindered success—hindered the journey to becoming the best version of herself—and when no one else was there, all she'd have was whoever she'd become.

She'd never liked having to justify chasing her dreams, getting into one of the best film schools in the world, and having the audacity to go. Still, if she let herself admit it, even she knew a cursory, *Hey, Kase. How are you?*, now and then, only to leave Kasey's reply unanswered for days on end, hadn't been good enough. Not knowing Kasey and Rafael had been broken up for two years already *wasn't* good enough. She didn't need the stretching silence or the disappointment shimmering in Kasey's eyes to know that.

She sighed, dropping back onto the couch. "I'm sorry. I should've called more. It was just hard, Kase."

"I don't think breaking up with the love of your life and moving to another continent alone is supposed to be easy."

Andy's eyes fell shut. An image of Whitney flashed in her mind—winded from chasing the dog circling Andy's feet, surprise scrawled on her face from her widened, brown eyes to her parted lips. Breathtaking, even in her shock. Then again, Andy had always found her breathtaking.

"I don't want to talk about that," she said, resting her cheek against the back of the couch as she opened her eyes. "I mean, you and Raf? Clearly, I have some catching up to do. Not that we have to talk about that either, but I really do want to know what's been going on with you."

"That's *a lot* of catching up, Andy."

"I have time."

Kasey shot her a look, brows raised, eyes knowing.

"I mean, I'll *make* time."

"Consider me cautiously optimistic."

"That seems fair." Andy laughed, and Kasey joined in, their harmony filling the studio apartment before Kasey's laugh tapered off into a smile.

"I hear you on not wanting to talk about it, so I'm only going to say this once. This amends tour better have a Whitney stop penciled in."

Andy dropped her chin, pressing the pad of her thumb against the blunt nail of her index finger. If the way Whitney had rushed off when they'd run into each other earlier that week was anything to go by Andy was right when she said, "I don't think she wants to see me, Kase."

"How would you know?"

"I just know."

"That's not an answer."

Andy rubbed at her own forehead. "Why do I feel like I'm missing something?"

"Something like what?"

"Like, that's the second time you've mentioned her, but there's something almost..." Andy glanced skyward, searching her mind for the word lingering just out of reach, unsure it was the one she'd been looking for even as she said, "*Protective* about it?"

Kasey shrugged, then stood, crossing into the kitchen. "We kind of started talking after you left. Plus, she saved me from having to pick up another job selling overpriced jeans to white-collar couples in AB Fits by hiring me to do marketing for the gym. Which also means I've finally saved enough money to leave this humble abode of paper-thin walls and lack of onsite laundry."

Andy furrowed her brows, blinking.

"Do you want a beer or something?" Kasey asked.

"Wait, was all of that code for you and Whitney being friends now?"

"The never-become-friends-with-your-best-friend's-ex rule doesn't apply when the ex is actually a decent human being, Andy."

Of course it didn't. It was a slightly tyrannical if absurd concept, but there were rare, powerful moments in Andy's twenty-nine short years where love and loyalty trumped logic. Agreeing to Kasey's rules of engagement with exes back in high school had been one of them. Still, Andy had always known Kasey and Whitney would get along, both being kind, perceptive, talk-with-their-hands types of people. They'd just always run in different social circles, Whitney straddling the athletic and artistic crowds, being both a gymnast and a theater buff, and Kasey preferring the company of her laptop almost exclusively. Who knew Andy leaving was all it would take for the two of them to become friends?

It wasn't a bad thing. Good people deserved good people in their lives, and Whitney and Kasey were the best Andy had ever known. She still felt a little smaller in her seat when she cleared her throat and said, "A beer sounds good. Thanks."

Two hours later, when Andy had walked to the end of the block and slipped into her Audi, her brain had already begun dissecting her and Kasey's conversation. She was glad to hear Mr. and Mrs. Santiago were doing well—sixty going on twenty-five, and always on the hunt for deals to make their next cruise affordable. Kasey still argued with her younger sister, Sienna, at least once a week, but they were closer than ever, even if "med school has turned her into a know-it-all little shit!" Andy still didn't know why Kasey and Rafael had called it quits. They'd sort of come to an unspoken agreement that Kase hadn't wanted to talk about her own breakup either. It didn't stop Andy's memories from wandering back to the night Kasey had shown up at her house, bursting with excitement when she hopped onto Andy's bed and squealed, "We're moving in together!"

Andy's eyes had widened until impulse forced her to blink away her shock. "You and Rafael?"

"No, me and Creepy Dan, *obviously*." A sarcastic eye roll had followed, but Kasey's smile had held the kind of incandescent bliss that didn't demand reason.

Andy had smiled and promised to be there for any and all move-in needs. She'd ignored the way her stomach hardened at the idea of moving in with someone at *eighteen*, because Kasey and Rafael beamed with forever whenever they so much as stood in the same room. Andy and Whitney would be doing their undergrad at separate colleges, but USC and UCLA were only forty-five minutes apart. They'd lain in bed and talked and talked and talked about it—weekend visits and spring break, how Andy would still come to all of Whitney's plays.

They'd never talked about forever.

Andy had just assumed they both knew *forever* didn't have to mean *right now*.

Then again, assumptions had never served her well.

She turned onto Beale Street, struggling between keeping her view on the road ahead and glancing out the window at the building her GPS signaled was Whitney's gym. When Kasey had grabbed her laptop to show Andy the designs she'd been working on for their latest marketing campaign, the first thing Andy's eyes had latched onto was the address strategically placed in the bottom right corner. Lucky break. Not that she thought she'd have to coax it out of Kasey one way or another. If anything, Andy had walked right into a well-placed trap—one orchestrated by someone who knew her well enough to remember that sometimes Andy was too stubborn to admit what she wanted. Needed, even.

She still wasn't sure Whitney wanted to see her, but she welcomed the ache of *this*. Of seeing a bit of Whitney's life, who she was and what she'd accomplished in the years since. Even if Andy herself was stuck on the outside now.

The letter *W* in a white, block font dominated one of two sleek beams by the building's entrance. A tinted window wall occupied the ground floor, muting the golden glow within, but she could make out three or four people milling around what she'd guessed to be the lobby.

The blare of a car horn drew her cruising scrutiny to a halt, and her gaze flicked toward her rearview mirror, a stark reminder that rush hour traffic was not conducive to whatever she was feeling. It should've jolted her right out of it, forced her to speed up and head back to her apartment to salvage an ounce of productivity from the day. Instead, she jerked her steering wheel left and turned into the darkened tunnel of the parking lot.

3

*W*hitney glanced up from her phone, stepping onto the central shaft of the revolving door before exiting into the lobby of W. Her phone buzzed, signaling another text message, and she redirected her attention to the open chat with her sister and brother, Avery and Landon. A year ago, she wouldn't have imagined she, who'd lived nearly all twenty-nine years of her life as an only child, would have a pinned text thread in her phone titled "Dimaano Sibling Soiree."

It had taken the risk of contacting a sister Whitney wasn't sure even knew she existed, a blowup between Avery and Landon once he'd found out Avery had known all along, and an emergency room heart-to-heart brought on by Landon's subsequent bar fight and resulting broken arm. Still, after Avery had suggested the idea of them having brunch or dinner a couple of times a month to get to know each other, Landon's name for the occurrence had stuck.

Some days, Whitney wondered how she'd gone so long knowing two living, breathing pieces of her family were out there who she'd never even met. Others, the thought that

Dad had tried to keep them apart to protect his own flawed sense of integrity stirred a resentment so quiet yet deep, she wouldn't even recognize it until the tightening vise in her chest made it too hard to breathe.

Landon (7:48 p.m.)
Please don't be late.

Whitney chuckled at the nervous energy emanating from her brother's words, her fingers already tapping out a response.

Whitney (7:48 p.m.)
Wow, Lan. Just @ me next time.

Avery (7:48 p.m.)
-laughing with tears emoji- self-awareness is important, Whit.
I also think we should take a moment to appreciate how seriously he's taking this meet-the-girlfriend dinner.
Dear brother, is that growth I sense?

Whitney (7:49 p.m.)
He has been exclusively dating this woman for three months. Maybe we can finally, happily lay Lothario Lan to rest.

Avery (7:49 p.m.)
Ugh yes
Lothario Lan leaves behind a mother, father, two sisters, and a string of broken hearts. He will not be missed.

Landon (7:49 p.m.)
-eye roll emoji- muting until you two are done.

Whitney sputtered a laugh. She'd never tire of their dynamic, of taking turns ribbing each other and, sometimes, double-teaming Landon like this. One of the things that had kept her away all those years was that she wasn't sure how she'd fit with them. Avery and Landon had shared their entire childhood, were twins on top of it all, but being their sister had come almost too naturally. They'd never treated her any other way.

Landon (7:50 p.m.)
Dress code's classy casual, btw.

Whitney was so busy smiling at Avery's *classy's a given, Lan* that by the time the abrupt panic that she wasn't paying attention to where she was going set in, a jolt of pain was already ringing through her shoulder, her phone skittering across the tiles.

"Shit. I'm so sorry." Her head snapped up at the victim of her unintended collision.

A smile fit for the tooth whitening ads plastered all over her dentist's office met her alarm. Auburn waves framed light gray eyes Whitney had stared into, been taken by in more ways than one. The woman rubbed her left shoulder with one hand, and for a second—just one—Whitney's guilt at crashing into her was offset by the sight of long, slender fingers ending in a clear-polished manicure. A night of drinks and conversation culminating in messy kisses, burning fingertips, and toe-curling orgasms flashed in Whitney's mind. Not that she'd gotten there herself. How the hell had she not been able to get there with this sculpted-by-the-gods, genius of a woman's fingers and mouth between her thighs for what had felt like hours?

On some level, she knew it had probably been too soon, but Isabelle's spontaneous request to meet up for drinks on Valentine's Day had been exactly what Whitney needed, especially after bumping into Andy. Isabelle had spent half the night talking in medical terms Whitney barely understood, but after two amaretto sours, Whitney didn't even mind anymore. She was just desperate to *feel*, well, anything but uncertain.

Sex had not been the answer.

"Anyone in there?" Isabelle waved a hand back and forth in Whitney's line of vision.

"Isabelle." Whitney blinked out of her haze. "I'm so sorry. I was—" She bent to pick up her phone, only for a hand to beat her to it.

"Must be a good text," Isabelle said, offering her the phone without breaking eye contact.

Whitney rolled her eyes. "My brother and sister."

"Ah." Isabelle bobbed her head in understanding. "How *is* my most temperamental patient?"

"Not getting into any more bar fights, thankfully."

"Good. He was worse than my peds patients with that cast. Never heard a grown man whine about the itching quite so much, and you can absolutely tell him I said that."

"Oh, gladly."

Isabelle joined in Whitney's laughter, her gaze drifting to Whitney's mouth before their eyes met again. The contact held, anticipation fluttering in Whitney's stomach, though dread twisted up her spine as she wondered what she hoped the next words out of Isabelle's mouth would be. Did she want it to be a request for date number five, or something along the lines of *It's not me, it's you*? It wasn't like Isabelle would be wrong. Either something was missing, or Whitney was just... broken. But Isabelle wasn't looking at Whitney like someone who was ready to admit that maybe they'd be better off as friends, and Whitney wasn't sure she hated it.

"I'm glad I ran into you. Even if it was a bit literal," Isabelle said with a laugh.

A glimpse of someone entering the lobby crossed the edge of Whitney's gaze, and she reflexively glanced their way before facing Isabelle. "Sorry. Force of habit. You were saying—" She cut herself off, brows scrunched as a flicker of recognition set in. She did a double take to assure herself the face her brain had conjured wasn't actually attached to the person standing a few feet away.

Her heartbeat stuttered, then sped.

Andy paused by the door, rocking back onto the heels of her Doc Martens as her hands disappeared into the pockets of her high-waisted jeans—fitted, cuffed, gaping at the knees. Even after their run-in last week, the sight of her hit Whitney like a bucket of cold water. Whitney had promised herself not to message or call or even wonder why Andy was in town. It had taken an initial call to her sister for support —ridden with panic on Whitney's end and questions mumbled through suspiciously erotic-sounding breaths from Avery—plus another hour-long call later that day, but Whitney liked to think she'd coped fine. She hadn't reached out to Andy. Her mind definitely hadn't wandered to their run-in when Isabelle had texted that night and asked if Whitney wanted to meet up for drinks.

"Someone you know?" Isabelle asked.

"Um." Whitney blinked as Andy moved toward them. "Something like that."

Isabelle chuckled, resting a steady hand on her arm. "Whitney, we did agree to keep things casual. It's okay if you're seeing her."

"Seeing her? God, no. She's just—" Whitney scrunched up her face. "Andy." She cleared her throat. "Andrea." Yes. That sucked the familiarity right out of it. Her mental rolodex of nicknames was reserved for people she thought about with fondness, not—

Fuck.

Andy halted in front of them, eyes trained on Whitney

as if there wasn't another person standing right next to her. "Can we talk?" she asked by way of greeting.

Whitney frowned, tilting her head. The Andrea Vahn she used to know had been a lot of things—driven, beautiful, infuriatingly brilliant, and, some days, just plain fucking infuriating—but rude had never been one of them. She side-eyed Isabelle, hoping she wouldn't have to spell out to Andy why now really wasn't a good time.

"I'm kind of in the middle of something," she said.

"Right." Andy pursed her lips, eyes scrutinizing Isabelle —head to toe to the hand still on Whitney's arm—before she took a reluctant step back. Something crossed her expression as her mouth worked open, then closed. Whitney could almost hear the apology roll off her tongue, but it never came. Instead, Andy dropped her gaze to the floor and asked, "Is it okay if I wait?"

Whitney's body tensed.

"It's okay." Isabelle's touch transitioned to a gentle squeeze before her hand disappeared. "My workout ran longer than planned, so I have to get to the hospital anyway. Can I text you later?"

"Yeah. Of course." Whitney released a breath, relinquishing her indignation to give Isabelle her full attention. "I'm sorry again. For crashing into you and for all of... *this*."

"Don't worry. I won't sue for damages." Isabelle winked. "Besides, if you can forgive me for leaving you twice in the middle of dinner, then I can forgive whatever nameless situation seems to be unraveling here."

"I mean, it's not like you were being paged to save lives or anything," Whitney teased.

A sound resembling a poorly suppressed scoff alerted her to Andy turning away and crossing the lobby to lean against the marble reception desk.

The soft brush of lips against Whitney's cheek drew her back, and her hands came up to Isabelle's waist only in time for her to pull away. "Talk later."

Whitney hummed her assent, watching Isabelle head for the door. She waited until Isabelle was on the curb and out of sight before she whirled in the opposite direction. She didn't stop by the counter where Andy waited, didn't ask her to follow, but within seconds Andy was on her trail. Whitney schooled her face into a hopefully genteel smile for every client traveling the hallway on their way out. Most days, she managed to fly under the radar without being pegged as the owner of the gym. She had classes and clients, wore the same branded athleisure gear as the other personnel. She liked it that way, and she wasn't about to jeopardize W's reputation for first-rate customer relations because Andy Fucking Vahn had waltzed in like *she* owned the place.

Whitney bypassed the elevator in favor of trudging up the two flights of stairs to her third-floor office. A few choice words were circling her thoughts, and she didn't want to express them in any place where they might be overheard by an employee or gym member. She pushed the door open and left it that way as an invitation, staring out the window with fingers pressed to her temple until she heard it close behind her.

She didn't waste a second rounding on Andy. "Are you fucking kidding me?"

For a moment, Andy just stared, her expression dissecting and direct in a way Whitney hadn't been prepared for, a way that chipped at her building rage and forced her to dig deeper for her resolve. It was bad enough Andy had shown up without invitation, but to hover around while Whitney was clearly in the middle of a conversation then go so far as to audibly scoff?

"You're just going to stand there?" Whitney demanded.

Andy's eyes fell shut and she drew in a deep breath, shaking her head as if to rid herself from a daydream. "I'm sorry."

"What was that out there?"

"I—I don't know."

"You don't know?" Whitney quirked a brow.

She knew what it felt like, but Andy had never really been the jealous type. In fact, she'd always had the quiet confidence of someone who never felt threatened by other people, romantically or otherwise. It had worked for them. Whitney performed in plays all throughout high school and university, and she'd needed someone who understood that kisses with costars were purely for show. If Andy had felt the need to kiss her a little slower, longer, deeper after every performance, Whitney never complained. But this... She didn't know what to do with this. She didn't know what to do with the irascible comportment of someone she didn't even know anymore.

"I saw Kasey today," said Andy, as if that explained everything.

Whitney sighed. "What is this, Andy?"

"I saw Kasey," she repeated, starting a slow pace along the room.

So that hadn't changed, the pacing.

"And after I left, I just kept thinking about you. About our run-in last week, and I know nothing's the same. I know why it won't ever be again. I know I can't just show up here. I didn't even mean to come in. I just—it didn't feel right. Being here and not seeing you doesn't feel right. It's like conjoined concepts." She framed her hands with her fingers parted, then slotted them together. "You and home." Her pacing came to an abrupt halt, and she dropped her hands to her sides with a grimace.

The words tugged at something caged deep inside Whitney's ribs. After their breakup, she'd fallen asleep wishing for this moment more times than she could count—the moment when Andy would show up on her doorstep and say words that vaguely resembled a plea for a second chance. This one felt like a parody of all her fantasies, a cosmic joke rambled six years too late from lips she still remembered the taste of. Things with Isabelle were casual and sluggish, and Whitney wasn't entirely sure she wanted it the way she should. But she didn't want whatever this was either.

"Andy, I'm seeing someone."

"No. I know. The roses, the banter with Dr. Redhead. I know." She shook her head. "I didn't mean like *that*. I just meant we used to be friends once. I guess what I'm trying to say is... I hope someday we can have that again, if you're ever open to it."

Whitney wasn't sure they'd ever been *just* friends, but they hadn't always called it something else either. It had taken years to even realize how truly, deeply, recklessly in love with her best friend she was. That didn't mean trying to go back to before would be easy. That didn't mean it *should* be easy, given how things had ended between them.

She tapped the face of her watch, desperate for an out. "I have to pick up Wes from the groomers." It would be another thirty minutes before they'd be finished with him, but Andy didn't have to know that. Besides, a long walk in the chill February night seemed like exactly what Whitney needed.

"Okay." Andy nodded, slipping her hands back into her pockets. "I'll let you get to that." She started for the door, eyes glued to her feet until she paused with a grip on the handle. The moment stretched, a noiseless debate seemingly raging in Andy's mind as Whitney watched. Andy glanced back at her, mouth open, then closing before she finally found her words. "I really am sorry, Whit."

4

Andy's fingers drummed along the smooth leather of her steering wheel as she examined the quaint building looming across the parking lot. Not much had changed since the first and only time she'd been here with her parents. It had the same taupe siding, same casement windows guarding the type of modest luxury Grace and Gordon Vahn had always been too focused on working and saving to enjoy. Andy had been the picture of stunned when they'd taken her here as a graduation present after she'd finished her master's in London.

They'd never been big on sentiment—being the kind of people who were comfortable talking to their only child once or twice every two weeks—and Andy couldn't cook for shit. She'd always been too busy to learn. Yet her love for food and wine had crept up on her over the years. This place, the gift of a meal requiring a stint on a four-month waitlist, one flagged by three out of four dollar signs on the Google price index, had been the most overwhelming indicator that her parents *did* care, even if they didn't always know how to say it.

Gia, San Francisco. Home to one of Andy's most private, dearest memories, owned by a woman whose prowess and success she'd always admired. And here she was planning to, what? Ambush Jenn Coleman in her own kitchen and hope to all that was holy that she just said yes to being in the docuseries because Andy asked nicely?

This wasn't a plan. This wasn't *the* plan. But what else was left? All their well-crafted email requests and calls had gone unanswered, and Jenn didn't have an agent or publicist or any other point of contact, really. Riva's suggestion to come up to San Francisco so they could help Andy felt rigged with the underlying assumption that Andy's failure to confirm Jenn's participation was the result of sheer incompetence. Which was absurd. Andy simply didn't want to ask Whitney for any favors. She didn't want to ask Whitney for anything, even if a forced introduction would be slightly more acceptable than just showing up here.

Memories of last night in Whitney's office pulsed in her mind, dredging up emotions Andy couldn't begin to unravel. Awe, pride, regret, yearning.

Whitney hadn't said yes to possibly being in each other's lives again, to being friends. She hadn't really said anything. Did that mean Andy was supposed to try harder? Do better? Or did it simply mean Whitney had given up on wanting anything from Andy a long time ago?

Andy forced the thought down and got out of her car. She needed to stay on task. Right now, all her thoughts had to be on Jenn Coleman.

As she crossed the parking lot onto the sidewalk, she mentally went over the speech she'd scribbled and crumpled up and scribbled again during her bout of insomnia last night. Words like *icon, role model,* and *younger generations of Black and brown queer kids* looped in her mind. But even as she made it to the door of Gia's, the elaborate praise leaping off the figurative page didn't seem like words that would appeal to Jenn. Andy wasn't sure what would.

That didn't stop her from gripping the gold handle of the main door and making her way inside. It smelled exactly like she remembered—like freshly baked bread and cheese with an herbaceous hint of tomatoes and basil. A faint instrumental lingered beneath muted conversation and clinking utensils, and hanging lamps bathed the sleek, semi-rustic interior in a mellow golden hue.

Andy's mind was already racing with all the angles she wanted to capture for Jenn's episode—the kitchen obviously, but the balcony dining area overlooking the main floor looked like a great option too.

"Welcome to Gia, San Francisco."

The greeting nudged Andy toward the host's podium, and her eyes flitted downward in search of a nametag. She'd always found people to be more receptive when referred to by their names. The "he/him" printed in smaller font above "Joey" was unexpected, but her muscles loosened at the sight. Somehow, it felt like reassurance that she owed it to herself and this dream of a docuseries to ask Jenn to hear her out.

"May I have the name for your reservation?" Joey beamed a smile that held none of the apathy of someone who didn't look a day over eighteen.

"Hi, Joey. I actually don't have a reservation, but I was hoping to speak with your boss. Jenn, I mean."

Joey flinched, skepticism creeping onto his face. "She doesn't talk to reporters."

"Oh, I'm not a reporter."

"O-kay. Are you someone she's expecting, or even knows?"

Andy considered saying yes, but Joey's squinting brown eyes suggested he was merely asking a question he already knew the answer to. Maybe it was a precaution against scaring off a friend or acquaintance of his boss. Still, Andy wasn't sure she could pass for either with Jenn's reputation for having a small circle, and she wasn't sure lying her way through the door would yield the best first impression.

The tap of heels drew her attention, and she glanced up to see a woman pause at the juncture between the main dining room and the waiting area, eyes glued to her phone. The waves of glossy, black hair cascading onto her shoulders and the impeccable silk blouse, pencil skirt, and red-bottoms ensemble she wore screamed Business Exec Out for Lunch, but there was something familiar about her, something niggling but persistent that Andy couldn't define.

"I'm going to take that as a no," said Joey, drawing Andy's attention back to his podium.

"No, I don't know her, and she's not expecting me, but if I could just have a minute of her time."

"I'm sorry," he said. "I really can't help you."

"Everything okay, JoJo?"

Andy's head snapped up to find the woman approaching them, her smile the picture of amiable as she rested a hand on Joey's shoulder but leveled her gaze Andy's way. Joey leaned closer to her, whispering an explanation, and the realization seeped in that the woman worked at Gia too. This didn't have to be a bad thing. She looked like someone Joey relied on for direction, someone who worked much more closely with Jenn than he did.

The woman nodded, mumbling to Joey that she'd take it from here before stepping forward. "I'm Avery. Admin manager. Would you mind coming with me?" She placed a hand across Andy's upper back, guiding her toward the door and onto the curb outside.

Andy would've taken it as a good sign that she now had the manager's ear, but sidestepping pedestrians to the soundtrack of midafternoon traffic didn't seem conducive to the pitch she'd planned. Avery studied the environment as if she was thinking the same thing, but then her lips tugged into a smile, her deep brown eyes alight with sincerity in a way that reminded Andy so much of Whitney.

Recognition coiled in the pit of Andy's stomach.

The woman on Whitney's Instagram. Photos and photos of her, dating back as far as the wedding, where Whitney had been pictured with Jenn.

"So, a sidewalk tête-à-tête feels a little gauche, but since I'm not clear on exactly what is happening here, you'll have to forgive me for guiding this conversation beyond the earshot of customers." She extended her hand. "Avery."

Andy tilted her head. Hadn't she already introduced herself?

"Avery Dimaano."

It set in like moisture through a sieve—quickly, with disquieting ease. Whitney's older sister, the sister she'd found out about at sixteen, after accidentally coming across a picture of a boy and girl who could've passed for twins in her father's wallet. Whitney's parents had never been together, though her dad, Pedro, had almost always been in her life. The revelation had definitely come as a shock, shock Whitney had processed through rage, tears, and a week spent in Andy's bed when she'd refused to go home after confirming her mother had known about her siblings all along. For Whitney, her parents neglecting to tell her about Avery and Landon was proof that she was a carefully sequestered aspect of Pedro's life, one he'd kept hidden to not blow up the image his other family had of him. "His *real* family," she used to say.

Andy had held and kissed her and whispered affirmations in her ear every night as Whitney fell asleep in her arms, but she'd never forgiven Pedro Dimaano for making the most wonderful person she'd ever known feel like a dirty little secret.

She'd never forgiven him. Even after Whitney had.

But Avery... Andy didn't quite know how to feel about Avery. If the pictures were anything to go by, the family drama was all water under the bridge now anyway.

She extended a tentative hand to accept Avery's handshake. "Andy."

"Vahn, right?" Avery asked. "I see your brain working, so I'm going to skip over the part where we both try to figure out whether we know who the other is. What I don't understand is why you need to speak with Jenn."

"I—um—" Andy closed her eyes, taking a second to remember the reason she was there. *Focus.* She reached into the pocket of her jacket and handed Avery her business card. "I've been trying to reach her to discuss a possible appearance in my docuseries."

Avery spared the card a passing glimpse before turning it over in her hand. "Docuseries?"

"*Queer Powerful Women of Color.*"

"Okay. And you thought you'd just show up and ask?"

"We've been emailing her. I—we weren't sure she was getting them. There hasn't been a response. We understand if she's not interested. I know media, public appearances, are rare for her. It's just..." Andy tried not to wilt under Avery's unwavering scrutiny. "She'd be perfect for this. Exactly the kind of person seventeen-year-old me needed to see to know my dreams were valid. To know there's room in this world for someone who looks like me, someone who is anything but a cis white man, to be taken seriously. To know I could, I don't know, accomplish more than the rest of the world thinks I should be grateful for because it's further than I should've gotten anyway?"

A ghost of a smile crossed Avery's face.

Andy tried not to read too much into the bizarre burst of approval blooming in her chest. She didn't know Avery well enough to decipher what her smiles meant. She didn't know Avery at all, and if her presence in Whitney's life was anything to go by, Andy really didn't know anything about Whitney anymore either.

Avery tapped the center of her palm with the tip of the business card. "Okay."

"Okay?" Andy drew out the question, fishing for more.

"I'll talk to Jenn and see how she feels about it. We'll get back to you."

"Wow. Okay, yeah." Andy's nod was too ardent, too fast, but Avery's response glimmered with possibilities that already had her head spinning. "I'll be in touch. Thank you, Avery."

"No worries." Avery made a half turn toward the door before spinning back in Andy's direction. "And Andy?" She paused, chuckling and shaking her head as if the incredulity of the moment had only just dawned on her.

Andy could relate. In fact, maybe she was too amazed by it herself to even imagine a turn in their conversation that would lead to the next words out of Avery's mouth.

"Whatever Jenn's answer is, however long you're in town, make sure when you leave my sister's heart is still intact."

"Avery, I'm not here to—I didn't—I know I—"

Avery shook her head. "It's okay. I don't need a rebuttal."

"Right." Andy swallowed against the tension in her

throat. She racked her brain for something else to say, another thank you, an explanation, something, *anything*. But the look on Avery's face suggested their conversation was over, so Andy slid her hands into her pockets, turned on her heels, and headed back to her car.

5

Whitney scoffed as the call disconnected and a silence echoed in her Bluetooth earphones. Wes tugged at his lead, desperate to move on from the five-minute delay brought on by Avery's call to inform his human of the surprise visitor they'd had at Gia that afternoon. If his insistent albeit futile attempts to continue his walk were any indication, he'd garnered all he could from the shrub he'd been pawing at to begin with. Not even the periodic coos thrown his way by the steady stream of pedestrians circling the Theater District were enough to keep him entertained.

Whitney's thumb was already scorching a trail across her phone screen, stringing letters together in an urgent text to Kasey: *Do you have Andy's number?*

An instant reply popped up, aided by Kasey practically being glued to her computer eighty percent of the time.

Kasey (4:13 p.m.)
I do?

Whitney (4:13 p.m.)

Can you send it to me now and ask all the questions I know you're dying to ask later?

Another bubble emerged on Whitney's screen—ten taunting digits—followed by:

Kasey (4:14 p.m.)

Will definitely be asking questions later.

But since your texts are emitting a particular energy, I'm just going to say, usually I'd totally be down to help you hide a body, but it's Andy we're talking about.

So maybe channel one of those post-yoga meditation sessions you offer at W?

A smile cracked across Whitney's face, and a bit of her rage lifted, floating away in a heavy exhale. She tapped out a quick reply: *Thanks, Kase, but no promises.* Then, she drew in a deep breath and clicked Andy's number.

Wes yanked at his leash again.

"Sorry, buddy." Whitney stumbled after him as he herded her down Market Street, listening as the phone rang once, twice...

"Hey, Whit."

Her steps halted at the serene acknowledgment—soft, almost expectant—and her forehead creased at the complete lack of surprise in Andy's tone.

"You still have the same number," said Andy, seemingly reading Whitney's silence.

Whitney didn't want to examine what it meant that Andy had recognized her number. Did Andy remember it? Or had it been sitting in her phone all these years, undeleted but undeserving of ever being used?

"I need to see you. I mean"—Whitney ground her molars, further irritated by her own poor choice of words—"we need to talk, preferably in person." She needed to look

Andy in the eyes to gauge the sincerity of her answers to the questions looping through Whitney's head. She needed to understand what had happened last night, needed more than what she'd detected to be the hopeless maundering of someone who was... lost?

"I'm at my rental at The Alexander right now," said Andy. "But I can meet you somewhere if that's what you want."

Reflex drew Whitney's gaze to the street sign at the end of the block. Her eyes fell shut in reluctant consideration. Four blocks on Sixth, then a turn onto Minna Street would lead her straight to The Alexander.

Wes yipped, standing on his hind legs to paw at the knees of her leggings. Another four or five blocks plus the walk back to her apartment would no doubt pacify him.

She sighed, shaking her head. "I can be there in twenty minutes, but I have my dog."

"Wes and I are friendly."

Whitney resisted the urge to roll her eyes, even if Andy couldn't see it. That didn't stop her brain from dredging up the recollection—Wes's leash slipping from her fingers as he darted down the rain-slick sidewalk toward a woman he'd never met but had allowed to pet him like they were best of friends. "Just... tell the front desk to expect me, okay?" Whitney clicked off the call, jangling Wes's lead as she resumed their walk. "Come on, Traitor Joe."

THE SECOND THE door swung open and Whitney laid eyes on Andy—barefaced and barefoot in a gray sweater and shorts—white-hot rage zipped through her. She allowed that to be the prevailing feeling coursing through her instead of the instant flutter in her stomach. It didn't matter how pretty Andy's eyes had always been in natural light. Whitney was on her doorstep for one reason and one reason only.

"Really, Andy? This is why you're back. To harass my sister and her boss at their workplace in the middle of the day?"

Andy beamed at Wes as she bent to take his face in her hands and ruffle his fur. "Hi, you."

Despite herself, Whitney warmed with mild affection. It would be cute how quickly Wes had taken to Andy if it wasn't so fucking annoying.

Andy stood upright again, though Wes still clamored at her feet for attention. Her tongue darted out to lick her lips as she steadied her gaze on Whitney, expression schooled in that doe-eyed, sloped-brow way that used to telegraph everything from remorse to understanding. "Harass? I'm sure that's not what she said."

"You have no way of knowing what she said. Because you don't know her, and you don't know me. So stop looking at me like that."

"Like what?" Andy asked, too calm and evaluating.

"Like *that*. Like you know exactly what I'm feeling and why I'm upset, and—" She dropped Wes's leash—he was a lost cause anyway—as she trudged farther into the apartment.

Beyond the sparkling floor-to-ceiling windows, the cloudless blue sky lounged over the nexus of cafes, parks, and cultural institutes this end of SoMa. It held all the quiet charm and modernity of a neighborhood Andy would fall head over heels for; less of the blatant, artistic chaos flanking Whitney's Victorian home in the Theater District. There were no beaming displays from Orpheum or the

Curran, no boisterous enthusiasm spilling out onto the street from the myriad of post-theater bars.

"Whitney."

"What?" She spun, her breath catching at Andy's unexpected proximity. It was like muscle memory—the way her eyes shifted to Andy's lips, soft and shimmering from a recent swipe of her tongue, the way Whitney's heart lurched, and a knot twisted in the pit of her stomach.

Something flashed in Andy's hazel eyes—a flicker of flames and dilating pupils—almost as if she remembered it too. Their second kiss. Only then it had been Andy who'd been worked up and needed answers, because they'd kissed once already in the pitch-black of Whitney's bedroom—a delicate exploration of something dangerous between friends—and Whitney hadn't wanted to talk about it. She hadn't wanted to talk about something that could shatter their friendship in ways that would make it impossible to collect all the pieces. She'd kissed Andy anyway. Somehow, the thought of never risking it had seemed twice as heartbreaking.

If only she'd known.

Andy took a step back, prompting Whitney to do the same as she ran a hand through her hair. "I'm not mad, Andy. I just... Be honest with me."

"Always," she whispered.

"Today at Gia, is that why you came to W last night? Did you know my sister works with Jenn? Because you could've just asked me. You didn't have to say all that about home and being friends, any of it. I would've introduced you."

"You don't think I know that? That's exactly why I *didn't* ask you. And last night..." Andy folded her arms, holding both elbows close to her torso as she backed away until her legs hit the sectional sofa. Wes scurried across the hardwood floors and leaped onto it. She sat down next to him, lifting a hand to scratch between his ears though her eyes never left Whitney's. "Last night *was* me being honest, Whit. I came here for work, to try to convince Jenn to be in the docuseries, but I couldn't be here without trying to see you. Maybe it didn't happen the way I would've planned it, but I meant every word I said."

The tension in Whitney's shoulders ebbed as she sat on the other side of Wes. "You and your plans."

Andy chuckled. "Fail to plan, you plan to fail, as depicted by my eloquent declaration last night."

Whitney had never liked how much emphasis Andy had put on that adage. Sure, it had fed her driven, meticulous nature, but it had also stifled a spontaneity and passion that made her so fucking beautiful. "The thing is, I'm not sure I know what you were trying to declare, Andy."

"That I miss you," Andy said without hesitation. "I miss my best friend."

Whitney pursed her lips, glancing down at her lap. "Now that you're back."

"I've missed you every second of every day of the last six years, Whitney. On this continent or the next. I just never thought it was fair of me to say it."

"And you think it's fair now?"

"No. But being here, seeing you that day, I didn't know how not to tell you anymore."

The words reached inside and touched a part of Whitney that understood them all too well. She stood, needing the refuge of more than a couch cushion and a tiny terrier between them. "How did you know Avery was my sister?"

"I didn't. I mean, I recognized her from pictures on your Instagram, but it took her saying her last name for me to put it together. The resemblance kind of smacked me in the face after that. Her eyes. Smile too."

Whitney quirked a brow, fingers trailing the veins in the wooden dining table as she glanced back at Andy. "You've been stalking my Instagram?"

"Only about once every three months. Moderation and all that." Andy laughed.

"Uh-huh." Whitney chuckled. She didn't want to admit that she'd skimmed through Andy's socials every now and then too, but she had to say, "Congrats on the IDA wins for *Conditional*. It's heartbreaking that so many kids wind up unhoused because families don't always take their coming-out well. For what it's worth, I think you captured their stories in a way that was both beautiful and evocative."

Andy's smile turned bashful. She ducked her head, eyes fixed on the hand still petting Wes before she looked back up at Whitney. "Did you cry? A film doesn't have the true Whitney Dimaano stamp of approval if a few tears aren't involved."

A laugh bloomed in her chest, full-bodied and free, and she felt weightless for the first time since she'd run into Andy. She couldn't say them out loud, but the words floated to the forefront of her mind. *I miss you too.* She missed the comfort of existing in the same space with someone who knew her better than she knew herself. She missed how simple everything had been before she'd quieted restless thoughts of her best friend with the taste of her lips.

"The most distinguished documentary association in the world gave you four awards and you're fishing for my approval?"

"Aren't all artists supposed to be narcissistic and needy?" Andy's gaze flicked down to Wes as if to ensure his faint yips were indeed a sign that he'd drifted off to sleep.

She stood and crossed the open floor plan toward the kitchen—all pristine, dark-wood finishes and shiny appliances, not a dirty dish in sight. Everything from the cookbook leaning against the cutting board on one counter to the three little jars of candy on another looked fit for a store catalog. The bizarre presence of sweet-and-sour, neon gummy worms amid the painstaking order of things was a perfect depiction of Andy Vahn.

"Can I get you anything?" she asked. "Juice or water or—"

Images flashed in Whitney's mind Andy's hands hot and low on her hips as she pressed Whitney against the door of her mom's old SUV to bite the dangling end of a gummy worm from her lips. Whitney's tightening grip on the bag of candy, toes curling in her sneakers in the middle of a 7-Eleven parking lot, caught up in a sugar high when she was already five minutes late for gymnastics training.

"Whit?"

Her fingers curled tighter along the edge of the table, and she broke her staring match with the candy jars to look at Andy. "Sorry, what?"

"Do you need anything? A drink or... gummies?" Andy rasped.

"Oh." A tingle crept through Whitney's fingertips, up her arms to her racing heart. "No. I, um—" She shook her head, ridding herself of the memory, the moment, whatever she was imagining in Andy's tone. "I actually have to go. I have to get Wes back home, then I need to stop by the gym before dinner later."

"Date with Dr. Redhead?" Andy smiled, the shift in her expression severe enough to give Whitney whiplash.

Maybe it was in Whitney's head, but there was a softness to the words, genuine interest or some kind of mental dispatch that who they were dating was something they could talk about, like friends did. Wasn't that what Andy had said last night?

She missed being friends.

"Isabelle," Whitney clarified. "And no. Landon, my brother, is having us all over to meet his girlfriend." She tried to suppress the unease that sharing a table with Landon and Avery's mother, Norah, stirred inside her, but tamping down her insecurities about the woman was a never-ending battle, no matter how well adjusted Whitney liked to think she was.

Andy tilted her head, eyes discerning as she leaned into the counter behind her. "How have you been doing with that?"

Two hours before sharing a meal with them wasn't the time for Whitney to delve into the complexities of loving her father, Avery, and Landon while feeling like an intruder when it came to *their* family. Andy shouldn't have been the person she wanted to explain it to; the person Whitney knew would understand, would say exactly the right words to make her feel better. She didn't know how to flat-out lie to her either. "Good. Mostly."

"That's great. I'm glad you found each other. Obviously I don't know anything about it, but Avery clearly loves you."

"What do you mean?"

"Just a feeling, I guess." Andy shrugged. There seemed to be more to it from the way her eyes purposely shifted to avoid Whitney's, but before Whitney could probe further, Andy smiled, aiming her attention across the room at Wes. "Sucks you'll have to cut his nap short."

"Yeah, well, naps were not on this walk's itinerary, but apparently you're some kind of dog whisperer now."

"Nah. I just think he's a good judge of character."

"Sure." Whitney beamed.

Andy stared, hazel eyes alight with emeralds and embers, and Whitney tore her gaze away to cross the room and rouse Wes. He woke with a growl that dissipated the second Andy swept over to ruffle his fur, whispering endearments of "Good boy" and "I'll see you soon."

The bit of annoyance still swirling in Whitney's chest intensified at Andy's assumption that they'd be seeing each other again, the assumption that Whitney even wanted to see her. As they exited the apartment, she told herself that if Wes did see Andy soon, it would be because Whitney had never been able to deny him anything.

6

A night on the Mediterranean.

Whitney had spent the last half an hour trying not to poke fun at the fact that her brother was the type of person who had committed to a themed dinner party, even down to the name. If anything, the decadent offering of fish, complemented by dishes of vibrant reds and greens, beans and nuts, was a sure sign that he'd planned the night with his girlfriend, Holland, in mind. Whitney had never known him to experiment with Mediterranean cuisine. Still, his talent and love for food were written over every artfully placed leaf of basil, from the eye-catching melee of shrimp, zucchini, bell peppers, and spices, to the tomato-cucumber salad that had her taste buds tingling with hints of citrus.

"So Landon tells us you're an actuary," their dad said, peering up from his half-finished bowl of vegetable tagine.

Holland dabbed at her lips with an ornate cotton napkin before replacing it in her lap. "Over at Guardian, yes."

"And I understand you're vying for VP," Norah chimed in. "Very impressive for your age."

Despite her affable tone, Whitney had always found

Norah's rigid posture and direct stare unnerving. It was as if she was constantly assessing everything and everyone for their worthiness to be in her presence. As Holland shifted, plastering on a smile and pushing a lock of light blonde hair behind her ear, Whitney wondered if the same unease was creeping through her right that second.

Avery's gaze briefly found Whitney's. "God, you two sound like a hiring panel. This is a dinner party. I want to know how Lan got Holland to agree to go out with him." She lowered her voice, faux-shielding her lips with one hand as she said, "Blink once for Stockholm and twice for hypnotherapy."

Chuckles permeated the room, and Holland shook her head, something more genuine in the curl of her lips as she turned to Landon and squeezed his hand. "It was nothing like that. The insurance company I work for is in the same building as his therapist's office. We just kept running into each other on his way to appointments. After almost a month of lingering looks and small talk, I got tired of waiting for him to ask me out."

"Wait, *you* asked him?" Kyla, Avery's girlfriend, leaned closer to the table, one arm stretched across the back of Avery's chair as she cocked her head to one side. "Lan."

Landon held up his free hand. "Okay, there seems to be some confusion over who asked who."

"Son, you either asked or you didn't." Dad took a sip of his wine.

"Okay. Let's settle this," said Avery, leaning into Kyla's outstretched arm. "Tell us exactly how it happened, Holland."

Holland squinted her blue eyes, her cheeks rosier by the second. "He asked if I usually grab lunch offsite, and I said yeah, because the options in the building are too sparse.

After which he nodded, mumbled, 'I get that,' then stared at me until *I* said, 'Would you like to join me sometime?'"

Whitney sputtered a laugh at the sheer ridiculousness of her brother trying to claim *that* as making the first move. "Oh my god, it was definitely Holland."

"Thank you." Holland mimicked a bow.

"So she may have been more direct..." Landon argued.

The debate carried on for another minute or two before the conversation focused on Holland again—whether she'd always lived in San Francisco, what her family was like and if she had any siblings, how her love for Mediterranean food had stemmed from her yaya's Greek heritage, and how she was so happy she'd met someone who inspired her to step outside the rigor of her job and dwell on simple things like good food and laughter. When Landon leaned in to kiss her, Avery and Kyla shared a longing stare of their own. Even Dad and Norah exchanged affectionate smiles, and a yearning so deep churned in Whitney's stomach, it had taken ten minutes before she'd even thought of taking another bite of her food.

WHITNEY FOLDED one leg onto the cushion of the wooden patio chair as she glanced beyond the balcony rail behind her. It wasn't the most striking view, with only the peeling paint of the adjacent building, the community market on the street below, and a string of passing cars to recommend it, but there was something calming about taking it all in amid the cool night air. If she had to guess, Landon had picked this apartment for its proximity to Gia, where he also worked as a chef, not the landscape.

On the opposite chair, Avery turned at a similar angle,

topping off both their glasses with more Riesling before lowering the bottle to the small patio table between them. "I think she's going to say yes."

Whitney frowned as she reached for her own glass. "Who's going to say yes about what?"

"Jenn. I mean, she practically broke out in hives at the idea of having cameras in her kitchen or having anyone follow her around for days. But after telling her what Andy said and her finally reading the emails she's been ignoring for months, I think she's going to say yes to being in the docuseries."

Whitney twirled the wine in her glass, getting lost in the pale, straw-colored swirls for a moment.

"Which means Andy might be around longer, orbiting your social circle," said Avery. "There's a high likelihood you'll run into her again."

"I figured as much."

"And you're okay with that?"

It wasn't as if Whitney had a choice. A documentary centering queer women of color at the height of their careers was something Andy had been dreaming about since they were teenagers. Whitney couldn't think of a better hometown candidate than Jenn, and she would never try to stand in the way of that over a few unresolved feelings.

"She came by W last night," said Whitney. "Then I saw her earlier. Before dinner."

"Andy?"

"Mm-hm." She nodded. "I called her after you told me what happened at Gia, and I wound up going by her place."

"I assumed by your tone that you weren't happy that she'd shown up, but let's table our examination of why you had to go to her apartment to resolve that. Did something happen?"

"Not really. We fought. Well, *I* yelled at her. She did that infuriating 'calm and level-headed' thing. Then we talked, with Wes practically falling asleep on her lap, and for a second it almost felt... easy?" Whitney's shoulders rose, then fell. "She said she wants us to be friends, that she misses me."

Avery raised her brows, concern scrawled in the downward tug of her lips and her unwavering stare. "*Can you* be friends with someone you're still in love with?"

Whitney shook her head. "I'm not in love with her."

"You're not?"

"No. Andy is..." She sighed, searching the star-speckled sky for the right words. "I'll always love her, Ave. I've given up on thinking I'm the kind of person who can just unlove someone I used to care about so deeply I would've given up anything for her. But I remember what it was like to be *in love* with her, that breathless rush of passion and impulse and feeling like I was going to burn right out of my skin whenever she so much as looked at me, and what I feel now... That's not it."

Whitney's phone buzzed against the patio table, drawing their attention. As she glanced down, the face ID initiated, revealing the contents of the texts that had just come in.

Andrea Vahn (9:11 p.m.)
I hope the dinner's going well.
I just wanted to say I'm here.
For the words and the silence.

Whitney drew in a breath, falling back into her chair. Of course Andy had picked up on something earlier. Six years ago, Whitney would've been impatient to head home, crawl into bed, and call her if only to fall asleep to the sound of her voice, but Andy wasn't her person anymore. Surely they both knew a fifteen-minute talk and shared laughter wasn't a time machine.

"I'm not going to ask," said Avery. "I know it's still hard when we all get together like this, that sometimes you still feel like..."

"An outsider?"

The slow purse of Avery's lips made Whitney want to take the word back in an instant. It wasn't like Avery could turn back time either. Besides, everything she'd done in the last eight months was so Whitney could feel the opposite of being stuck on the outside. Still, sometimes, good intentions were like Band-Aids for feelings, and Whitney didn't want Avery to take on the responsibility of mending things that had been broken before they'd even met. All she needed was this, a glass of wine between sisters and the security of knowing the bond they were building was neither fleeting nor temporary.

"Sorry." She smiled, resting a hand on Avery's arm. "I think tonight it was more about being a seventh wheel to all of you wonderfully-in-love people. Which is weird. You know how much I love *love*. I think lately I just miss feeling like..." She gestured toward the open balcony door to the clear view of the living room. Landon slipped his hands around Holland's waist from behind as they both laughed at something Dad had said. "*That*. I miss that."

"Things with Isabelle have been... *anticlimactic*, then?"

Whitney's jaw dropped, and she stared at her sister before slowly shaking her head. "I can't believe you just said that."

"That was low-hanging fruit. I had to." Avery sputtered a laugh. "But really, do you think it was just too soon, maybe? You said it yourself that you usually have better sexual chemistry with someone you feel an emotional connection to. Maybe you're not there with Isabelle yet. Doesn't mean you won't get there. It's also okay if it just doesn't feel right, Whit."

"No. I know. I just... She's literally perfect, Ave."

"Doesn't make her perfect for you."

Whitney closed her eyes, pushing the thought back. "Enough about me. Since when are you leaving Ky alone with Norah?"

Avery glanced toward the living room where Kyla and her mom sat, caught in their own quiet conversation. "Since she and Dad ran out of the typical background check questions. Mom has graduated to treating Ky like she's her personal travel consultant, and since talking about all the places they've visited is a travel influencer's wheelhouse, Ky eats up all the attention. I figure it's harmless bonding. The more Mom sees her, talks with her, the more she'll realize Ky isn't a phase for me."

Whitney bobbed her head. "So coming out in your thirties isn't so different from doing it in high school."

"Not when it comes to moms."

Whitney stared up at the sky, her mind a rumble of memories. She expected an onslaught of images from the night she'd told her own mother she was queer. Instead, younger versions of her and Andy flooded her mind—Andy tugging her up the steps toward the Vahns' front door, her eyes alight with the kind of incandescent bliss that made Whitney's heart stop, then race, bolder and braver than Whitney had ever seen her when they stumbled to a halt in the living room and Andy's parents looked up, expectant yet reserved. *We're going on a date,* she'd said. *With each other. I'll be back by curfew.*

Avery reclined in her own chair, gaze trained on Whitney. "So, are you going to call her?"

A swift *no* lingered on the back of Whitney's tongue. She didn't have to ask to know Avery had circled back to Andy, to the texts from earlier, and she swallowed the lump in her throat with another sip of wine.

"I don't know, Ave."

7
———

There were perks to living in cities that never slept. LA, New York, London...

Andy had forgotten that San Francisco held glimpses of it too. As she adjusted the pair of throw pillows beneath her head, staring out at the panorama of sporadically lit skyscrapers and the faint glimmer of stars, she was content with the company of this place she used to call home and her favorite narrator voicing another sapphic romance into her earphones.

The clock ticked closer to midnight.

Whitney still hadn't replied to the texts Andy had sent almost three hours ago, but she took that as a good sign. Maybe she'd imagined the insecurity in Whitney's eyes and words when she'd mentioned dinner with her siblings. Or maybe words like *I'm here* just didn't fall within their purview anymore. Hadn't Andy seen enough to know that if Whitney needed to talk she had people? A brother and sister, Kasey, probably Jax too.

Andy's eyes drifted close as she tuned back into the love

story unraveling through her earphones. The constant push and pull and seething tension was her favorite part, but she'd always been a romantic voyeur of sorts—an avid consumer of love, terrible at actually being in it.

Warm breaths hit Romy's face, fingers lighting a path from the edge of her sports bra to her navel to pause, letting the sensation spread like wildfire through every inch of her body. Her eyes fell shut, and she dragged in a breath, an undertone of coconut permeating the air, pushing her closer to something that wasn't right, no matter how good it felt.

"Don't fight it," Jordyn whispered, breath tickling at Romy's lips—

The narration cut off with the announcement of an incoming call, and Andy's eyes sprang open to check the name on her phone's display. She breathed a quiet laugh to herself, cradled by relief as she slumped into her spot on the couch and tapped the answer button. "Hey."

"Hi," Whitney murmured. She heaved a sigh. "You were supposed to be sleeping."

"Do you want to hang up and call again so I can pretend I was?"

For a moment, the only response was the faint sound of rustling sheets, and Andy imagined Whitney rolling onto her back to stare up at the smooth, white plane of her ceiling the same way Andy was. "No. I don't want that."

"Can I ask about dinner?"

"Dinner was good. Landon made Mediterranean. His girlfriend, Holland, seems great. Dinner was great."

Andy hummed, contemplating the scant details and Whitney's detached tone. Her calling didn't mean she was ready to talk about it. Though Andy had already decided the Whitney on her phone wasn't the same person she'd known back then, she did what she'd always done whenever Whitney had called her late on sleepless nights. She reached into her vat of random, potentially useless facts. "Did you know newborns can't breathe through their mouths?"

A sleepy melody of a laugh filled Andy's ears. "They can't?"

"Nope. But their nasal passages are really tiny. That's why they sound so stuffy all the time."

"I guess that makes sense." Whitney hummed, the tenor of her voice dropping slightly when she said, "Tell me another one?"

"Elephants are one of the only land mammals that can't jump."

"Is that because they're so heavy?"

"Yeah. Plus, all the bones in their legs point downward, so they can't leap off the ground anyway, even when they're running," said Andy, her tone laced with awe and amusement. "And now you're trying to remember every elephant you've ever seen."

"I mean"— Whitney sniggered—"I wasn't *not* trying to remember. How do you retain any of this?"

Andy shrugged, though Whitney couldn't see it. "I like to be prepared."

"For what? Your debut on *Jeopardy!*?"

"Well, I don't know about *Jeopardy!*, but having them for moments like this doesn't hurt." She let the ambiguity hang in the silence between them, neglecting to specify that she loved her brain's capacity to retain random drivel because it gave her something to distract Whitney whenever her lips and hands weren't an option. If it wouldn't be so messy and complicated and doubtlessly unwelcomed, Andy would've offered those too. Besides, it was like that song said—friends don't know the way you taste—and maybe they were too far gone for that, but bolstering her memories with all-new encounters...

Andy didn't even want to think about it.

"Andy?" Whitney whispered.

Andy perked up, grounding herself in the moment before her brain wandered too far into dangerously reminiscent territory. "Hmm?"

"I missed my best friend too."

ANDY SHIFTED IN HER SEAT, sparing a second to scrutinize the white walls and blond-wood furniture around the room. Traces of amber lingered in the air, mixed in with the earthy scent of the two potted plants in her line of sight and something more inscrutable, a fruity elegance owed to one or more of the three women seated in front of her.

She hadn't planned for three people. When she'd woken early Saturday morning—Whitney's even breathing still echoing from the speakers of her phone—the text on her screen had left her buzzing with excitement as much as anticipation. So much so she'd read the words four times before the weight of them had sunk in.

Hello, Andy. It's Jenn Coleman. Are you available to meet on Monday at 9 a.m.? There are a few things I would like to discuss before confirming my participation.

The squeal Andy had let out, though suppressed, had stirred Whitney awake before Andy's finger made it to the mute button. Whitney's sleepy, answering purr of Andy's name had yanked on her heartstrings with such an unintended ferocity that her brain had undergone a full-time lapse before remembering that "I'm here, baby" wasn't the right answer. They'd hardly spoken the rest of the weekend, which had given Andy time and space to focus on her meeting. She'd prepared for all angles and situations imaginable, and yet she hadn't considered having three people in front of her instead of one.

"You've met Avery," said Jenn, rolling her chair closer to the sparsely occupied oak-finish desk.

Avery's gaze narrowed almost imperceptibly, ever scrutinizing despite the smile on her perfectly lined lips. An empty chair identical to the modern rustic sets Andy had passed in main dining lurked to the left of Jenn's desk, but Avery seemed more at home standing, even in pointed-toe stilettos.

Andy managed a quick nod to Avery before Jenn gestured in a sweeping motion to the woman on her right. She had dark chestnut hair down to her shoulders, striking brown eyes, and a constellation of beauty marks dotting her olive complexion. "This is Valentina, my partner."

Andy's brain snagged on the word. *Partner as in business or...*

"I know this may seem unorthodox," said Jenn, "but I have to admit that if I'm going to be convinced to let you come in here with cameras, these two women are your best bet."

So Jenn Coleman didn't have a publicist but she had a... *squad*?

"Okay." Andy nodded, clearing her throat. "Vahn Productions is putting on—"

"Sorry. We've read the proposal. Just..." Jenn sighed, tilting her head as something that vaguely resembled kindness crept onto her face. "Tell us what you would need, what your process entails."

"Well, like you said, I'd like to come in with my team, or just me, if that's what you're comfortable with. I have experience with lights, cameras—"

"Action?" Valentina grinned.

Andy chuckled. "Well, I was going to say editing, but that works too. What I'd like more than anything is to capture *you*, Jenn. Who you are in this space, to these people. A lot of that I can get with your team hardly even knowing I'm here. I mean, I can also acquire some chef's whites if this"—Andy gestured to her own leather jacket, button-up shirt, and dark jeans sans holes—"is too distracting. But I *would* love to explore your journey to becoming a famed, world-class chef who happens to be both queer, if you don't mind that definition, and Black. And I think *that*, though beyond valuable, might take a lot more vulnerability."

"Right." Jenn's expression turned contemplative as she leaned back in her chair.

It occurred to Andy that maybe the very mention of having to share her experience was enough to make Jenn feel exposed. But if Andy, a Black woman herself, couldn't mention it in front of Avery, whom she knew to be half-Filipino, and Valentina, whom she'd guessed was Latinx, possibly Jenn's closest confidantes, then this would never work.

"And this would happen over the course of a week?" Jenn asked.

Andy bobbed her head in assent. "Ideally."

"Which is code for more if necessary," Avery chimed in.

Andy took a breath. Clearly, Jenn wasn't intrigued by the idea of having a full crew lurking around her restaurant for days on end, which was fine. Andy could get the necessary footage, but she wouldn't get the chance if she didn't come up with *something* to convince Jenn to be in the docuseries in the first place. "Look... I understand that Gia is one of the premier restaurants on the West Coast, certainly here in San Francisco. I know your feet are on the gas a hundred and ten percent of the time. Jenn, if you say yes, this happens only within your parameters. Will I try to push my luck a bit?" Andy breathed a laugh. "Probably. But I *will* always get your consent first."

One corner of Avery's lips twitched, stirring the same inexplicable yearning for approval—Avery's approval—that Andy had felt last Friday. She'd left that sidewalk feeling like Avery had already been sold on the idea of showcasing Jenn, and despite Avery's stoicism so far, Andy was almost positive she was still on board. Why wasn't that enough? Why did she still feel so fucking desperate for Avery Dimaano's endorsement?

Valentina reached across the table and placed a hand on top of Jenn's, the passing glance that followed speaking to *more* than business partners, especially when Jenn flipped her hand to squeeze Valentina's.

"Would this filming extend to my home?" Jenn asked.

Andy's mind blanked. "Um. It's not in our current plan, no."

Jenn's answering hum made Andy shift in her seat, especially when Jenn exchanged looks with both Valentina and Avery. Did Jenn *want* her home life to be captured? Andy couldn't imagine it. A home visit seemed too tangential, anyway.

"Well, do let me know if that changes," Jenn said. "How soon does filming start?"

Andy's brows shot up, her lips parting in anticipation.

She fought to keep her tone steady, her phrasing careful, when she asked, "Sooo, it's a yes?"

"It's a yes." Jenn beamed.

"Holy—I mean, *wow*. Thank you. Thank you so much. I can't begin to tell you how important this is to me."

Jenn waved away Andy's rambling gratitude, rolling her chair back as she stood. "Avery's an excellent paraphraser. And I have to say your words to her last Friday resonated much more than the platitudes and technicalities in your team's proposal, though those, too, have a place, I'm sure."

A gulp slid down Andy's throat as she chanced a glance at Avery. "Well, thank you. All of you. I'll get back to my team and have a proposed filming schedule sent over. But I'd like to do a proper walkthrough later this week if that's okay. Just me," she added quickly, one hand shooting up in a cringeworthy display of scout's honor.

Amusement crossed Valentina's face, followed by a mouthed *relax* Andy was certain she'd only imagined.

"Just you is perfect," said Jenn. "Valentina and I are in the kitchen practically twelve hours a day, so Avery will be my point person for all necessary communication before, during, and after filming. That includes legal."

A lot of talking to Avery then. Andy pursed her lips. "Perfect."

"Can I assume you'll have the contract sent over by the end of the week?" asked Avery. "None of this happens without one. I'm sure you can understand that."

Andy nodded. "Yeah. No, of course. You'll have it by tomorrow." She offered a handshake to each woman before working both hands into the pockets of her jeans. "I'll let you get your days started."

"Thank you, Andy," said Jenn, guiding her toward the door.

Andy scoffed a smile. "Thank *you* for even considering this." She'd have a meeting with Riva later—a follow-up to last week's discussion—but she exited Gia with her phone already in hand, tapping out a text.

Andy (9:18 a.m.)
Jenn Coleman -check mark emoji-

8

Whitney held her smile as the last set of people from her advanced yoga class exited the ground-floor studio. It had been a while since she'd led any of the beginner classes on their roster, but having an instructor out with a cold had required a last-minute sub. Since Mondays had always been her designated day to hole up in her office with music, focusing on more administrative tasks, that sub had turned out to be her.

She glanced down at her watch, slipping out of the room as another horde of people streamed in, mats slung over their shoulders, a muddle of murmured exchanges about their days, kids, and partners trailing in their wake. The promotional flier mockups Kasey had sent over were waiting, unreviewed in her email, and she still hadn't called the repair technician about the squeak being emitted by one of the leg abduction machines on the strength floor, but she turned right toward the juice bar instead of heading to her office. If she was going to finish the day strong, she'd need the refreshing boost of a vanilla almond milkshake.

"Finally escaped the yoga bees?"

Whitney paused, glancing over her shoulder to find Jaxon headed her way, his tablet in one hand, a purple shake in the other. As usual, he was garbed head to toe in W athleisurewear, but with the red fleece hoodie thrown over his T-shirt, he emanated all the energy of a cozy, six-foot teddy bear.

She rolled her eyes as he dropped an arm around her shoulder. "I told you to stop calling them that. Someone could hear you."

"No one's going to hear me. So, who was it today? The music teacher or the tag team blondes?"

"The blondes." Whitney sighed. When she'd first started leading classes, she'd underestimated how chatty some people were after they'd spent fifty minutes under her guidance, attempting to replicate her form. She'd been ogled and complimented on her flexibility in ways that left her feeling stripped naked and very uncomfortable. But four years of practice had helped her perfect the art of a polite shutdown while maintaining her client list.

"They want to do things to you." Jax shook his head, only mildly scandalized by the idea. "Many bad, bad things."

"Sleeping with clients is bad for business."

"You don't have to tell me. I have a pregnant wife at home and eyes for no one else. It's just fun to watch you squirm. Besides"—he faked a cough—"Dr. Ramon."

Whitney pushed his arm off her shoulder, unrepentant even as he scrambled not to spill his smoothie on the spotless lobby floor. "We met before she became a member here."

"But you didn't start seeing her until she *was* a member."

"Fine. Report me to management for breach of conduct."

Jaxon laughed. "Why are you prolonging it anyway? It hasn't clicked."

"We're not in college anymore, Jax. In a year, I'll be thirty. I don't know if *clicking* should be the litmus test for relationship longevity."

His brows rose. "Is that what you're looking for? Longevity?"

"Have you met me?" Whitney shot him a look, joining the line of three people waiting by the juice bar.

Jax slid in next to her despite already having his own drink. A quick check of the time—6:03 p.m.—confirmed he was done for the day. No doubt he was sticking around to prod at her love life, but they'd known each other since they were both sports science majors at UCLA, so no one was more familiar with her dating history: the post-Andy heartbreak, swearing off dating forever, experimenting with hookups only to circle back to her inherent desire to be committed to the person she was sleeping with. Although she'd agreed to Isabelle's proposal to keep things casual, Whitney needed the comforting potential for *more*. Before Isabelle, there'd been a time when Whitney had thought she found that, but this metaphoric more had failed to materialize beyond a year-long stint with someone whose laugh eventually made her want to rip her own hair out. They'd also tried to kick Wes in a misguided attempt at discipline. If Whitney had ever felt murderous at any point in her life, that had to be it.

"Right." Jax held up his shake in lieu of an empty palm. "So the Whitney Dimaano Never-Ending Quest to Find Her Soulmate continues."

Whitney huffed. "I don't need a soulmate. I just need someone who gets me as well as I get them, who knows what I need even when I don't. Extra points if I want to rip their clothes off and double if they don't turn out to be a pet-kicking sociopath."

"I see we're still unpacking the Jeri trauma."

"Wes never liked them," Whitney grumbled, folding her arms beneath her chest. "I should've trusted him more."

"Sure. Let your dog pick the person you spend the rest of your life with."

An image of Andy holding Wes's face and whispering sweet nothings to him flashed in Whitney's mind, and okay, not even her beloved pet son could be allowed to wield that much power. His instincts were still developing, after all. Besides, Friday night had been nice. Whitney hadn't meant to drift off with the soothing, tired husk in Andy's voice as a lullaby, but talking the way they used to before everything had shattered was nice. It was almost as nice as waking up to find the line still open, then to have Andy share that Avery had gotten her a meeting with Jenn.

Soothing, simple, nice.

Anything else would complicate that. Whitney liked knowing Andy would be gone the second she'd wrapped filming with Jenn. For someone always seeking more solid ground, knowing any resurrected feelings between her and Andy would be temporary held a bizarre comfort. At least this time, when Andy left, it wouldn't feel like Whitney had been catapulted into the stratosphere without ever seeing it coming.

The person in front of her moved toward one of the lounge chairs in the sitting area, and Whitney stepped up to the counter.

Daphne the smoothie barista grimaced in her standard feigned annoyance, the flush against her alabaster skin most likely thanks to the mini surge in customers. "Anyone could forget you actually own this place with the way you *insist* on waiting in line."

"We've been over this, Daph," said Whitney. "If I hop to the top of the queue, actual customers have to wait longer."

Daphne's green eyes narrowed. "Isn't that one of the perks of being the boss?"

"I'm perfectly fine with waiting, and you better not be letting this one"—Whitney hooked a thumb toward Jax—"jump ahead either."

"No need to skip when you text beforehand and pick up when it's ready. Gimme a sec." Jax dug into the pocket of his track pants, came out with his phone, and pressed it to his ear. "Hey, babe."

"So a vanilla almond shake?" Daphne asked, brows raised expectantly despite her knowing Whitney's order by heart.

"Yes, please."

"Wait, now?" The pitch of Jax's voice—panic and shock—yanked Whitney's attention back to him. "Is your mom there?" Pause. "Okay. I'll meet you. I'm on my way. I'm on my way!"

Whitney moved closer to him, following as he rushed toward the main doors. "Jax—"

"Michelle's in labor."

"Oh. Wow." Whitney's eyes widened and her hands shot up in reflex as Jax tossed her his car keys. She'd missed the birth of his first child, Sky, while on a week-long vacation in Medellin with her mom. After a run-in with another car's fender had almost caused Jax to miss the birth himself, they'd agreed if they were together the next time Michelle went into labor, Whitney would be the one behind the wheel. She spared a quick glance over her shoulder, yelling,

"Raincheck on the shake, Daph!" before she and Jax both disappeared onto the central shaft of the revolving door.

They made it to UCSF Medical Center in twenty-five minutes—a feat in rush hour traffic. Not that anyone would be able to tell with Jax's endless leg tapping and running commentary of "Whit, I love you, but my eighty-year-old granny could maneuver this traffic better," and "Fuck, Whit. You could've made that," every time she slowed on an amber light. Never mind that Whitney hadn't driven standard transmission since she was, what, nineteen? Even so, her sole purpose in those twenty-five dreadful minutes was to get him there alive and without incident.

As a nurse ushered Jax off to Michelle's room, Whitney considered that missing the birth of their child was probably the one thing no parent wanted to do. She certainly never would—even if she wasn't the one to carry—and she tried not to think about how her mother's reluctance to tell Whitney's father about her until she was six meant he hadn't been there when she was born. She liked to think he would've been, despite the illicit nature of her conception. She liked to think he would've still shown up, like he'd done every day since he'd known she existed. But mostly, she didn't like to think about it at all.

A rumble of chatter permeated the sterile waiting area. Muted exchanges traveled from the nurses' station, and someone's adorable albeit restless extended family took up as many as six chairs in one section.

Whitney reached for her phone and absentmindedly swiped to her messages. Her gaze caught on Andy's name. Their last exchange had been Saturday morning when

Whitney had sent a simple *thanks* that garnered an *always* in return. Her thumbs hovered over the keyboard. Based on Avery's earlier update, congratulations were in order. Jenn had agreed to be in the docuseries, the same one Whitney had listened to Andy dream about out loud while she lay awake, losing herself in the spectrum of colors glimmering in Andy's eyes—the golden strands of a meadow; the soft green of grass slick with morning dew; flickers of burnt orange.

Sending her well wishes seemed like the least she could do, though Andy hadn't told her directly. Revealing that Avery had done so might send the wrong message—that Avery was being unprofessional, or keeping tabs on Andy *for* Whitney, which she absolutely wasn't, and—

"Whitney?"

Her head jerked up to the sight of Isabelle meandering across the plain white tiles of the waiting room. In her pristine doctor's coat and navy scrubs, red hair in loose waves down to her shoulders, she was the spitting image of the night Whitney had first seen her, the night Landon had been admitted with a broken arm and a concussion eight months ago.

Isabelle's brows drew closer, her gaze shifting around as if in search of an explanation to why Whitney was seated alone in the Obstetrics, Gynecology and Reproductive Sciences waiting area. "Is everything okay?"

"Yeah. Michelle, Jax's wife, is in labor. He's in with her now. I'm just hanging around in case they need anything."

"How nice." Isabelle beamed, but the hint of reservation in her tone suggested she wasn't one of those people who bought into the whole miracle of childbirth thing. "Rest assured she's in excellent hands."

"I bet." Whitney squinted, returning her smile. "Are you

sure you're an ortho surgeon? Between the red hair and these scrubs, I think I might be sensing some Addison Montgomery vibes."

A frown wrestled with the amusement still glinting in Isabelle's eyes, her confusion evident when she tilted her head and asked, "Who's Addison Montgomery?"

Right. Because *real* doctors didn't watch *Grey's Anatomy*. Now that Whitney thought about it, Isabelle didn't understand half her pop culture or musical references. She'd never seen *Chicago*, *Hamilton*, *Les Mis*, or *The Greatest Showman*, and when Whitney had gushed about *Encanto*, Isabelle had chuckled in her refined, sexy way then asked, "Isn't that a children's movie?"

Whitney smiled, refusing to dwell on how it felt so similar to the practiced grin she used to turn down advances from gym members. "Never mind. How's your day been?"

"Good," said Isabelle. "Better, now that I've run into you. Although I do find it mildly concerning that you didn't mention you're here."

"I've been pretty"—Whitney shook her head—"distracted. But I do have an appointment here tomorrow. Maybe I can make up for it then?"

Unease crossed Isabelle's features again. "Should I be concerned?"

"Just a routine yearly checkup." Their spur-of-the-moment hookup two weeks ago was the first time Whitney had been with anyone in months, and Isabelle had promised to mention it if she started seeing anyone else. But since they were still calling their arrangement casual, maybe Whitney would take the opportunity to get tested too.

Isabelle scrunched up her face, her expression playful. "Nothing like having a physician prod at your body *and* your sex life."

"Aren't you supposed to give me a speech about how important these appointments are?" Whitney narrowed her gaze.

"Well, you're already going, so my guess is you *do* know how important they are. Besides"—Isabelle peered over her shoulder before closing the gap to bring her lips to Whitney's ear—"if you're up for a follow-up exam after, consider me at your service."

Whitney's stomach fluttered. This was one of the things she liked about Isabelle: her unwavering confidence, the fact that she hadn't been deterred by Whitney not having an orgasm the first and only time they'd slept together. Maybe she understood that it happened more often than people liked to admit, or maybe with almost a decade more experience than Whitney, she was so secure in her sexuality that it hadn't once occurred to her that she'd done anything wrong. After all, she hadn't. Whitney had been sure to murmur that reassurance against her lips before she'd gotten dressed and left Isabelle's apartment.

It wasn't anyone's fault. It just hadn't... *clicked*.

Despite the mounting tension coiling tighter and tighter in Whitney's body as the days went by, stumbling into this gorgeous woman's bed for a do-over didn't feel right. Why wasn't her skin on fire at the mere thought of getting Isabelle naked again, the thought of kissing and touching her until her body convulsed with release?

"Am I being too forward?" Isabelle's smile faltered.

"No. I like forward," Whitney said quickly. "And I like you."

"I like you too..." Isabelle trailed off, the lilt in her tone giving away her growing confusion.

"It's just—" Whitney's eyes fell shut.

This was cruel. Another week and even someone with

Isabelle's poise wouldn't be able to rationalize Whitney's wavering. Despite the fact that they'd now seen each other naked, their relationship felt grounded in the same place it had been when they'd started seeing each other almost two months ago. Whether that was because Whitney wanted more or because she didn't was still to be determined. Maybe Isabelle didn't expect her to know that yet, but until Whitney figured it out, taking things further with Isabelle felt... wrong.

Whitney opened her eyes, sighing. "I'm not sure I'm in the best place for this right now."

The dip between Isabelle's brows deepened, and she moved closer in a direct effort to keep their conversation from being overheard. "The best place for sex? Because I had an incredible night with you, Whitney, but we don't need to go there again until you're ready."

"No, I know. The thing is, I'm starting to feel like I'm stringing you along, which might be patronizing to even consider when this is supposed to be casual, and we have sporadic dates every two weeks that sometimes get interrupted because your job is literally life-or-death."

"So this is about my job?" Isabelle flinched back.

"No." Whitney winced. "Fuck. I'm really making a mess of this. Isabelle, you are *perfect*. Everything I should want—"

"Sorry." A small, black device emerged in Isabelle's hands, and she dropped her gaze, lips twisted in an apologetic frown before their eyes met again. "I'm being paged. I'm sorry. I want to finish this, but..."

"Duty calls." Whitney laughed. The universe and its impeccable timing.

Isabelle pressed a kiss to Whitney's cheek, her feet already shuffling in retreat when she said, "I'll text you. I promise."

A breath escaped Whitney's puffed cheeks as she fell back into her chair.

"Well, that didn't look good."

Her eyes widened as Jax emerged in the chair next to hers. "What are you—is he here?"

"Nah. Little buddy's taking his time. Although the doctor said something about slow effacement of the cervix. Basically, it could be hours, so you can head home if you want."

Whitney shook her head. "I'm good for a while. Do you need anything? Does Mich?"

"All good, but if you're still here when we get to the screaming and growling stage, just check that she hasn't turned me to stone with the sheer force of a death stare."

Amusement laced Whitney's reply. "Sure, Jax."

He braced both hands on the arms of his chair and got to his feet. "Seriously, though. Is everything all right with the good doctor?"

Whitney dropped her head back against the wall with a mild thunk. "I might have to get back to you on that."

9
———

The lights on Andy's car flashed as she hit the lock button on her key fob and stepped onto the curb of the two-story Edwardian she'd grown up in. Its gray siding and white trim gleamed with a fresh coat of paint, though the three stories of scaffolding encasing the adjacent building left it looking twice as distinguished. Never mind the London plane tree, ever sturdy and well tended, in the single patch of soil at the edge of the concrete driveway.

Visions of her parents maintaining it all themselves slinked through her mind. Dad had spent so much time out in the yard with garden shears and paintbrushes as Mom hovered by the ladder with a steadying hand. Andy had been permitted to help only if all her schoolwork had been done. After all, they'd insisted school was her job. They would take care of everything else. Wasn't that why she hadn't been back all this time? Because after school came a career, and with hers being in LA and their emphasis on success, they'd always been content to come to her instead.

Thanksgivings. Christmases. Birthdays, not so much.

As she started up the stairs to the front door, she had the

strangest feeling that maybe if she'd insisted, if she hadn't thought it easier to stay away, a lot of things might've been different. Her quick raps against the white-sheathed oak provoked an indiscernible yell from within the house.

She smiled to herself, comfort and nostalgia coursing through her like a burst of adrenaline.

The door swung open, and her mother stared up at her, one hand drying the other with a checkered towel. The crow's feet by the corners of her eyes and mouth had deepened since Andy had seen her two months ago, but her ochre complexion, broad shoulders, and wide hips spoke to the same imposing woman Andy had known all her life—even if Mom *was* barely over five feet tall.

"Hey, Mom."

A close-lipped smile stretched across her face, and she reached up to pull Andy in for a hug. Andy bent, meeting Mom's steady pats against her back and letting herself be studied when they both pulled away. "Good. You look good."

Andy sniggered as Mom turned and started down the short hallway to the kitchen. She shut the front door, then followed, glancing right into the open dining area, left into the living room, refamiliarizing herself with the house's pale-yellow walls. Parted white curtains let in the fading daylight, bathing the white sofa, simple wooden coffee table, and organized shelves of tiny boxes and frames in a soft glow.

"Dad still at work?" Andy asked once she made it to the kitchen.

By the stove, Mom glanced up from a steaming pot. The fragrance of red peas, coconut milk, and Scotch bonnet peppers lingered even after she replaced the lid. "He's finishing a trip nearby before he heads home."

"Remember how mad he was when rideshare apps

started getting popular? Ranting about how taxi drivers would become obsolete? Now he has a five-star rating on Uber."

"Hmph." Mom hummed a laugh. "He likes his routines. Big changes scare him, but he's adaptable. You two are the same that way."

Andy dropped her gaze to her boots for a second, the new angle allowing her a glimpse of a beige bandage on Mom's left foot. She knitted her brows as she moved closer. "Did something happen to your foot?"

"I had a little slip." Mom waved it off, eyes locked on the gathering of lettuce, tomatoes, and cucumber on the counter in front of her.

"What do you mean a little slip? Did you get it looked at?"

"Andrea, I have been a registered nurse for thirty years. I can take care of my own sprain."

Andy rolled her eyes. "Of course, Mom. That's not what I meant. Should you even be standing this long?"

"Wash your hands. Can I trust you with the salad?" Defiant eyes stared back at Andy.

"What do you mean? It's a salad."

"And eating at all those fancy restaurants doesn't mean you know how to make one."

"Ha-ha. You're terrible." Andy moved to the sink and pumped some soap into her palm. "But don't think I've forgotten about your foot."

The faint click of a lock signaled Dad's arrival seconds before he bellowed, "Some birdbrain park them stush car in the driveway and block me out." Even after more than thirty years, the playful jab held traces of his Jamaican accent, and Andy was grinning before he even set foot in the kitchen.

"Who are you calling a birdbrain, old man?" Andy gazed

up at him, his gangly height and hazel eyes a mirror of her own despite his lighter complexion.

He tossed his head back in a lively chortle before squeezing her shoulder. "Good to have you home."

"Good to be home, Dad."

"Need any help, Gracie?" He moved toward Mom.

"You can set the table. The rice should be ready in five minutes, but the oxtail needs another ten."

"All right." Dad pointed a finger Andy's way. "Don't burn that salad."

Andy took their ribbing at face value. They'd never been good at I-love-yous, but seeing them happy in the rare moments when they weren't both exhausted from sixty-hour workweeks had never failed to fill her up and leave her yearning all at once. She made a mental note to bring up their work schedules at dinner, to make sure they'd slowed down a bit now that they were older—now that they didn't have to take care of *everything* by themselves anymore.

Maybe she'd gotten lucky. Few documentarians made a living doing the thing they loved, but winning four awards for her first project plus all the connections she'd made during her time in LA, London, and New York had set her up to work with some of the country's leading production companies. Then there was all the freelancing and how much of the actual work she'd done as a one-person film crew before it was even possible to pay herself.

Maybe it had been luck, but it had also taken twenty-hour days of hard work, sweat, and unshed tears. Still, as her dad exited the kitchen, his gait slower and more strained, she turned to measure the slight hunch in Mom's posture, a stark contrast to her melodic humming and fluid steps from counter to stove. Andy couldn't help feeling that, though they'd equipped her to chase her dream with everything she had, she wasn't prepared for the cold awareness seeping in whenever she thought of everything she'd given up in the process.

"Atticus Finch, Aster Grey, Jay Gatsby?" Kasey studied her cocktail menu, her pitch hinting of excitement, though her squinted eyes were giving skepticism.

"Yeah, I think I'm just going to order the strawberry mezcal." Andy laughed as she scanned her own list of options.

Kasey hummed, cataloging the ingredients aloud. "Strawberries, grapefruit, lime—ooh, but the mango rum looks *good*."

Three hours earlier, when Andy had sat down to have dinner with her parents and Kasey had texted to ask if she wanted to get a drink, Andy had been surprised to say the least. Beyond a check-in text over the weekend, they hadn't talked much since their catch-up at Kasey's apartment nearly two weeks ago. Andy had extended the offer to hang out again sometime, but she'd mentally accounted for the possibility that Kasey might've been too skeptical of rebuilding their friendship to take it. Sitting next to her at a bar, eclectic black-and-white zigzag flooring beneath their feet and a hazy cover of "Wicked Games" streaming all around them, it almost felt like nothing had changed. Like they were just best friends catching up between semesters at colleges in different cities.

"How full are you?" asked Kasey.

"Full." Andy cradled her stomach. "I'm literally here for the cocktails and company."

"Ugh. Did Tía Gracie make oxtail?"

"Yup." A wistful smile tugged at Andy's lips as warmth coursed through her. "You still call her that?"

The cutting glare Kasey shot her said it was absurd to even ask. "I love your parents. That didn't change because you ghosted."

"I didn't"—Andy winced—"ghost. *But*... I'm here for all the processing, especially if it means we can do this more often."

"You mean until you're done filming with Jenn Coleman?"

"No. I mean..." She let the thought hang, mulling over it for the third time since she'd left her parents' house. There was still so much to consider. She didn't even know if she'd be able to make it work with her career and the company she was trying to grow in LA. She'd never been impulsive either, but that didn't stop her from messaging her Realtor on the way over. There was something about being back, about seeing her parents, Kasey, and Whitney, that had her all wound up and wired to *just do it*. Maybe that was her brain regurgitating years of Nike ads, but she was terrified of what would happen if she didn't do *something*. It was a haunting sensation, like she'd blink and everything that mattered outside of filmmaking would be well and truly gone. "I think I might stay a while," she hedged. "After filming wraps."

Kasey raised one hand to signal the bartender, her tone casual when she asked, "What? Like an extra weekend or something?"

"No. I mean I have a call with my Realtor this Friday."

Kasey's head spun so fast Andy thought it might snap right off her neck. She tilted her head, squinting as if to gauge Andy's seriousness. "Are you okay? Because if this is one of those make-everything-right-because-you-have-a-rare-and-deadly-illness things, you need to tell me right fucking now."

Andy sputtered a laugh that faded the second her eyes caught the person entering the lounge. "Whitney."

"Dios, Andy. You can't just pick up and move for a woman you used to date six years ago. This isn't a Hallmark movie."

"What?" Andy scrunched up her face. "No, I mean, you didn't tell me you invited her."

Kasey's thick, dark brows sloped downward, her tone telegraphing her perplexity when she shifted on her stool to follow Andy's gaze. "Because I didn't."

Whitney stepped forward, messy waves framing her face in a sleek, layered bob Andy still wasn't used to. Whitney's hair had fallen well beyond her shoulders all those years ago. Still, she wore the new style with an air of grace and maturity that replaced Andy's yearning for the past with new intrigue. The first two or three buttons of her long-sleeved shirt were open, revealing a double-chained gold necklace that dipped toward her cleavage. Even halfway across the room, servers crossing their vision to and from tables, Andy registered the exact second Whitney noticed her—her slowing steps, the subtle yet perceptible part of her lips, the way Andy's own skin tingled with awareness and something that fluttered low, *low* in her stomach.

A flash of red hair emerged in the same instant a hand settled on Whitney's jean-clad hip, guiding her left toward the row of two-tops along one wall.

Cold realization crept through Andy. "Oh."

Behind her, the bartender materialized, drawing her attention back to the bar as Kasey rattled out her order. A mumbled request for a strawberry mezcal and chips left Andy's mouth as compulsion drew her attention back to

Whitney and Isabelle getting comfortable in an intimate booth setting toward the back.

For a second, Whitney peered up and their gazes held, the intensity in her eyes making Andy more aware of her own racing heart. She schooled her expression into a smile, set to raise her hand in a wave when Kasey's palm slapped against her arm. "Stop that."

Andy grimaced, soothing her injured flesh as she turned back to Kasey. "Stop what?"

"Ex returns to town. Cue longing stares across dark room. We've literally seen this movie like fifteen times."

"That is not what is happening here."

"I know you remember what the two of you were like together. We all do. But there's a reason it didn't work, Andy. Whatever's going on with Isabelle, you need to let her have this."

There was something in the words "whatever's going on with Isabelle" that suggested maybe things between her and Whitney weren't as serious as they seemed. Andy hadn't garnered much from the one other time she'd seen them together—that night she'd shown up at the gym—but she'd overheard enough of their conversation for the idea of them dating to seem even a bit baffling.

A memory pulsed in her mind.

Whitney stood in front of her in a seamless sports bra and shorts, her sleek, black hair swept up in a high ponytail. The combo never failed to leave Andy awestruck and dizzy with want, even as Whitney absentmindedly flexed her taped ankles by pressing her toes against the carpeted floors of her dorm, rambling about how bizarre it was that Andy's mom was working on her dad's birthday.

"It's just... people like your mom, nurses and doctors, they're invaluable. The world would literally collapse without them. But I can't help but wonder if she and your dad work as well as they do because he works crazy hours too. I don't know if I could do it. Be with someone who had to be gone that much, which"—her eyes fell shut and she released a heavy breath—"probably sounds really selfish."

Andy slid closer to the edge of the bed and pulled Whitney onto her lap. Arms wrapped around her neck as she mapped every inch of exposed skin with her eyes, in love with the muscles and curves, thinking how absurd it was that anyone could ever consider Whitney's body "not ideal" for a gymnast because her shoulders and hips weren't narrow enough.

Whitney hummed a laugh, tracing the hinge of Andy's jaw with a thumb. "Are you even listening to me?"

"Of course I am. I'm just used to my parents being workaholics. Besides, you know they never make a big thing of birthdays, even when they don't have to work."

"I know. And I know you have goals, dreams. We both do. Just promise I get to be right here when they all come true."

"Right here?" Andy quirked a brow, dropping a hand to Whitney's ass as she shifted beneath her.

"I mean, together, the two of us. But..." Whitney chuckled, nudging Andy to lie back onto the bed before brushing their lips together. "You know I never say no to being on top."

Kasey's voice drew her back to the present. "I'm serious, Andy."

"I know, Kase." Andy squeezed her eyes shut, forcing the recollection back into the mental lockbox that had been threatening to implode for years before looking at Kasey again. "Why do people keep saying that to me like I came back to destroy her life? I'm here for *work*. And weren't you the one who said she should be on my apology tour or whatever you called it? That kind of requires me to talk to her." She let her rising annoyance drift away with a sigh. "Look, I'm glad she's doing great. I'm glad she has someone. Is it so hard to believe I want all those things for her too?"

"No, it's not." Kasey shook her head. "Because you loved her. You *still* love her. That's exactly why I'm telling you, Andy."

"Of course I love her. She was my best friend."

Kasey pressed a palm to her chest in faux hurt. "Pretend for a second I'm not wounded you said that to my face."

"You were both my best friends." Andy rolled her eyes.

"Can you honestly say she's not the reason you suddenly want to stay longer?"

"My parents are getting old, Kase. My mom was thirty-four when I was born. Dad, even older. I'm going to be thirty this year. You do the math."

"Andy, tonight is supposed to be fun. No one said anything about math."

"My point is, seeing them three times a year for the last six years doesn't feel like enough anymore. Never seeing you, and yes, never seeing..." She trailed off, her throat tight with a whirlwind of unprompted emotion. "Whitney is part of the reason, but not all of it. I am under no illusions that she wants me in her life that way again. Like you said, there's a reason it didn't work. So you can all stop worrying so much."

Drinks emerged in front of them, and Kasey immediately reached for her bright yellow cocktail, a slice of dehydrated lime fixed to the rim. She took a sip, smacked her lips, then bobbed her head in approval. "What *did* you mean earlier? Who else has said something about it?"

Andy reached for her own rocks glass, the amber liquid

inside it tinged red with floating strawberry bites. "I may have had a run-in with her sister."

Kasey's brow shot up. "You riled up Avery? Shit. She's literally the nicest person in San Francisco."

"Right. I'm sure that's a verified assessment." Andy clenched her jaw, petulant. "And she wasn't riled up so much as she was... shrewdly menacing?"

"I could see that." Kasey sniggered.

Andy smiled, taking another sip of her drink. If it wasn't because Avery seemed to be straddling the line between indifference and not liking her at all, Andy might've been a little more impressed too. Still, tonight wasn't about Avery—or Whit. It was about rebuilding her and Kasey's friendship. "Are you ever going to tell me what happened between you and Rafa?"

"Andrea Vahnnn," Kasey drew out her name in a way Andy could've easily mistaken for a drunken slur if they weren't only halfway through their first round of drinks. "What part of 'fun night out' didn't you understand?"

"Fine." Andy held up a hand. "I just—I know I was the one who..." She cleared her throat, still coming to terms with referring to her leaving this way. "Disappeared. But I want you to know—"

"I was pregnant."

Andy stilled, mouth slightly agape as she blinked at Kasey. "Oh."

"Then I chose not to be. It was—" Kasey gulped, picking at her nails as she stared down at the bar. "Do I want to be someone's super cool aunt someday? Absolutely. But I'm not a mom, Andy. I've never wanted to be a mom. And I know that wasn't the only option. I know there's adoption and—"

"Hey." Andy reached for Kasey's hand, dipping her head to meet Kasey's eyes. "You made the decision that was best for you. You don't have to justify that for me. You shouldn't have to justify it for anyone."

Kasey scoffed. "You'd think so."

"I'm guessing Rafael didn't agree."

"No, he did. To a point, anyway."

"What do you mean?" Andy frowned, tilting her head.

"I mean, for some people, two decades of Sunday mass and letting his mom weigh in on everything comes with a heavy dose of guilt. We stayed together after. I guess he just... never got over it."

Andy's eyes fell shut. "I'm so sorry, Kase." She wanted to say she was sorry she hadn't been there. She *was* sorry, but she was also acutely aware that her being there probably wouldn't have made it any easier for her friend. Maybe she should've been there anyway. What were friends for if not to hold each other up in the moments when life got in the way of love?

"It's fine," Kasey mumbled. "Some days I don't even think about it anymore. Not like I used to. Whit really kept me afloat then. Held my hand, dried my tears, checked in like clockwork every single day. So if it seems like I'm being hard on you, it's because I know firsthand that she has a heart of gold but it shatters like glass."

Andy glanced across the lounge floor to find Whitney's eyes still trained her way, scrutinizing yet strangely vulnerable. She returned Whitney's stare, powerless to do anything else. But it lasted all of two seconds before Whitney pushed a strand of her dark hair behind one ear and focused on Isabelle.

Andy turned back to Kasey, her chest clenching as she locked eyes with the shimmering pair awaiting hers. "I promise I'm not going to hurt her," she murmured, "and I promise to never not be here for you again."

Kasey glanced skyward in an attempt to keep the tears rimming her eyes from falling. "Fuck, Andy. We really need to reassess your definition of a girls' night."

Andy laughed, sliding forward on her stool to swipe her thumbs beneath Kasey's eyes. "Hey, 'no crying in the club' was always your mantra."

Kasey dropped her head back in a vibrant laugh, taking Andy's wrists in both hands when she looked at her again. "I'm really glad you're here."

"I'm really glad I'm here too."

She pointed a stern finger Andy's way despite the grin still lighting her face and her glimmering eyes. "But I'm still mad at you."

Andy scoffed a laugh. "Wouldn't have it any other way, Kase."

10

Isabelle got to her feet, her close-lipped smile graceful if somber as she smoothed the front of her gray bodycon dress with one hand. The other held on to Whitney's. "If I'm being honest, I invited you here tonight knowing how this talk would end but hoping you would change your mind."

Whitney's brows drew together. Their conversation had gone as well as she'd imagined, even if the waiter had taken both her plate of flautas and Isabelle's chopped Caesar salad back to the kitchen almost completely untouched when they'd requested the bill. She was almost afraid to ask, afraid to disrupt the tenuous maybe-we're-better-as-friends balance that lingered between them, but she had to know. "What do you mean?"

Isabelle glanced down at their loosely linked hands before meeting Whitney's gaze again. "At the hospital, before I got called away, you said I was perfect. Everything you *should* want. Not everything you do."

"Isabelle, I—"

"It's okay. I understand, trust me." She spared a glance

toward the bar, prompting Whitney to notice that both Kasey and Andy were no longer there.

Compulsion had lured Whitney's gaze toward them more times than she cared to admit. She wasn't sure if it was because, even from a distance, the visual tone of their conversation seemed to have run the gamut from cheerful banter and slaps on the arm to something more subdued before looping back to Kasey's vibrant cackle of a laugh and Andy's subtler, enthralling one.

"I guess I'll be seeing you around at W," said Isabelle.

Whitney blinked, the words drawing her attention back to the woman in front of her. "About that. I can have your membership fee reversed if you'd rather not—I mean—"

"Don't be ridiculous." Isabelle's smile stretched wider, though the slight tilt of her head seemed almost condescending. "We're both adults. Besides, I'm not ready to give up those steam rooms."

Whitney hummed a laugh. "In that case, can I interest you in our latest promo? Thirty percent off your next annual membership."

"Nice try." Isabelle reached for her clutch, winking as she turned on the heels of her Louboutins. "Good night, Whitney."

"Bye, Isabelle." Whitney watched her leave before pressing her fingers to her eyes and dropping her head back, groaning a frustrated, "Oh, Whitney," to herself. Even knowing she'd made the right decision, the hint of disappointment slinking around her head left her feeling like she hadn't tried hard enough. Still, she'd been telling herself that for almost two months, and the romantic connection she craved with another person felt so far out of reach she was afraid she'd never truly experience it again.

As she started for the restroom—a quick stop to wash

her hands and check her reflection—she tried to remember if it had always been this hard, connecting with someone. Had dating always been a whirlwind of fleeting hits, lasting misses, and resounding doubts? Or had time and experience exaggerated her expectations to the point of self-sabotage?

A rush of running water greeted her as she stepped into the bathroom. The whiff of sweet citrus in the air—lemons or bergamot—was a welcomed surprise, especially when she walked up to the first available vessel sink and drew in a long breath. Full-length mirrors spanned the entire wall, reflecting the pair of women two sinks down as they swapped lipstick shades, then went to work applying them. The buoyancy echoing from their exchange held notes of a night still brimming with possibilities—it *was* barely ten— but Whitney's mind was already leaping toward the simple comforts of a long day coming to an end. She was eager to curl up on the sofa with Wes and watch videos of her favorite gymnastics floor routines, or indulge in the cuteness overload of Jax's daily picture of baby Maddox, which always came with a caption along the lines of "This kid never sleeps, I swear."

Had Andy and Kasey turned in for the night too? Or had Kasey swayed Andy toward a night of midweek barhopping that would leave her grouchy and adorably hungover in the morning?

"Hey."

For a second, Whitney resented her brain for so perfectly capturing the delicate tenor of Andy's voice. Then someone emerged at the sink next to hers—long fingers adorned with mismatched rings on the thumb and middle finger steady beneath the running tap, smooth arms left on display by a cropped racerback tank, and only a sliver of skin bridging the gap to high-waisted jeans that hugged subtle curves.

Whitney's own hands went still beneath the water as their eyes locked in the mirror, Andy's soft with traces of a smile, her pupils on the verge of swallowing the ring of meadowy brown that never failed to hold Whitney's attention a second too long. Her brows twitched in awareness that she was staring, and she shook her hands, stepping toward the paper towel dispenser. "I thought you and Kasey already left."

"We're about to. She's already outside." Andy crossed the tiles and stopped in front of Whitney, close enough for the sweet and spicy hints of cardamom on her skin to flood Whitney's senses. A curly, dark strand from Andy's pixie cut nestled against her brow, teasing the tips of her thick lashes, and Whitney fisted her hand against the urge to reach up and sweep away the lock of hair. "I, um—" A visible gulp moved down Andy's throat. "Can I just...?"

"What?" The word left Whitney's lips faint as a whisper.

Andy reached up, locking Whitney between her arm and the wall as she yanked a towel from the dispenser. "Grab one of these."

"Oh. Sorry." Whitney dropped her own towel in the trash and jolted backward, needing to put some space between them. Even so, her eyes insisted on studying the subtle flex of Andy's biceps. The missing leather jacket that would've completed Andy's ensemble was inconvenient if not outright distracting. Yet it wasn't nearly as astounding as the small, dark scribble of a word next to Andy's clavicle. *Brave.* Since when was Andy Vahn into tattoos?

"Good date?" Andy asked.

Whitney tilted her head, frowning.

"With Isabelle. I'm guessing she's waiting for you."

"Oh. No." Whitney blinked, clearing the haze in her mind. "She already left."

"Hmm. Well..." Andy hooked a thumb over her shoulder, her free hand disappearing into her back pocket. "I should probably get out of here before Kasey starts getting impatient. I'm sure you know what that's like."

Impulse spurred Whitney forward. "Wait, what was that?"

"What was what?" Andy asked slowly, eyes squinted.

"That hum. When I told you Isabelle left already."

"Nothing." She shrugged. "Just a hum, I guess."

"You never just hum, Andy."

Her lips parted, then closed, eyes wandering as if in search of the right words. "It's really nothing."

"Then just say it."

"Whitney—"

"Just say it, Andy!"

"She's a doctor!" Andy licked her lips, and the muscles in her jaw tensed, suppressing the outburst two seconds too late. "I guess... I don't know. I can't really see it. Someone like you with someone like her... which is stupid because I don't know her at all."

"You're right," Whitney snapped. "You don't know her, and as someone who hasn't been in my life for six years, I don't really think it's your business to *see* anything in my relationships, Andy."

"You asked," she said softly.

"I did. My mistake." Whitney whirled toward the door, only then realizing that the two women who'd been debating their lipstick choices had left, abandoning her and Andy to the solitude of old patterns and too many unsaid words.

"Whitney, wait!"

She knew her reaction wasn't fair—she *had* asked—but the familiarity, maybe even judgment, in Andy's tone had poked a hornet's nest of emotions that had been dormant for years. Maybe that was the worst part about tonight. She hadn't even been able to give a hundred percent to her own fucking breakup because apparently there were no other lounge bars in all South of Market and Andy just had to be here.

She tugged on the handle of the bathroom door, yanking it open a second before Andy's palm forced it shut with a thud.

The moment stretched, audible breaths in the stillness of the room, Andy so close Whitney could lean into her without having to take a single step back. The hairs on the back of her neck rose at Andy's whispered, "Whit, I'm sorry."

Andy's hand fell from the door, and Whitney turned, her four-inch booties leaving them at eye level. The moment felt fraught with déjà vu—not because of their proximity or the race of Whitney's pulse, but because she wasn't sure what Andy was apologizing for, like she hadn't been sure that night at W.

"I was out of line. I shouldn't have said that. I don't know anything about it. I don't know anything about anything. Just—" Her tongue darted out to lick her lips again, and Whitney's eyes clung to the sheen left in its wake. "I was never any good at this."

"At what?" Whitney asked, this breath a little shorter than her last.

"Fighting with you."

"That's not what we're doing."

Andy's gaze drifted to Whitney's mouth before flicking back to her eyes. "Then what are we doing?"

Whitney's stomach clenched as something treacherous swelled within her, nudging her closer to an exploration of dormant desires and certain danger. She surrendered to the aching need to reach up and brush away the lock of hair threatening to impede Andy's vision, ignoring the shiver down her spine when the tips of her fingers grazed Andy's jaw and a faint catch of breath echoed between them.

Then she turned for the door. "Say hi to Kasey for me."

BETWEEN ANOTHER FAILED SHOT at romance, having her cervix prodded and examined, then losing three more trainers to the cold Robbie had assured Whitney was an "allergy flare-up," this week was kicking Whitney's ass. She'd never been more grateful for having Friday evenings be one of W's slower periods, but she was nearing ten hours of back-to-back classes from spin to Pilates to peewee gymnastics. She still had two hours left in her day, including an hour-long one-on-one with her least favorite white-collar client. With some clients, conversation during personal training came almost as naturally as instruction, but she wasn't sure she had it in her to pretend to care about one more monologue on how "game-changing" NFTs and crypto were.

She was beginning to think White Collar didn't even need one-on-one sessions. Half the men who walked into W with serious aspirations of getting fitter or bulking up took one look at her five feet, four inches frame and decided Jax or any of the four other male trainers on staff would be a better fit. She'd been in the business long enough that the occurrence no longer provoked her to grumbled debates over whether sexism or her being sexualized was to blame, but there were moments in the three months since she'd been training White Collar when she'd decided he hadn't requested her out of any lack of prejudice. He just preferred the captive audience of a woman.

With less than an hour left before she had to meet him on the strength floor, she debated whether her time would be better spent catching up on emails, running down to the juice bar to see how Kasey and Daphne had been juggling Jax's managerial duties, or locking herself in the free studio downstairs and blowing off some steam with an unchoreographed dance.

Her phone skittered across her desk, and she glanced down at it to find an incoming video call from her mom. *Shit.* A quick tap of the answer button launched her mom's face into focus—full, round cheeks, snub nose, and gleaming, brown skin almost identical to hers.

"God, Mom, I'm so sorry. I was about to call earlier, and then the repair technician showed up. *An hour late,*" she emphasized. "I would've rescheduled, but we really needed that leg abduction machine looked at and—"

"Breathe, honeybee." Mom's soft laugh echoed through the speakers of her phone, and it occurred to Whitney, not for the first time, that there had only ever been two people who could quiet her overwhelmed rambling with a mere utterance and a laugh. Thankfully, her mother was still the only one who insisted on calling her *honeybee.* "It's okay," said Mom. "I know you wouldn't have missed our call if it wasn't important."

"Well, is there still time?" The glimpse of a navy blue, collarless blazer and crisp, white shirt gave away that Mom was still dressed for work, especially with her makeup tastefully but purposefully understated and the springy curls of her black-to-gray ombre hair artfully swept into a bun.

"Wait, you just got home? I thought you said he'd be there at eight."

A quick peek at the clock said it was barely after seven, which was plenty of time for most people, but there was a reason Mom had requested Whitney's help getting ready for this date—her first in ten years. Perpetual lateness had yet to be classified as a genetic trait, but Whitney was pretty sure her tendency to be at least ten minutes behind schedule had come from one Catherine Hughes.

"What do you mean?" Mom dropped her chin, studying her own appearance before looking up at the camera again. "This isn't what I wore to work today."

One corner of Whitney's lips ticked up in a smile. "Mom, you were literally wearing that blazer when I came by the hotel for lunch last month. It's a work blazer, not a date blazer."

"Well, can't it be multipurpose?" Mom grimaced, flinching back.

"Sure, but date-night blazer outfits are kind of tricky territory."

"Maybe I should just cancel." She sighed.

"No, no. Let's not do that. You're a knockout in anything you wear, anyway. That's why you're always fighting off all those wealthy tycoon types."

"Hotel staff isn't permitted to fraternize with guests, Whitney. Being a manager doesn't exempt me from that."

"Yes, but Cillian isn't a guest, and you said it yourself: no one has made you laugh like he does in years. It doesn't matter what you wear as long as you're comfortable."

Another self-inspection accompanied Mom's resolute, "I'm comfortable."

Whitney raised her brows. "And you feel sexy?"

"Whitney, I am fifty-six years old. Feeling sexy isn't on my list of priorities."

"Halle Berry, Kelly Hu, Salma Hayek, Laverne Cox, Gillian Anderson—"

"Are you naming women in their fifties?"

"*Hot* women in their fifties, Mom. You're a hot woman in her fifties. Own it. And considering you're literally not allowed to leave me for another four decades minimum, I refuse to aid and abet this one-foot-in-the-grave, self-depreciative gibberish."

Mom tossed her head back in a contagious laugh that left Whitney no choice but to join in. Maybe she'd had the worst day—week, even—and maybe she was still frustrated over how things had ended with Isabelle. Maybe she was over failing at dating and not knowing why, but her mom deserved everything good the world had to give. If an Irish man ten years her junior who insisted *Seinfeld* was still the funniest show he'd ever seen happened to be one of those good things, Whitney would sit on an endless number of pre-date calls until Mom felt comfortable enough to get back out there. In his own way, Dad had done his best by Whitney, but this woman was her day one. This woman had somehow managed to both work full-time and *always* be there. She'd put her own life second so Whitney could come first more often than she even realized.

Mom's laughter faded with a whimper of mirth, and shimmering dark eyes stared back at Whitney. "Fine. Yes, I feel sexy."

Whitney snapped her fingers in approval. "That's what I like to hear."

A moment passed, Mom's expression undergoing the slow but brief trek to a more somber one, and Whitney could almost guess the question before it came. "Have you been sleeping okay? You look a little tired."

"I've been sleeping fine. I've just had a few longer days this week. Should be more settled by next Friday."

"Right." Mom nodded. "Well, I'll take Wes this weekend if you need a break. I got him one of those puzzle things that dispenses treats when he gets it right."

"He has enough toys, Mom." Whitney laughed. Every time her mother got Wes a new toy, which tended to be about once a month, she'd both lament and warm at the thought of how spoiled her future children would be, having two grandparents who'd let them have whatever they wanted. She used to think at least Andy's parents would level it out, being more practical, frugal people, but she hadn't allowed the thought to cross her mind in years. Why had it slipped in now?

"This is the last one, I promise," said Mom, a flagrant if endearing lie. "They said it's good for brain development."

"Wes is entirely too smart for his own good, but who am I to stand in the way of a grandmother and her grandpup's brain development?" A banner notification popped up at the top of her phone screen, previewing a text from Avery. She tapped it, mumbling, "One sec, Mom."

Avery (6:21 p.m.)
We may be losing Val to the dark side -eye roll emoji-

Whitney's lips curved into a skeptical smile despite the dip between her brows. Before she managed to type out a reply, her phone buzzed again.

Valentina (6:21 p.m.)
I trust you to see whatever Ave just sent you for exactly what it is.

Slander on my good name.

It took a moment for the realization to set in that both

texts could only be about one thing, especially since Whitney had purposefully ignored the knowledge that today was Andy's first official walkthrough at Gia in preparation to start filming next week. Knowing Andy, she'd studied every inch of the restaurant, mentally prepared her angles and shots, and formulated a strategy for how it would all work with the restaurant at full occupancy. Knowing Andy, she'd already won over at least three employees with nothing but her cool, leather-jacketed demeanor and unwitting charm, with the rest of Gia's staff to fall like dominos within the coming days.

But it wasn't until Mom casually uttered, "You'd never guess who I ran into yesterday," that Whitney decided it was all a goddamn conspiracy.

Andy Vahn was inescapable.

11

*A*ndy exited the revolving door into W's lobby, scanning it for any sign of Whitney. The person standing behind the black marble desk perked up, their eyes trained Andy's way in anticipation of a professional greeting, but she glanced left toward the juice bar on the off chance that Whitney might've been there instead. No luck. She tightened her grip on the cappuccino in one hand and the bag of pomegranate dark chocolate bites in the other.

A casual comment from Kasey about how swamped they all were at the gym since Jax's baby had been born two weeks early, and how Whitney had been spiraling to keep everything in perfect order, led Andy to believe she might still be at work, even if it was after seven on a Friday. Still, the same part of her that had left Gia thinking a surprise visit with Whitney's favorite coffee and chocolatey snack might be what she needed to close out a long week was starting to think this was a terrible idea. They weren't show-up-with-snacks people in each other's lives anymore. In fact, they were so far from it, Andy wouldn't be surprised if her presence only pissed Whitney off further, especially after what had happened at the bar earlier that week.

They hadn't talked about it, but Andy couldn't just do nothing. Doing nothing wasn't in her DNA. Besides, the constant push and pull was the only familiar thing about them.

"Welcome to W," the clerk said. "I'm Robbie. How can I help you today?"

"Is Whitney still around?"

"I think so, yeah. Probably holed up in her office, though." Robbie grimaced, holding up one finger before swiping up a landline receiver in his other hand. "Who should I say is asking?"

"Andy. But if it's okay," she blurted out, then paused as he abandoned his dialing to look up at her. "If it's okay, I'd rather you not call her away from what she's doing. I was just hoping to drop these off and maybe say hi."

"Andy." He mulled over the name like he was trying to place it in his mind, verify whether he'd ever heard it before.

"I'm an old friend."

Robbie quirked a brow. "An old friend who knows where her office is?"

"I do, actually. I was here just last week." The circumstances of which were need-to-know. Andy decided Robbie did not need to know.

"Awesome. She could use the pick-me-up." He gestured Andy closer, one hand shielding his mouth as she cautiously moved within whisper range. "She's been a little... *intense* this week. We had our fifth gym baby, and Jax is out. You know Jax, right?"

Andy nodded, struggling to keep her expression neutral despite her rising skepticism about where Robbie was going with this. She already knew the part about Jax's baby from

Kasey, but should Robbie be telling her—a virtual stranger—personal details about why his boss had been, as he'd coined it, intense?

"Him and Whit go, like, way back," said Robbie. "I think she may be a little sad he'll be out for a while. Plus, I'm kind of worried she hates me for getting half the trainers sick. But I thought it was allergies, you know? Pollen season isn't for another month and a half, but I *never* get sick. Like, ever. It was an honest mistake."

"Mm-hm."

"So maybe do me a solid and tell her I personally sent you up?" He grinned, pressing clasped hands to his mouth.

Andy debated telling him how ill-advised this plan to get back into Whitney's good graces was when she herself wasn't sure how it would unfold. But unlike Robbie, bless him, she was not in the business of spilling her guts to people she'd met two minutes ago. She shot him a smile, starting toward the short hallway off the lobby. "I'll let her know. Thanks, Robbie."

She bypassed the elevator, hoping the two-floor walk up to Whitney's office would quell a bit of the unease creeping through her. Their relationship had always been a delicate balance between pushing too hard and pushing just enough. Maybe applying the rules of engagement from back then wasn't the answer, but it wasn't like they could meet in the middle the way they usually did either. Not that they hadn't gotten close. There were moments in the brief time they'd shared together when the look in Whitney's eyes said a bruising kiss, ripped clothes, and sure yet trembling hands were the only right answer. But Andy wasn't immune to the vortex that was wishful thinking, no matter how hard she tried to avoid it. She didn't need that anyway—the craving, the fire, the unbridled lust. She just wanted

Whitney back in her life in whatever capacity Whitney was okay with.

Andy's steps slowed as she neared the office, eyes glued to the dark shades shrouding the otherwise clear view afforded by walls made almost entirely of glass. Did that mean Whitney wasn't inside or simply that she didn't want to be bothered?

Andy bit the inside of her cheek, glancing up and down the empty hallway. Maybe she should've called. No, she *definitely* should have called. The warmth seeping through the cardboard sleeve on the coffee cup intensified as if to signal that carrying it around indefinitely had not been the plan. She could head back to her car and drink it herself. Pomegranate chocolate bites didn't exactly appeal to her sweet tooth, but maybe she could make an exception.

She turned to leave before clenching her jaw and whirling back toward the door.

Get it together, Vahn. It's just Whitney.

Whitney, who had been her best friend for years before Andy had even allowed herself to consider how her lips would feel; the way they pillowed, plush and soft, against Andy's before pressing firmer in tandem with Whitney's tightening grip on Andy's hips...

Andy squeezed her eyes shut, grasping the paper bag tighter as she lifted the same hand to knock on the door. Three days. It had been three days since she and Whitney had argued in the bar's bathroom, and the haze of underlying emotions still hadn't cleared. It wasn't only that the fleeting brush of Whitney's fingers against her jaw had left Andy's skin burning for hours that night. It was that, for a second—Andy could've imagined it, really—Whitney's gaze had swept along her body like it was something she wanted to reacquaint herself with in the most intimate detail. Andy couldn't shake the phantom of it, which was problematic for her quest to revive their friendship, but—

The door swung open. "Robbie, it's really okay—" Whitney cut herself off, lines creasing her forehead. "Andy?"

Andy questioned exactly how many times Robbie had tried to talk to Whitney today, but decided she'd do him a solid by *not* mentioning he'd been the one to send her up. Her concern for him all but dissipated when her eyes drifted to the sports bra hugging Whitney's chest, her open track jacket leaving the toned muscles of her abdomen on full display, especially given how she was standing with one hand still braced against the door. High-waisted leggings and neon pink sneakers completed the look. Andy's eyes snapped back to Whitney's in a desperate attempt to make her appraisal of Whitney's body seem a little less obvious.

"Hey." The husk in her voice was a dead giveaway.

Whitney's firm eye contact and slightly parted lips said as much. She turned, crossing the tiled floor back to her desk. "I'm busy, Andy."

"I know." Andy rushed in, shutting the door behind her. "I just wanted to drop these off and maybe make sure we're okay. After the other night."

Whitney ignored the high-back chair in favor of hunching to click at the cordless mouse seemingly connected to the open laptop on her desk, a position that made her cleavage too much of a focal point from where Andy stood. Her eyes flicked up to Andy's before narrowing to the laptop screen again. "Is that a cappuccino?"

"Your favorite." Andy bit down on a smile, slipping both the coffee and the paper bag onto Whitney's desk in offering. "I also got dark chocolate pomegranate bites."

"I'm off coffee. It's a New Year's resolution thing I'm

doing with my sister." Her hand shot up, and she squeezed her eyes shut as if to reject her brain's impulse to explain. "Never mind. I'm at work. I may own it, run it, whatever, but I'm still at work. You can't just show up here, Andy."

"That's fair."

"Don't. You cannot just show up here with your sneaky rational charm and expect me to drop everything for you."

"We both know I'm not sneaky, and I'm definitely not charming. Andy chuckled.

Whitney shot her a look.

"Okay, okay." A breath escaped Andy's lips, and she took a moment to choose her words so her frustration didn't get the better of her. She hadn't expected it to be easy—coming back home, talking to Whitney—but it was beginning to feel like every small step in this uphill climb was being thwarted by Andy's ruthless tendency to put her foot in her own mouth, which wasn't even an inclination she'd thought she had. If anything, Whitney had always been more prone to rambling or saying things she'd later wished she hadn't. This new Whitney radiated a quiet confidence and not-so-quiet rage guarding walls Andy no longer knew how to get past. She was almost intimidating, which Andy somehow found... excruciatingly sexy?

Warmth spread beneath Andy's shirt, her leather jacket exaggerating the sensation. "You're right. Clearly this wasn't a good idea. I'm going to go."

A scoff drowned out the dull echo of her first step. "Of course you are. Let me get the door." Whitney rounded her desk, brushing by Andy to take the handle of the door in her grip and hold it open.

Andy's laugh slipped out with a razor-sharp edge. "You don't want me to stay, but now you're mad I'm leaving?"

"No." Whitney's lips pursed. "Because the thing is, Andy,

you are brilliant at a lot of things, and leaving isn't the least of them."

A boulder settled in Andy's stomach. She'd taken all the jabs from Kasey—*leaving, disappearing, ghosting*. It's not like she could blame her. There were times in the last six years when she'd quieted her yearning only with the idea that she'd done what she had to in order to become who she'd always dreamed of being. She'd told herself it was okay if people didn't understand. Still, in her most sincere moments—late at night when her brain was too exhausted to fight off the ever-looming nostalgia—memories of the touch and smell of Whitney's skin and the melody of her laugh would coil around Andy's heart like barbed wire. Every muscle in her body would ache with *knowing*.

Leaving the way she had was probably the one thing Whitney could never forgive.

She hadn't consciously avoided talking about it. She'd said *I'm sorry* twice already only for the rest to get stuck in the back of her throat and for apprehension to poison her resolve. Perhaps there was also a part of her that was content, hopeful, that Whitney would want to leave it in the past.

Andy took slow steps to close the gap between them. "Fine. Then let's talk about it."

"I *don't* want to talk about it."

"Then what, Whit? Tell me what to do. Tell me what you want. Whatever it is, I'll do it."

"Just go, Andy."

"No." Andy dipped her head to meet Whitney's gaze, both hands coming up to cradle her face. Tense muscles and glossy, brown eyes met Andy's touch. She braced herself for the backlash, for Whitney to pull away, scream at her, remind her that she didn't get to have Whitney this close.

Not anymore. Maybe never again. It didn't make her sound any less breathless when the plea rolled off her tongue. "Please just tell me."

It happened all at once—the hand darting to the back of her neck, lips crashing into hers, Whitney relinquishing her grip on the door to back into it and pull Andy against her. Andy gasped, and a groan rumbled between their lips as fingers threaded through her tapered curls to scratch at her scalp. Whitney's free hand dropped to her hip, slipping beneath Andy's shirt to provoke the heat rapidly unspooling between her thighs.

"Whit—"

Showing up unannounced had played out in several ways in Andy's mind on the way over. Fire and fury among them. But this... The hot glide of Whitney's tongue slipping into her mouth as blunt nails bit into the skin at the small of her back was way beyond the scope of anything she'd imagined.

"I feel like we should really"—her breath caught at the brush of lips beneath the lobe of her ear—"*really* be using our words right now."

Whitney pulled back, pupils pitch-black and blown, lips Andy's favorite shade of red. "Are you asking me to stop?"

"Is that a trick question?" Andy's brows snapped together, breaths escaping her in shallow pants. "I mean, no. I don't want to stop." They probably should. Stopping seemed about the smartest thing Andy could do to preserve an already tenuous reconciliation, but being smart required the kind of fortitude she simply didn't possess with Whitney's hand still on her waist and her lips so close Andy could smell the hint of vanilla on her breath. "I'm just... a little confused?"

Darkened eyes narrowed to Andy's. "About what?"

Andy braced one hand against Whitney's tensing abdomen, then circled her navel with a finger. "This, for starters."

"Well, I was kissing you. It kind of felt like you were enjoying it."

"You know I was."

"We're on the same page then." Whitney pushed off the door and pressed Andy against it in one fluid motion. Between Andy's four-inch height advantage and the deliciously insistent pressure of Whitney's body, Andy was ready and willing to be climbed any second now.

They *were* on the same page. Just... "Maybe in different books?"

"Remember our second year in college?" Whitney panted. "When you spent a week holed up in your dorm finishing your film for that showcase? I was getting up at four every day to get in extra training for the NCAA championships. We just kept snapping at each other. Three fights in three days, but I *needed* to see you."

"Whitney." Andy squirmed, pulse throbbing between her legs. The memory flickered into focus, severing her dwindling grip on reason with visceral visions of herself pressed against a wall, desperate as a palm dragged up her inner thigh beneath the flimsy cotton of her shorts to find her wet and aching.

"Remember how you begged me to fuck you? How you came shuddering with your eyes rolled back and my hand over your mouth? How much better we both felt after getting it out of our systems?"

"Is that what this is? Getting it out of your system?" Andy asked, unsure what she wanted Whitney's answer to be.

"I can't *think* straight, Andy. I want to be over it. I want us to be friends, but all I want to do is scream every time we're in the same room, and I'm too emotionally exhausted to scream or fight or—"

This time it was Andy's mouth cutting off the explanation, Andy's hands tugging at Whitney's track jacket to caress her warm, silken skin and palm her breasts over the smooth fabric of her sports bra. Her nipples peaked, the echoing moan reverberating through Andy's body straight down to her core.

Fingers worked at the button of her jeans, undoing her zipper in a blur as she discarded her own jacket to the floor. "Tuesday," Whitney mumbled.

Andy swallowed hard. "What?"

"My last checkup. All good."

"Oh. *Fuck*. Um." She fumbled through the fog in her mind for a date. "Six—no, seven. Seven months ago. I haven't been with anyone since. Work has been—" The words choked off as fingers slid over her trimmed curls to circle her clit. She had the strangest feeling there was something she was forgetting to say or ask.

Not that she could summon an ounce of focus on anything but the pressure between her thighs and Whitney's murmured, "You're shaking."

"I know, I know." One hand curled into the waistband of Whitney's leggings in search of something—*anything*—to hold on to. The other wove through her silky, black hair, coaxing a whimper from her. It was too soon for Andy's body to be this on edge, but Whitney didn't have any intention of going easy on her, and apparently, six years hadn't left her any less susceptible to how outrageously good Whitney was at taking her apart. All unassuming dominance and skilled fingers and—

"Do you want me inside you?"

"Now, please." Andy pushed at her own jeans and underwear, shoving them farther down her thighs and stepping out of them, groaning when the pressure of Whitney's fingers disappeared from her clit.

Something slotted into place, something like a door being latched, then Whitney was pulling her forward. "Come here."

Andy closed the gap between them, pressing her lips to Whitney's as they stumbled across the office, only breaking their kiss when her fumbling hands garnered a grip steady enough to yank Whitney's sports bra over her head. Her gaze dropped to the full, round breasts, lips parting at the nipples awaiting her tongue and teeth.

Whitney fell back onto the sofa, dark eyes trained up at Andy as she patted her lap in silent command.

Andy held her stare, positioning a knee on either side of Whitney's hips to straddle her. The heat from her thighs and the smooth fabric of her leggings signaled that even in the haze of kissing, grappling hands, and discarded clothes, there was still a full outfit between them both. Andy's top was still on; Whitney's pants too. Instead of fixating on the absurdity of it, Andy cradled Whitney's jaw, thumb tracing her kiss-swollen lips as a prelude to her mouth.

A hand settled on her ass as the other slid between her thighs, two fingers gliding through her slit and into her with zero resistance. "Fuck, Andy."

"Oh my God." Andy pressed their foreheads together, hips grinding down of their own accord. She dropped one hand to Whitney's breast and tweaked a nipple, in love with the moan it elicited, the way Whitney's grip tightened and she crooked her fingers before driving them deeper. Heat bore down on Andy's back despite the air conditioning fighting to combat the buildup of sex and writhing desperation in the room.

"You're already so close. You're so close I can feel it."

Andy's thighs quaked, and she scrunched her eyes shut.

Whitney breathed a chuckle against her neck, almost as if she'd deciphered Andy's desperation to stave off the crash. She didn't want to think about what came next, what came after the shock wave of pleasure surging through her veins. She wasn't ready to go back to not being able to have Whitney like this, and maybe this hadn't only been reckless, but it had been really fucking stupid. Getting it out of their systems could never apply to this. Not to them. Not for Andy.

Whitney's thumb circled her clit, and she mumbled the words against Andy's mouth. "It's okay, baby. You can come for me. I *want* you to come for me."

Spots flashed behind Andy's closed eyes. She crumpled forward, biting down on Whitney's shoulder as a cry rose in her throat. The orgasm crested and rippled through her, curling her toes as she clenched around Whitney's fingers. The hand between her thighs went still, and aftershocks darted through her body to speckle her skin with goose bumps. She opened her eyes to find Whitney already staring, her expression reverent, lips parted in awe, emotions so out of place considering what *she* had just done to Andy's body.

Still, it was the delicate press of her lips and brush of knuckles against her cheek that cracked Andy's chest open, forced her to stop, to rewire her brain before the three words clawing up the walls of her throat tumbled out. Whitney had been clear on what this was. However reminiscent of their past this felt, it wasn't *that*.

There was still one thing she needed to know. "Tell me I

get to reciprocate that. Tell me I get to make you feel even a fraction of what I'm feeling right now."

"Andy, I..." The way Whitney squirmed beneath her had Andy's imagination running wild with thoughts of getting on her knees and finally getting Whitney out of those tights, kissing and biting a trail to her center.

"I just need you to say it, Whit. Say it and I won't stop until my name is the only thing you remember."

A faint ringing and buzzing stirred up, snapping both their gazes to the watch on Whitney's left wrist.

"Shit." Whitney's eyes fell shut, and she dropped her head back against the sofa, the expanse of her neck taunting Andy with a light sheen of sweat. Her eyes darted back to Andy's, the urgency in them clear. "I, um—"

"You have to go." Andy never thought words whispered from her own lips could hit like a sucker punch. The idea of Whitney leaving *now* when Andy's limbs still felt like Jell-O and she was seconds away from reacquainting herself with the taste of Whitney had her body wound tight with lingering desire. But it wasn't just that. The immediacy of her having to go before they'd even caught their breaths made what they'd just shared feel somehow... transactional? She stood from Whitney's lap with as much composure as she could muster, keeping her eyes glued to the floor when she went in search of her jeans and underwear.

"Andy."

"It's okay. I get it. You're at work. You said that earlier."

A hand wrapped around her arm, tugging so they were face to face. "Stop. Please? I want to talk about this. We should—fuck, Andy. I'm so sorry. I should never have—"

Andy shook her head, cutting Whitney off. "I can handle you having to go. I hate it, but work I understand. What we just did... I could never regret that. No matter what we are to each other now. The one thing that would hurt is if you did."

"I don't regret it, Andy. I just don't want you to—" She dragged a hand through her hair, neglecting to finish the statement.

Gears in Andy's mind worked to uncover the missing words. Whitney didn't want her to what? Get the wrong impression? Drive herself crazy trying to decode what it meant, like she had the first time Whitney had kissed her, then spent weeks never wanting to talk about it? It wasn't like they were seventeen anymore.

"Let me make it easy. Sometimes, sex is just sex. It doesn't have to be more than that." The words left an acrid taste on her tongue probably because, for the Whitney Andy used to know, sex *always* meant something more, always came with an emotional connection that transcended physical intimacy. But so much was different now. *She* was so different now. "Let's just call this residual tension or something. We were together for a long time. The lines got blurred for a second. It's—"

"Normal," Whitney husked.

"Exactly." A part of Andy was grateful Whitney had finished the thought. It felt less like her trying to rationalize for her own benefit if they were both in agreement.

Another alarm went off, but Whitney neither looked at it nor moved to turn it off. Instead, she stared, her pupils giving way to some of the walnut brown of her irises. Her hair framed her face in messy, dark waves Andy was desperate to run her fingers through all over again, to guide her back onto the couch and finish what they'd started. But she took Whitney's wrist and stopped the alarm bizarrely titled *White Collar*. Then, she pressed a hand to Whitney's tensing stomach, reveling in the feel of her skin as she found the will to nudge her away. "You're going to be late."

"Yeah." Whitney blinked before glancing down at her own still bare chest, the wet mark on her leggings. "I need to, um—I need to wash up and change real quick." She hooked a thumb toward the door at the back right side of her office.

Andy nodded, watching her disappear into what she assumed was a bathroom. She was glad Whitney hadn't asked her to wait. The second she'd gotten her clothes on, the tightness in her throat and her constricting lungs told her she couldn't stay.

12

A soft morning glow stretched over Golden Gate Park despite the sixty-degree chill in the air. Whitney tugged at the shawl collar of her draped knit jacket with one hand, the other locked in a firm grip on Wes's lead. His episodic sniff inspections and steady gait were surprisingly subdued. Walks in the park always had him darting through every patch of verdant lawn and field of wildflowers in a relentless quest to catch that single bee that managed to evade him. Then again, he'd never been much of a morning dog. If anything, he always regarded Whitney's scheduled stumbling out of bed at six a.m. with a low growl and heavy dose of stink eye before burrowing back into the padded comfort of his own oversize bed. Was ten on a Saturday just as bad, or had he sensed that Whitney didn't have the energy to chase him this morning?

Last night, Mom had called to recount her "perfect" date with Cillian, everything from the bouquet of pink and red Asiatic lilies he'd greeted her with to the private music performance and four-course hibachi dinner served between sets. It'd been a welcome reprieve from the thoughts spiraling through Whitney's head, but an hour later, when Mom had said goodbye with a dramatic yawn, it had left Whitney with nothing to distract her from what had happened in her office with Andy.

Visceral recollections of Andy's lips and tongue, hot hands on Whitney's skin and desperate fingers plucking at the waistband of her leggings, crackled through her mind like lightning—sudden, yet so breathtaking she couldn't get the afterimage out of her head if she tried. The bruise on her shoulder hadn't helped. The ripple of pain and pleasure still surged through her when she thought of how Andy only ever bit her that hard when it was so good she wanted to scream. Never mind the traces of vanilla, coffee, and *sex* in the air, or that Whitney had been right on the edge of combusting from the sheer indulgence of it all. She'd lain in bed restless and achingly aroused, and she hadn't done a single thing about it.

As she approached the bench where she'd promised to meet Andy, dog walkers and joggers all along the trail, she reminded herself why they needed to talk, even if talking was the last thing she wanted to do. No signs of Andy, she settled onto the metal-framed bench and gazed down at Wes. "Looks like we're early."

Wes squinted, barking twice.

"Don't even start. You're running on a full eight hours. If anyone should be complaining, it's me."

He cocked his head to one side.

"Now you don't understand what I'm saying?"

A breathy laugh drew Whitney's attention, and she glanced up just in time for Wes to dart toward Andy, skipping and barking and prodding at her knees with tiny paws. One hand swept back the hood of her sweatshirt, revealing messy, dark curls and beaming, hazel eyes as she bent to greet him, ruffling his fur and murmuring private endearments that made Whitney entirely too warm inside.

"Should I be offended you always greet him before even acknowledging me?" she asked.

Andy's brows snapped together. "No? I mean..." She trailed off, waving a hand toward Wes's wide-eyed, tongue-dangling, blissful face. "Just look at him. Besides"—she met Whitney's eyes—"this is only our second planned encounter. Your use of *always* feels a bit hyperbolic."

"Sure." Whitney suppressed a smile, studying the angles of Andy's face, the sharp edge of her jawline and cupid's bow of her lips, the thick brows hooding eyes ringed darker around the edges now that Whitney allowed herself a closer look. Despite the dark circles, Andy seemed surprisingly light, given how they'd left things last night. "Should we sit, or do you want to walk?"

If Andy's mindset was anything close to Whitney's, she'd want to be on the move—pacing or walking, anything but standing still. "Walking sounds nice," she said, eyes locked on Wes.

Whitney offered her the leash with a quirk of her lips. "Here. He's just going to spend the time distracted by your presence anyway."

"You say that like it's a bad thing."

"Should it be a good thing my dog, who I raised since he was an anxious mess of a rescue pup, likes you more than me?"

"He doesn't. I'm just the shiny, new human in your life. Besides, I'm sure these are at least half the reason he's so stuck on me today." Andy reached into her pocket and came out with a small ziplock bag half-filled with mini bites that looked suspiciously like Wes's favorite treat.

Wes hopped onto his hind legs and yipped, echoing his excitement.

Whitney's stomach fluttered at the sight. It reminded her of a time when they'd been the center of each other's worlds, reminded her that, at her best, Andy had always been about the details. She was the kind of person who made it her mission to learn everything she could about someone, then show them how attentive she'd been by never ever having to put it into words, which made it that much more heart-shattering when she decided they weren't worth it anymore.

An old ache clawed its way up Whitney's throat.

"Sorry," said Andy. "I hope this is okay. It was an impulse buy."

"You never impulse-buy."

"Okay. It wasn't, but the day you came by my place, I guess even though you were pissed, a part of me was hoping we *would* see each other soon, and I know this guy is part of the deal. So I walked into that pet store on Sixteenth, and I kind of"—Andy cringed, as if she wasn't sure how her next words would be received—"ran into your mom. She might've mentioned these were his favorite."

"Of course she did."

Mom *had* mentioned seeing Andy, not so much the where or that they'd apparently had an entire conversation that would lead to this, a moment where the anger of two weeks, a few days ago even, didn't flare at Andy being so infuriatingly lovely. Two weeks. Was that really all it had taken for Whitney to fall into bed with her again? Fall into couch? *Fuck.* How would she ever look at that elegant, faux-leather upholstery again without recalling how Andy had clenched when Whitney called her baby, without thinking about how Andy would've come all over it if not for the shield of Whitney's lap?

Now that she thought about it, she should burn those leggings and hope by some miracle the memories went up in flames too.

"I think..." Andy's steps slowed, and she turned to Whitney, brows furrowed, eyes averted. "I think I've been so desperate to be in your life again, a part of me has been reverting to old habits. Showing up with coffee you don't even drink anymore, getting your dog treats without your permission. Commenting on who you're dating—"

"Andy—"

"Wait, please." Her eyes darted up to Whitney's. "There were a lot of reasons last night shouldn't have happened, the least of which isn't that you're seeing someone, Whit. And I —I promised I wouldn't—" She shook her head. "I don't want to ruin that for you. Maybe it sounds selfish, but last night, I didn't consider that. I can't think of anything else when you look at me, or kiss me, especially when you touch me like *that*. I know it's probably just history, tension, whatever. There's *still* so much between us, but I don't want my being here to turn you into someone you're not."

"You can't take credit for my decisions, Andy. Good or bad." Whitney stepped closer. "Last night *was* my decision. I wanted..." Her muscles tensed in a physical warning for her to reconsider her words. Really, she didn't know what she'd wanted. To shut Andy up so she didn't have to rehash how dark everything had been those first weeks after Andy had left?

The worst part had never been the tears. It hadn't even been questioning if shards of glass were actually stuck in her chest or if the piercing tightness was just her brain's way of saying her heart was still beating. It was wondering what she'd done, why everything they'd shared wasn't enough anymore.

Or maybe she just *wanted* Andy. It's not like her body had ever craved anyone with the same untamed fervor. It's not like anyone else had ever made her dizzy with a single swipe of their tongue across their lips.

"You had a tough week," said Andy, ever rational. "I was there. Isabelle—"

"And I have decided to be just friends."

"Oh." Andy gaped, blinking and shaking her head. "Fuck. Whit, I—"

Whitney held up a hand. "It's not because of last night. It happened before that. It's not even because you're here. I guess…" Her eyes wandered skyward in search of an explanation. "The whole opposites-attract thing hits differently when the person you're with doesn't like anything you do and asking about their day results in a twenty-minute exposition about acetabular fixation surgery, as if the average person even knows what that is. Not that it was all bad. Her passion was intriguing, even if I didn't always understand it. It didn't hurt that she's gorgeous and sexy and—" Whitney dropped her hand, abruptly aware of her wild, meaningless gestures. "I don't know. I don't know why I'm telling you any of this except to say we tried. Or maybe I didn't try hard enough. Romance, *love*, just doesn't make sense to me right now."

A shadow of emotion crossed Andy's face, her expression growing more pinched, but the discontent fled before Whitney could decide whether she'd only imagined it. The rise and fall of Andy's shoulders was so casual Whitney figured she had. "I'm all for logic, but when it comes to love, it took me a really long time to understand that it's nothing we can control. You know when you know."

"I guess," Whitney said softly.

"I am sorry it didn't work out, though."

"Are you?" She didn't mean for it to slip out, didn't mean to keep existing in this never-ending cycle of hurt and want and yearning.

The sudden intensity of Andy's stare spurred a banging in her chest and a sickening unease in her stomach, especially when Andy's lips parted and she said, "I am. All I've ever wanted is for you to be happy, Whitney."

Whitney clenched her molars, resolute in her efforts to prevent a second slip. She still thought it, though. Her throat still sweltered with the acidity of treacherous words she refused to unleash. *Then why did you leave?*

"That being said," Andy went on, seemingly oblivious to the whirlwind of past conflicts brewing in Whitney's chest.

Strange. Last night, after the blessing and curse of Whitney's alarm, there had been something so acute, so pained, in the slope of Andy's brows and gleam of her hazel eyes, in her rationale for why burning fingertips, searing kisses, and scattered clothes had been almost inevitable between them. Whitney hadn't *wanted* to see it. Andy being hurt by the less than ideal conclusion of that moment signaled something Whitney didn't want to be true. She needed last night to be the zenith of escalating desires between two people who were simply too familiar, too adept at making each other come. If not for that alarm, if not for the undeniable fact that Andy would've taken her apart in seconds—always knowing exactly how hard to bite before soothing Whitney's nipples with her tongue, too precise in the press and drag of her fingers against that one spot Whitney had never been able to reach on her own—Whitney wouldn't have hesitated when Andy asked to reciprocate. Even in the haze of her orgasm, legs still tremoring, it was almost as if Andy knew

Whitney wasn't sure she'd be able to minimize last night as a quick fuck between exes if things went that far.

Whitney had done all the touching. She'd stroked Andy through gasps of intensifying pleasure, kissed away her mumbled, sexy nonsense, watched the vulnerability flower in her shimmering eyes. Last night, Whitney had been okay with that, selfishly relieved, even. This morning, with none of the same exposure in Andy's tone or gaze or demeanor, Whitney wasn't sure what she was feeling.

"Whit, are you still with me?"

Her eyes snapped up at Andy's question, at the abrupt realization that she'd missed something crucial. "I'm sorry." She pressed two fingers next to her brow as signs of a headache thudded at her temples. "I, um—can you repeat that?"

Andy tilted her head in concern. "Which part?"

"All of it?"

"Um, okay." She dropped her gaze to Wes, seemingly trailing the invisible path of his tiny paws. "I did mean what I said last night. It doesn't have to be more than something that felt good in the moment. But I think we can both agree that we probably shouldn't do it again."

"Right. Of course."

"Not that I wouldn't *want*—" Andy glanced up, eyes sweeping down to Whitney's mouth, then lower before she jerked her head back toward Wes.

Warmth bloomed below Whitney's navel before spreading north, creeping up her abdomen, between her breasts, and up her neck to heat her face.

"Things are complicated enough as it is, and I don't—I'm not sure I could focus on us being friends again while constantly maneuvering the dynamics of when it would be appropriate to kiss you."

"That makes sense," said Whitney with a slow nod. Leave it to Andy to shoulder the responsibility of a sexual encounter Whitney had been the one to initiate. She hadn't thought that far, hadn't thought about *again*. Not when she was still so stuck on yesterday. What did it say that Andy was the one who felt the need to address the possibility?

"Besides," said Andy, "you said it yourself. It was just to get it out of our systems."

Sure, because sex had always been that simple.

"Is it?" A recognizable rasp coated Andy's words, her boldness sprouting only long enough for her to look Whitney in the eyes. "Out of your system?"

The hairs on the back of Whitney's neck stood on end, and a shiver crept down her spine, sparking every nerve ending down to her toes, making her acutely aware of how not out of her system it was. She cleared her throat despite the lingering fog in her brain. "Completely."

A smile snuck onto Andy's lips, the glimmer in her eyes leaving her so soft in the midmorning glow, Whitney didn't dare debate its sincerity. "Yeah. Me too."

13

A bittersweet blend of milk and espresso warmed Andy's tongue as her eyes narrowed at the storyboard reflected from her laptop screen. She lowered her coffee cup to the wooden two-top, the mild thud and faint rush of traffic beyond the walls of Gia her only company in the main dining room. At barely nine a.m. on a Monday, the restaurant projected a calm completely at odds with the early dinner service rush she'd gotten a glimpse of last Friday.

It almost seemed choreographed. Every flaming pan and sizzling grill, the careful yet harried movement of each chef, and the meticulous care taken by Jenn at the expo station. The dance of servers, twirling between main dining and the kitchen with fragrant dishes of Mexican chicken parmesan, enchilada ravioli, Italian fajitas, and spaghetti tacos. Bussers flipping tables in seconds to accommodate the never-ending stream of patrons by the hostess stand. Soft music, clinking glasses and utensils, laughter. Perfect and precise and so, so alive.

Yet there was a charm to the stillness, something magical in the idea of transforming cold ingredients and fresh produce, systematized bottles of liquors and wines, into sheer human joy.

Andy's mind had been overflowing with mental B-roll takes the whole walkthrough. She'd envisioned an establishing shot of the building's exterior—this quaint corner of Mission, San Francisco; wide angles of main dining; full shots of Jenn in the kitchen, tight enough to capture the fierce concentration on her face but wide enough to frame her imposing posture and impeccable chef's whites. She'd even imagined the interview.

She had it all laid out, but it had taken nearly the last twenty-four hours to piece it together with the precision she needed to go into filming this week. Plus, as Riva had rightfully pointed out, they were now a week behind schedule according to the production calendar. A niggling thought lingered that she should've pushed harder to get Jenn to agree to allow a crew to come in instead of just her. Then, she could focus on telling the story she wanted to capture—the direction, the journey—but something told her a full crew trudging through Gia for a week was non-negotiable on Jenn's part. Hadn't she said as much?

Painstakingly detailed. Focused. Insular. That was the Andy she'd needed to be this weekend to ensure there was nothing she'd miss in the next couple of days. But that Andy would've gone straight home to work instead of stopping by the gym on Friday. Whitney wouldn't have kissed her or taken her on that couch or—

Andy pressed the heels of her hands to her eyes, shaking her head. "Head in the game, Vahn." She didn't have time to spiral into another all-consuming memory of that night, or the morning after. She didn't have time to consider how adorably sleep-addled Whitney had looked, how she'd smelled like jasmine and petitgrain, or how the soft plush of her lips turned Andy's stomach to mush at the very thought of them against her neck. "Fuck."

The tap of heels echoed against hardwood, and she yanked her hands away from her face to be met by Avery's skeptical stare. Her presence shouldn't have been startling. She *had* let Andy into the building before disappearing to her own office less than twenty minutes ago, but for reasons Andy had yet to make sense of, the sight of Avery's silk blouses, pencil skirts, and stilettos unsettled her every goddamn time.

"Should I leave you to the privacy of whatever is happening here?" Avery asked with a lilt in her tone. Humor and condescension, maybe a hint of indifference.

Andy sat up straighter in her seat, as if it was even possible. "Minor pep talk."

"Ah." Avery nodded. "When Whitney mentioned you were good at those, I imagined something a bit more nuanced than forceful swearing. At yourself, no less."

A breathy scoff escaped Andy. "She's the only person who would ever say I'm good at pep talks." Andy's primary forms of self-motivation had always been opposite sides of the same coin: an overwhelming drive for success and a crippling fear of failure. If she'd managed to give Whitney any form of pep talk in the past, it'd only ever been because she'd rambled the truth of her admiration whenever Whitney needed to hear it. The night before a gymnastics meet or seconds before she sauntered onto stage for a breathtaking performance that showed none of her insecurity.

Avery hummed.

Silence descended between them, Avery's gaze scrutinizing, Andy wondering when she'd find whatever she always seemed to be searching for. Her skin prickled at the thought, and she resisted the urge to shift in her chair.

"Jenn and Val will be here in a couple of minutes." Avery's eyes dropped to her phone, thumb swiping across its screen.

"Oh. Thanks."

"Mm-hm."

Andy's own eyes scanned the empty space for some kind of clue. A reprieve, maybe. She'd never felt the need to fill every silence with impulsive drivel, especially not when she had work to do. There were few things that made her more uncomfortable than aimless conversation with someone she barely knew. She took another sip of her coffee, wrapping both hands around the paper cup and grounding herself in the heat against her palms as she cleared her throat. "So, how long have you known Jenn?"

Avery's eyes shifted, though her chin remained dipped toward the phone in her hand. "Almost eight years."

"Since she opened this Gia then?"

"Yeah. It was my first job after leaving the firm."

"Pedro's?" Andy's brows scrunched together, her brain instantly rejecting the familiarity in using his first name. As far back as the night she'd met him, Whitney's dad had always insisted on it. Dressed in a crisp, blue button-up, face and smile the kind of charming built for a *Forbes* cover, he'd tried to dad-joke his way into his daughter's best friend's good graces when all she could think about was why her stomach did that awful flip when Whitney leaned in and whispered, "Two minutes and we'll go to my room, I promise."

"Our dad's firm, yes," said Avery.

Andy's curiosity piqued. "So you're a lawyer, then?"

"According to the State Bar of California."

"Doesn't that make you a little overqualified to be working restaurant admin and HR?"

"I'm sorry. Are these questions about me or about Jenn?" Like everything Avery said, the words left her mouth with a polite evenness and the undercurrent of something else.

Something Andy was growing more incapable of ignoring by the second. She pursed her lips, redirecting her attention to her laptop. "Thanks for the heads-up on Jenn's arrival."

"You already said that."

"Look, I get it, okay?" Her head snapped up, eyes locked with Avery's, her frustration flaring at the perplexity reflected back at her.

"Get what?" asked Avery, eyes squinted in a textbook display of cluelessness.

"Why you don't like me."

"Like you?" The dip between her brows deepened. "Andy, I don't *know* you."

"Yeah, well, you don't seem to want to."

"Is there a reason I should?" Avery shot back. A fire flickered in her eyes, though it disappeared in a flash. She drew in a deep breath, all her poise and power returning at once. "Listen, we have to work together. The little I do know says you're a professional, so I'm guessing that won't be a problem for you. And, if I'm being honest, I'm sure you're an incredible person. My sister wouldn't have fallen for you if you weren't. If I would've met you then, I would want to know all about the person you used to be."

Andy's brain snagged on the words *used to be*. Was that what Whitney thought? That she'd returned so irrevocably changed that the Andy of their teenage and undergrad years was a mere phantom?

"I haven't always been there for her, as I'm sure you know," said Avery. "But the day I hugged her for the first time I decided I would never not be there again. I know you two have been talking, fighting, rediscovering your friendship. I would never stand in the way of whatever closure she needs. But however things turn out between you two, when it's all over, I need her to know there's still *one* person she can tell anything without wondering where they stand. My answer is with her. Always."

Andy didn't know what it was like to have siblings, let alone the type of fiercely protective older sister who would talk about her the way Avery spoke about Whitney. No remorse. No compromise. Until Whitney had found that picture of Avery and Landon, Whitney hadn't known what it was like to have siblings either. Even then, it had taken years before she'd had any kind of contact with them. Maybe this was why Avery's perception of Andy bothered her so much.

From the moment she'd pieced it together, outside on the curb of this very restaurant, she'd known Avery was important. Maybe it was in the pictures on Whitney's socials. Maybe it was just a fucking feeling. Maybe, even in her subconscious, Andy had associated winning over Avery with getting Whitney to trust her again. Hadn't Whitney always turned to the people she loved whenever she felt incapable of trusting herself? Hadn't Andy used to be the person she turned to, the one who would face anyone for and with her without blinking?

"I think, um..." Andy swallowed the lump in her throat, fumbling for the strap of the bag housing her standard lens and camera on the adjacent chair. "I'll get a few shots out here before opening, then head to the kitchen around prep if that's okay."

"That's fine." Avery nodded. "And you still want to save your sit-down with Jenn for Friday?"

"Yup. Unless that no longer works."

"I'm sure she'll say something if it doesn't."

"Great." Andy slid out of her chair. "Thanks."

"Andy..." A weighted sigh lingered between them that left Andy wondering if Avery had reconsidered her earlier words. "You don't have to thank me every time I'm about to leave a room."

"Not for that. For being someone Whitney can count on."

One corner of Avery's lips quirked into a soft smile. Then she turned on her heels, heading back in the direction she'd come. "I'll be in my office if you need anything."

WHITNEY SLID to the edge of her chair, hunching over the phone on her desk in her best attempt to bridge the distance by sheer willpower. The focus of Jaxon's camera shifted, and tiny, brown feet came into view, the near imperceptible movements hinting at Baby Maddox riding an invisible cycle. Warmth flooded her chest cavity, a smile splitting her face though she'd yet to see his. "A bit higher, Jax, unless the aim of this video call is for me to reaffirm that he has ten beautiful little toes."

An off-screen grunt countered her cooing before the camera shifted again, revealing a forest-green onesie, searching little hands, and beaming, brown eyes that stole Whitney's entire heart. "Oh my gosh, he's perfect."

"You realize you say those words at least once a day," said Jax, his voice brittle with exhaustion.

"Yes, I do realize that, and I'll keep saying it because he

is. Besides, my two-minute daily interactions with him are the only thing that brings me peace right now."

"Peace?" Jaxon scoffed, the camera jerking toward his surly face. Dark-ringed eyes glared at her. "Whit, the boy doesn't sleep."

Whitney squinted at him. "Sky is only five years old. How have you forgotten how to do this already?"

"No." Jax returned an ardent headshake, Maddox cradled in one hand as he prepared for a tirade Whitney was too distracted by the baby's perplexed face and adorable squirming to heed with the seriousness her friend required. "Sky slept. She slept through the night. A miracle, I'm sure, but it's like he's trying to make up for lost time. I mean, the time we didn't lose. What am I even saying? You know what I'm saying, right?"

"Oh, totally." Whitney did not know what Jax was saying, but her wiggled fingers yielded a purse of blubbering little lips and a spit bubble from Maddox, so she took that as a win.

"He'll stay down for an hour, tops. Then it's three a.m. and he's wailing, and you think he just needs a diaper change or he's hungry. No." Jax's eyes widened, and he shrugged, Maddox bouncing with the motion. "He just wants to hang out. Just stay in Daddy's arms. The second I put him down, he's back to waking the neighborhood. I tell you, he better be a singer or something because the pipes on him."

"I'm guessing the tag team strategy hasn't been working with Michelle."

"Depends on how you define 'working.' We switch off, yeah, but between Sky and the order of five dozen artisanal soaps Mich promised a retailer for *this* week, we're both wrecked." He scratched his collarbone, stretching the already slumping neckline of his plain white T-shirt. "She sneaks out to the studio when she can, and I want to help her, but the last batch I had a hand in came out looking like an ugly space rock. I'd only be in the way."

"Yeah, you probably would be." Whitney grimaced playfully.

"Wow, Whit. Thanks for the leap of faith." Jax sneered. "How are things over there, anyway?"

"Not horrible. Kasey's coming in five days a week starting today, and Eli and Lexi are both back, no thanks to patient zero." Having two of her best trainers out for three days each last week was an inconvenience, if necessary, contingency. It wasn't like she'd had a choice after one of them had all but hacked up a lung on a gym member in a kickboxing lesson and the other had accumulated a pile of snot-filled tissues the size of Mount Davidson on the strength floor. Them being back at work would allow Whitney to tackle some of the admin chores she'd had to ignore by filling in. Even working yesterday—on a Sunday, which she'd made a point to do as infrequently as possible—she still needed to complete this month's payroll and review inventory for the juice bar before the day was out.

"Patient zero?" Jax asked through a chuckle. "Do you mean Robbie?"

"Yes! Because we all knew it wasn't fucking allergies, and he insisted on staying both times I sent him home."

"Sounds like Robbie." Jax nodded. "Just take a few deep breaths every time you're about to talk to him. You know he takes everything personally, and he'll only try to overcompensate if he thinks you hate him."

"I *don't* hate him. I'm just... peeved."

"Whatever. You're really not as good at hiding your feelings as you'd like to be. Definitely not from the people who know you best."

Whitney's mind wandered back to two days ago. Golden Gate Park. The serenity of the brisk air and redolent medley of wildflowers juxtaposed with the mental minefield of experiencing it next to Andy the morning after they'd had sex. Was Andy still one of those people who knew her best? What feelings had she given away with her compulsive staring and soft-spoken words? Even with the words she hadn't said? Beyond that, what had she given away when she'd kissed Andy in this very office instead of just letting her leave?

Her eyes shifted to the sofa, phantom moans and breathless pleas prickling her skin, making the hairs on the back of her neck rise.

"No." She blinked forcefully enough to shatter the looming recollection. Not for the first time, she figured maybe she should talk to someone about it. Jax or Avery or Val. Not Kasey. If Andy had told anyone, it would definitely be Kasey, and her knowing both sides of the story would only leave her in the middle. Should they have agreed to not tell anyone?

"No isn't an applicable response," said Jax. "I wasn't asking. You *are* bad at hiding your feelings."

"I wasn't debating that. I was..." Whitney shook her head. "Nothing. The gym is fine. I am fine. Now go back to whining about how tired you are. Or just angle the camera toward Mads. He might be better company."

"I'm going to ignore the reason you're so desperate to avoid talking about yourself, because it's only a matter of time before you spill whatever it is, but also because I need a kid favor."

"My favorite kind."

Jax rolled his eyes, as if Whitney's enchantment with kids, especially his, hadn't always worked in his favor. "Mich and I promised to take Sky to an *Encanto* ice-skating show. Like, budget Disney on Ice."

"Say more." Whitney beamed, planting both elbows on her desk.

"That was before this guy"—Jax pointed an accusing finger at Maddox—"came early, and she had actual people for parents instead of two high-functioning zombies who can't even fathom taking a baby to an hour-long show that includes a souvenir picture with the cast after."

"Right. So you want me to take Sky."

"Exactly."

"Jax, you had me at budget Disney on Ice. No, it was the moment you said *Encanto* ice-skating show. Besides, I haven't seen Sky since she decided only nuggets are dinner food. We're due some hangout time."

"Yeah. She keeps asking when Aunt Whitney is coming to meet her baby brother. Michelle is the one who doesn't want anyone physically near him for another couple of weeks, but I'm the one who had to explain how germs and shots work to a five-year-old."

Whitney laughed. "Sounds about right."

"Anyway, we did get two adult tickets to this thing, so you can take a plus-one if you want. How friendly are you and the good doctor since the whole maybe-we're-better-as-friends talk?"

"Not *that* friendly." Whitney and Isabelle hadn't so much as exchanged a text since they'd called things off at the lounge last week. They hadn't run into each other at the gym either, which was sort of a relief if Whitney was being honest. She didn't know what she'd say if they *did* run into each other, so as a healthy manner of dealing, she'd settled on avoidance. "Musicals aren't really her thing, anyway. I don't think kids are either, although that's more of a vibe than something she actually said."

"Well, I guess you could take someone else."

A stack of imaginary playbills flipped through Whitney's mind, every page printed with Andy's name in varying fonts—Andy who loved musicals as much as she did, who'd watched all her plays when they'd been together, learned the lines and songs just to help her practice. *Andy, Andy, Andy.*

"Yeah, I think Sky and I will be good on our own," said Whitney. "Unless you really don't want the ticket to go to waste."

"I mean, it only cost close to a week's worth of groceries."

Whitney's face contorted with disbelief. "You spent a week of groceries for *budget* Disney on Ice?"

"Not the point, Whit," Jax deadpanned.

"Got it. Will find someone or donate."

"Thank you. Sky's been ranting about taking pictures with Mirabel for weeks."

"Oh my gosh, same."

A basso chuckle resonated from the speakers of her phone. "You're ridiculous. You know that, right?"

"You love me."

"Yeah, well, those things aren't mutually exclusive."

"I can live with that." The time at the top right of her screen caught Whitney's eyes—3:17 p.m.—and she narrowed her focus back to Jax with a sigh. "I have to go. I want to walk Wes and make it back in time for my peewee gymnastics group at five."

"Okay. I'm going to see if I can get this guy down for a nap." He angled the camera toward Maddox's face one last time, and Whitney laid a hand on her own chest at the curious eyes beaming up at her.

"Hey, Mads. Give Daddy a break, okay?" she pleaded. "He's kind of a grump when he's tired."

"Goodbye, Whit," Jax drawled, lips twitching with the faintest hint of humor before the screen went black.

14

Andy zipped her camera case shut, glancing around Jenn's desk to ensure nothing had been left out of place. The room tended toward minimalism in a way she hadn't been able to fully appreciate the first time she'd set foot in it more than a week ago. Her own office back in LA was a glass structure of clean, simple lines and cool grays, a functional beacon of natural light set on the sixteenth floor. By contrast, Jenn's private corner of Gia maintained an earthy elegance that relied on the soothing presence of pine floors and potted plants.

Functional *and* warm.

Even having been here since before the restaurant opened to garner more footage of the pre-shift ritual—updates, tips, and a "newbie initiation" that included dancing, of all things—Andy had barely spent more than thirty minutes in this space that probably said more about Jenn than she'd even realized. She'd gotten great B-roll of the back-of-house staff from lunch until dinner service tapered off at just after eleven—clips of immaculate, mouthwatering dishes perfected by Jenn's finishing touches and heated debates among Val, Landon, and another chef, Warren.

Unlike Avery, Landon either didn't know the intricacies of Andy and Whitney's relationship or he'd shelved his feelings about it in favor of tossing a wink and a moneymaker grin whenever the camera happened to fall on him. A glorified TV chef in the making if Andy had ever seen one. It was a relief nonetheless. She couldn't even begin to think about having to maneuver around the disapproval of both Whitney's siblings, while trying to focus on the job she was here to do.

Steady raps echoed from the door, and her chin jerked up seconds before it swung open. Jenn walked in, still garbed in her chef's whites with a Gia-branded to-go bag in hand. "Sorry, did I startle you?"

"No." Andy shook her head. Minutes to midnight was not the time to be getting lost in thought, especially in an office that wasn't even hers, especially not when she still had work to do at home. "I feel terrible you're knocking on the door to your own office."

"It's just a courtesy," said Jenn. "And having you here is much more practical than you waiting in main dining every morning, then packing up before service starts. This way you have a desk to return to at any given point in the day."

"Yeah, but it's *your* desk."

Jenn waved away the thought. "Between Avery and my head chef, Mel, I hardly ever need it. I actually prefer not to need it."

"I might've noticed that you like being in the kitchen more."

"You've noticed that in two days?"

Andy shrugged. "It's something on your face." Nothing as transparent as a smile or typical expression of joy. A quiet confidence, serenity almost, amid the ordered chaos of yelled directives, sizzling pans, and people who never ever slowed down.

Jenn hummed, placing the bag on her desk. "This is for you. Valentina mentioned you don't seem to take breaks much, and I can't have you passing out here even if it is almost midnight already."

"Oh. No, I'm fine. I really don't—"

"It's no problem." Jenn pushed the bag closer to Andy. "They're from the leftovers. The rest gets picked up by Postmates for shelters. Besides, Valentina insisted. I forget to take breaks too, and though we're both around food more than twelve hours a day, she thinks it's her job to remind me to eat."

Andy dropped her chin, a smile creeping onto her face at the sheer domesticity of it, something as organic as Jenn's girlfriend reminding her to eat. How had this woman—someone whose success Andy venerated down to her reputation for being meticulous and misanthropic—wound up in a relationship with a woman who was virtually an intern when they'd started seeing each other? Her *own* intern. Never mind the fact that Jenn didn't strike Andy as the type of person to volunteer personal details of her relationship to a virtual stranger.

"It's easy to get lost in it," Andy said. "The work."

Jenn nodded. "It is, which makes us exceptional at what we do and close to terrible at everything else."

Andy tilted her head. *Us?*

"Anyway," Jenn went on, skating past the allusion of kinship before Andy could decide whether she'd imagined it. "I know we didn't see much of each other yesterday. I had to leave early. My son had a soccer game, and there are hardly ever any seconds to spare during the days here, but I wanted to make sure everything's been okay. Though I have no doubt Avery has it all under control."

"Yeah." Andy fidgeted with the zipper on her camera case. "She's great. Really."

"She is." The lengthening silence nudged Andy to look at Jenn directly, just in time for Jenn to say, "I should get back to the kitchen. We're still closing, but I'll see you tomorrow?"

"Of course."

"Great. Good night, Andy."

"Night, Jenn."

As Andy exited the office, she considered making a stop in the kitchen to thank Val for whatever tasty offering awaited her in the takeout bag Jenn had brought her. Instead, she stayed on course to the main doors, mumbling a casual "thanks" to the front-of-house staff who saw her out before closing the door behind her. Tomorrow, she could have a quick chat with Val before they both started working. A niggling thought sprouted at the idea—Avery's voice inside her head looping notes from the conversation they'd had yesterday.

"I need her to know there's still one person she can tell anything without wondering where they stand."

It wasn't as if Andy had set out to befriend any of these people, but Val projected an affability that made her easy to like. Maybe that was the problem. Val, Landon, Avery... They were Whitney's people. Did that make them all off-limits by principle?

She made a mental note to ask Kasey about it.

The lights on her car animated with a click of her key fob, and she unloaded her equipment and takeout bag onto the back seat before attending to the buzzing phone in her jeans' pocket. Her stomach flipped at the notification. Six years and the sight of Whitney's name on her phone still commanded her body like she was a doe-eyed teenager.

Whitney (11:47 p.m.)
You up?

Andy tucked her bottom lip between her teeth, one thumb swiping across her screen as she slipped into the driver's seat and slammed the door shut.

Andy (11:47 p.m.)
That depends.

Whitney (11:48 p.m.)
On what?

Andy (11:48 p.m.)
Whether that's millennial for: come over so I can do bad things to you.

The *typing* bubble appeared, then vanished, only to reemerge seconds later and fade again. Andy drummed her fingers along the steering wheel, glancing around the parking lot. Only the red Acura she'd come to identify as Landon's kept her black Audi company, with Jenn's SUV parked in the alleyway outside Gia's side door. A trio of cackling women stumbled by on heels that were too pointy to be kind to their coordination, especially after what Andy assumed had been a few drinks.

After a last-ditch attempt—and failure—at picking out constellations across the blue-black sky, she surrendered to the urge to look down at her phone screen. Still no reply. Before she could overthink it, she thumbed her way to the call button and hit "Speaker." The dial tone reverberated in the silence of her car, ringing once, twice—

"I thought we agreed we wouldn't do that again."

Andy's eyes drifted shut at the soft rasp in Whitney's voice, and she reminded herself to lead with her brain instead of the clench in her lower abdomen. Though, she couldn't help but wonder if maybe Whitney had taken that long to reply because she'd actually been considering it.

"I was kidding," said Andy.

"Which time?"

"Just now. You know I say stupid things when I'm tired."

"Sometimes," said Whitney. "Sometimes your tired mumblings are kind of genius."

Andy let the comment hang in the silence, waiting for more. Was that Whitney's way of saying Andy showing up on her doorstep at midnight was one of those genius ideas? Or was it an allusion to their past?

"Working on today's footage?"

"Not"—Andy pressed a palm to her mouth, suppressing a yawn—"not yet. I'm just about to leave Gia."

"Andy, it's almost twelve a.m."

"Yeah, well, according to Jenn, Mondays and Tuesdays are when they close earliest. So it won't get any better the rest of the week."

"Do you *have* to be there until close?"

"I just started shooting, Whit. We're already behind on the production schedule, and I only have one week. A week to capture all her nuances and how she relates to her staff, to make sense of the journey of how she came to be Jenn Coleman. Shooting twelve hours a day probably still won't be enough."

"Just..." Whitney hesitated. "Don't burn yourself out, okay?"

"Either my body doesn't know what that is, or my brain forgot how to recognize it."

"I'm serious, Andy." The whispered reprimand reached into Andy's chest and stirred a quiet yearning, one akin to Val reminding Jenn to eat. The feeling retreated in an instant, almost as if a single ray of light would leave it petrified, frozen and forever exposed.

Whatever form her and Whitney's relationship took when they managed to collect the scattered fragments of the past, it wouldn't be what Jenn and Val had. Even Andy knew that. "Don't worry." She conjured a smile, though Whitney wasn't there to see it. "I'm good at taking care of myself."

"Maybe a little too good."

Andy was more than willing to let that slip like she hadn't even heard it. "Can't sleep?"

"No, I'm getting there. I just wanted to, um..." Whitney trailed off.

"Tell me," Andy urged softly.

"It's kind of ridiculous. You've seen *Encanto*, right?"

"Twice. Loved it."

"Well, I have these tickets. Actually, they were Jaxon's tickets. Him and his wife, Michelle, but now they have Maddox and they're practically zombie people, or so he says. And Sky really wanted to see it."

"*Encanto*?"

"Yeah. On ice," Whitney clarified.

"Right. And Sky is..."

"Jax's daughter. She's five and probably way too smart for her age but so freaking adorable."

Andy warmed at the adoration in Whitney's tone. "I bet she is."

"Anyway, it would be a shame for the other ticket to go to waste, and no one else I know would be into it like you would, so will you—would you like to join us?"

"You and Sky, for *Encanto* on Ice?" Andy asked, only

because she hadn't heard this Whitney in a while. The unbridled confidence of the woman she'd been getting to know the last three weeks intrigued her to no end, but flustered, rambling Whitney had a special place in her memories.

"Yes. Me and Sky."

"And she's okay with a stranger crashing your time together?"

"You wouldn't be crashing. I ran it by her this afternoon, although I *may* have talked you up by saying you make movies too."

Andy furrowed her brows. "I do make movies."

"Not the kind a five-year-old knows how to appreciate yet. So, if she asks, you know the people who made *Frozen*."

"Whitney Dimaano." Andy faux-gasped. "Lying to children is very unbecoming."

"Yeah, I'm not proud of it."

Laughter erupted from her phone's speaker, and for a second she stared at it, wishing she could capture the melody and cradle it in her thoughts forever. Then she remembered this was the same laugh that had been fading in and out of her memories for years, the soundtrack to all her daydreams of *home*.

"I'll be there," she said.

"Before you agree, it's this Thursday. As in, the day after tomorrow. And I know you're already swamped with shooting and—"

"Whitney..." Andy smiled. "I said I'll be there."

"Okay."

"What time should I pick up you and Sky?"

"Oh, you don't have to do that. I can just send you the details, and we can meet at the rink."

"Two cars emitting greenhouse gases all the way to the

same location with people who are going to meet there, anyway? Sounds bad for the environment."

"Of course," Whitney deadpanned. "Does six work?"

"Six is perfect."

"Good, but I'll pick you up at Gia, so you lose as little filming time as possible."

"Even better."

Another group of laughing strangers passed by, and a single car zoomed down the street. Andy almost felt ready to lean into her headrest, close her eyes, and fall asleep to Whitney's subtle breathing. She could fall asleep anywhere with Whitney next to her, or on the phone, as it may be, but she still had footage to log. She still needed to review as much of it as possible. "You should get some rest," she said.

"Yeah." Whitney drew in an audible breath. "Will you let me know when you're home?"

"I wouldn't want to wake you."

"Andy..." The delicate it's-not-up-for-debate laced into the mere utterance of her name gave away Whitney's next words. "Text me when you're home."

Andy grinned. "I will."

15

"So, I did a thing."

Whitney grimaced, drawing one leg beneath her onto the booth-style chair opposite Kasey. The lounge area of the juice bar wasn't ideal for their weekly meeting. Whitney had certainly never met here with Jax, but between Kasey's insistence that office spaces made her feel stuffy and the fact that they'd already met at least once every day this week, Whitney had conceded with little confutation.

Today was Thursday. She'd promised herself she wouldn't freak out about it. She hadn't freaked out—not the day before, not even last night when Andy had texted her to confirm they were still on—but her insides hadn't stopped quivering since she'd woken this morning with her heart racing and cool beads of sweat rolling down her chest. She couldn't remember the dream, though the persistent throbbing between her thighs had led to a few deductions. Still, that wasn't the unsettling part. It was the whispered name that left her lips when she rolled onto her back and stared up at her ceiling. Andy's name.

Now the graphs on her laptop screen, her own fucking

expense reports, were a muddle of colors and digits her brain didn't even recognize.

Kasey's eyes flicked up from her own computer, brows drawn low in wary skepticism. "You did a *thing*," she repeated, separating the words down to the syllables. "An Andy thing?"

Whitney's head flinched back, and she said a silent prayer that the warmth fanning from the tips of her ears to her cheeks wasn't a visible blush. It wasn't like Kasey had ever been the oblivious type, but she hit that nail on the head way too fast. "Why are you so sure it's an Andy thing?"

"Isn't it?" Kasey leaned back in her chair, crossing both arms over her chest.

Whitney sat up straighter too. She would cling to every last thread of composure even if the quirk of Kasey's lips made her feel like her skin was made of cellophane. "Well, yes, but I'd like to know why you'd immediately come to that conclusion. Has Andy said something?"

"Should she have said something?"

Whitney huffed. "You're really not helping, Kase."

"I don't even know what I'm supposed to be helping with!"

The shift in pitch drew no less than four pairs of eyes their way, forcing Whitney to aim a practiced smile and an apology at the man seated in the green tub chair toward the center of the lounge. "Sorry. She's a morning person." The man scowled, adjusting the Air Pod in his ear before apparently returning to his phone call. Whitney turned back to Kasey, hissing, "This is why we have meetings in offices," across the table.

Kasey's eyes narrowed to slits. "Whitney, out with it."

"I invited Andy to a musical ice skating show with Sky

tonight, and now I need you to come." She spewed it out in one breathless confession, then bit down on her bottom lip.

"No." Kasey held up a hand, face contorted as if the mere suggestion caused her physical pain. "You know I can't do musicals."

"Yes, and as someone who loves you, it's a character flaw I selectively ignore. As someone who loves me, you can do this."

"I really can't. There's too much random singing and dancing and overall campiness. I don't see what the problem is, anyway. A musical on ice and an adorable kid to entertain sounds right up you and Andy's—" She cut herself off, realization wrestling its way onto her face as her eyes fell shut. "Oh, Whitney."

"I know, I know."

"Okay." Kasey exhaled a heavy breath. "You two clearly share a proclivity for self-sabotage, but surely this falls more on the friends side of the elaborate emotional scale you've been tiptoeing around? It's not like a circus performance will give you the sudden, inescapable urge to rip her clothes off."

Whitney's gaze flicked up in consideration. Should she mention that the urge to get Andy naked wouldn't be sudden at all? If she was being honest with herself, had Andy leaned into that text the other night about coming over so Whitney could *do bad things* to her, Whitney would've welcomed her in with a fistful of her leather jacket and a bruising kiss. They wouldn't have even made it to the bedroom, which might have been mildly traumatizing to Wes, but—

"Are you actually considering it right now?" Incredulity swept onto Kasey's face. "Because we can both think of about thirty-seven reasons why you two sleeping together would not be a good idea."

Whitney sighed. "I know. Top of the list, she'll be gone by next week."

"Wait." Kasey tipped her head to one side. "She hasn't told you?"

"Told me what?"

The moment dragged, Kasey's brows squishing closer together as her brain worked, leaving Whitney to wonder, her heartbeat sluggish with dread, stomach roiling.

"Told me what, Kase?"

"Nothing." She gave a slight shake of her head, her bewilderment vanishing in place of casual conviction. "I'm sure it will come up."

"I don't understand. You're sure what will come up?"

"She has to be the one to tell you, Whit. But don't worry. It's a good thing." She paused, scratching her chin. "I think?"

"That sounds really promising," Whitney shot back, her tone dripping with sarcasm. "You're really not going to tell me?"

"Nope. As for your problem with seeing her later, just try not to think any sexy thoughts. Aren't all those kids that will be around a natural anaphrodisiac anyway?"

"I don't know if it works like that."

"Then go home half an hour early, charge up your vibrator, and get it out of your system before you two meet up."

Right. Because the last time Whitney had decided to get *it* out of her system had worked so well. She rubbed a hand across her forehead, dropping her gaze to her laptop screen. "It's fine. I'll figure it out."

"Sure you will. Which folder did you say the vendor contracts are in again?"

Take Two

COLD, wooden siding braced Andy's shoulders as she leaned against Gia's façade, the heel of one boot angled against the wall, eyes skimming through her work emails. She made a habit of checking her messages at least once every hour whenever she wasn't filming, always too on edge about missing something that might make or break her next project. With Whitney about to arrive any second, she figured she'd take the opportunity to check one last time for the evening. The last thing she wanted was to spend her time with Whitney and Sky preoccupied with work, even if her checklist was mounting by the minute.

She couldn't remember the last time she'd cut shooting early to go do something that had nothing to do with her current project, but this was Whitney. She'd asked at their favorite time of day, just before midnight when the weight of hours past could still be allayed by the sound of her voice, her tone laced with the kind of endearing fluster that reduced Andy's vocabulary to a single word.

Yes. Yes, yes, always yes.

The front door of the restaurant swung open, and Andy shuffled farther left to accommodate the exiting customers, though her eyes never left her phone.

"You're still here!"

The buoyancy in the words jolted her chin up, and her eyes landed on Val dressed in a Gia sweatshirt and jeans instead of the chef's whites she'd been garbed in when Andy had left the kitchen fifteen minutes ago.

"Only for a bit longer," she said.

Val tipped her head to one side, pushing a lock of chestnut-brown hair behind one ear. "Is something wrong with your car? I have to be back in an hour, but I could give you a ride somewhere."

"Thank you, but no. My ride should be here any second. Actually..." A platinum gray compact SUV emerged in Andy's periphery, and she shifted to look past Val as the car rolled to a stop by the curb. "I think this must be her now."

The window retracted to reveal Whitney, hand poised in a wave, her smile the kind of heart-stopping that had kept Andy awake at night, wondering if she'd ever see it aimed at her again.

"Oh." Val shot Andy a questioning yet amused glare before doubling back to Whitney. "Hey, Whit!"

Andy shifted her weight from one foot to the other, clutching at the single bag strap slung over her shoulder. "I should get going. I'm pretty sure she's parked in a tow zone."

"Don't let me stop you. That's not the kind of woman you want to keep waiting either way." Val winked, taking a step back to let Andy by.

The words vined through her brain, inciting perilous thoughts. Was that Val's way of not so subtly nudging Andy to make a move? Was Whitney *waiting* for her?

No.

She squeezed her eyes shut, perished the thought. That had never been their dynamic. Whitney had always been the one who'd known, who'd dived headfirst into what they could've been with breathtaking bravery. Even in her office last week, she'd been the one to kiss Andy, pin her against that door, and give them permission to have something they'd both been craving. Maybe Andy had been the one to leave, but Whitney had always been the one with all the power.

"Andy?"

She paused on the steps, glancing back to see Val

doubled over before righting herself with a silver barrel fountain pen in hand.

"I think you dropped this."

"Oh, yeah. Thank you." Andy scoffed at herself, accepting the pen and slipping it into the pocket of her jeans. "For someone who digitizes all her notes, I have a strange fascination with these things."

Val's shoulders shook with a laugh, and Andy's eyes drifted, catching the gold chain that seemed to have escaped the neckline of Val's sweatshirt when she'd bent to retrieve the pen. But it wasn't the necklace so much as the ring attached to it that had Andy's curiosity standing at attention —a dazzling, six-pronged diamond floating above a gold band, clinging to every ounce of light even in the dim glow of an overcast March evening.

An engagement ring?

Andy's eyes darted back to Val's as if to flee the very observation, as if, somehow, she'd deduced something no one was supposed to know. At least not yet.

The conspiratorial grin etched across Val's face as she tucked the chain back under her shirt and pressed her index finger to her lips said as much. "You two have fun." She turned on the heels of her well-worn Chucks, ducking her head to address Whitney again. "Would love to stay and chat, Whit, but I have to see a lady about some fairy lights!"

Still processing, Andy descended Gia's front steps at half Val's speed, trying to make sense of exactly what had transpired between them. Were Jenn and Val secretly engaged? Was Andy somehow the first to know? A sense of ambivalence pulsed through her—happiness radiating through her chest, though she hardly knew them at all—and a memory slinked to the forefront of her mind.

Andy stood in front of Whitney's dresser in a pair of

bikini-cut underwear and nothing else, fumbling through the top drawer in search of a T-shirt—the same Cranberries band tee Whitney refused to give back, going so far as to demand Andy wear it periodically.

"So it always smells like you," she'd whispered against Andy's mouth.

Coming up empty on her first attempt, she opened another drawer, calling, "Hey, babe! Where's that shirt I always borrow?"

Whitney's answer reverberated from within the adjoining bathroom. "It's in the wash. Just wear the backup!"

"The backup?" Andy murmured to herself. Leave it to her girlfriend to designate a backup shirt for when Andy slept over and *not* mention it before now. She continued her careful rummaging, prepared to settle on whatever looked like it would fit, given that Whitney was at least a size smaller than she was. Her eyes latched on to a dark velvet box nestled in the back corner of the drawer, a stark contrast against the hot pink tank top offering scant coverage to something Andy wasn't sure she was meant to see.

Blood rushed in her ears, the slow thud of her heart rattling her ribs as she reached for the box and flipped it open to reveal a ring—two tapered baguette diamonds framing a classic center stone that screamed *forever*.

She shoved the memory back into her brimming mental box as she slipped into the passenger seat of Whitney's car and slammed the door shut.

"You okay?" Whitney asked.

"Yeah. I'm good." Andy nodded, lowering her gear onto the car floor before reclining against the headrest. A hand landed on hers, the pressure gentle yet unexpected.

"You look like they just announced the wrong film at the 2017 Oscars. Did something happen with Val?"

"That was weirdly specific." Andy chuckled. "But no. Nothing happened with Val. I'm just..." She wet her lips, overcome by the relief rushing through her at having Whitney next to her despite the recollection still swirling in her head. Her eyes drifted to their linked hands, and she allowed herself a second to refamiliarize herself with the touch of Whitney's palm, to revel in how casually affectionate it was before looking back up. "I'm really glad I'm here. With you."

Whitney's stare softened, the steady eye contact reaffirming the dark coffee swirl of her pupils in Andy's memory, the smooth planes of her jaw, the dip and curve of her full lips.

"Are you Andy?"

Andy startled, spinning toward the back seat to find a little girl staring back at her. Her curly, dark hair was caught in two puffs. She wore an *Encanto* T-shirt and a purple tutu, tiny feet garbed in unicorn-speckled sneakers dangling from her car seat.

A grin spread across Andy's face. "I am. And you must be Sky."

"Sky Melissa James."

"That's a pretty name. I like your outfit," said Andy.

Sky dipped her chin, pinching the fabric of her shirt between her index finger and thumb. "Aunt Whitney gave me this shirt."

"Oh, she did? That was really nice of her."

"She's nice," Sky affirmed.

"The nicest." Andy glanced up to find Whitney's eyes still trained on her, though the intensity in them had altered.

"As adorable as this meet-cute is, I kind of need you to put this on..." She trailed off, leaning across the center console to reach for Andy's seat belt. This close, the scent of jasmine flooded Andy's senses. Her fingers ached with the desire to thread through thick, wavy hair and close the inches between them with her lips, which wasn't very PG, but it wasn't like the five-year-old in the back seat could read her mind. The faint tinge of a blush creeping up Whitney's cheeks said maybe she could. Maybe she was thinking exactly what Andy was.

The seat belt clicked into place.

Whitney backed into her own seat. "Safety first, right?"

"Right." Andy's throat felt tight. "Thank you."

"Don't mention it." Whitney's gaze flitted up to the rearview as she shifted into drive. "Ready, Sky?"

Sky kicked her unicorn sneakers in excitement. "Ready, ready!"

They made it to the indoor rink in twenty-three minutes, Sky chattering all the way, her line of questioning for Andy never-ending.

"Do you know Anna and Elsa?" she asked, having exhausted all her questions about Moana.

Andy had shot Whitney a sidelong glare, her bottom lip trapped between her teeth in a terrible attempt to suppress a laugh. "So I've heard."

"What about Olaf?"

"Oh, Olaf and I go way back."

"What does 'way back' mean?"

"It means..." Andy considered it, too amused to regret the endearing interrogation Whitney's white lie had gotten her into. "I've known him a long time."

"Since he was little like Mads?"

"Mm-hm. Since he was a tiny snow baby."

Sky's eyes had gone wide, mouth agape in wonder until they'd made it to their seats in the front row and the rink captured her attention instead. A banner complete with a portrait of the Madrigal family against a backdrop of the casita hung above a smooth expanse of ice, the rink flanked by flickering graphics and dancing lights all around the border.

Whitney leaned closer, her breath a visible puff of air in the freezing space. "Since he was a snow baby? Really?"

"Don't even start. You set me up."

She dropped her head back, her laugh the perfect chord amid the cacophony of excited babbles from kids of all ages, mediating adults, and the cinematic instrumental playing from out-of-sight speakers. "Maybe a little," she admitted. "But think of the cool points you've gained by being the only adult she knows who's friends with Olaf."

"When you put it that way..."

"Not that she wouldn't have loved you, anyway."

The moment stretched, both staring at each other, Andy's thoughts more treacherous by the second. It was so easy to be there with her, so easy to want it all. The screaming kids—no—*their* screaming kid, brimming with excitement in the cutest mismatched outfit they'd probably insisted on assembling themselves, and this, the simple joy of a life she was too afraid to have. Not that she'd ever been able to stop wanting it. "Whit—"

"It's starting, it's starting!" Sky leaped onto Whitney's lap in lieu of her own seat, shattering the moment and making it that much more whole all at once.

Whitney squealed, arms tight around Sky's waist as she nuzzled her neck in an act that had Sky squirming.

Andy's heart cracked right open.

"You're staring," said Whitney, eyes trained ahead at the darkening rink.

Andy wanted to say she knew—she *did* know she was staring—but it wasn't as if she could help it.

A round of "Mirabel, Mirabel!" erupted from the audience, and Andy reluctantly tore her gaze from Whitney in time for an older model dressed in an identical costume to glide onto the ice, accompanied by the first song. It occurred to Andy that she hadn't given much thought to how the entire film would play out on ice. She'd been too content by the idea of Whitney inviting her to care. As the skaters glided through one sequence to the next, the performance came together in a seamless reimagination, never sacrificing any of the film's original charm or the mannerisms of the characters. They watched the intro of the entire family, felt Mirabel's determination despite her insecurity about being different, and awed at Luisa gliding from one town chore to the next, carrying a herd of cattle on her shoulders.

Halfway through the show, still completely absorbed by every lift, spin, and twirl, Sky crab-crawled onto Andy's lap without breaking her bellowing sing-along to "We Don't Talk About Bruno." All Andy could do was warm and melt and belt out the lyrics, too, even with Whitney's eyes on her. This time, she didn't return the stare. That way she wouldn't feel tempted to perfect this little glimpse into what could've been by leaning in and sealing it all with a kiss.

Two hours later, after the show had wrapped and they'd gotten their pictures with the cast, they pulled up in front of Jaxon's quaint Edwardian in the Mission. He descended the front steps wearing fuzzy house slippers—coral, of all colors—a pair of sweats, and a half-zip pullover sullied with a yellowish blob that suspiciously resembled puke. As Whitney's only close friend Andy had yet to see since her return home—the one who'd been with her all through university—Andy expected a skeptical look, if not an outright scowl, at Jax realizing she'd been the one to join Whitney and his daughter at the show that night. Instead, he beamed, hunching his well-over-six-foot frame to...hug Andy through the passenger side window?

Her forehead scrunched as she patted him on the back, the only reciprocation her body managed to process. "Hey, Jax?" she said, skeptical, her voice low so as to not wake Sky, who had crashed almost the second they'd strapped her into her car seat back at the rink.

Jax pulled back, resting his forearms on the belt molding of the door. "You're back in town and my five-year-old kid has seen more of you than I have? Don't seem right, Andy."

How could Andy put into words that she didn't think he'd *want* to see her without sounding bitter or self-pitying? Because she wasn't. Her friendship with Jax—if she could even call it that—existed entirely as a consequence of her relationship with Whitney. She could probably count on one hand the number of conversations they'd had without Whit being present. So why did he seem so genuinely happy to see her?

She dredged up a smile. "Work has been a little intense, but it was really fun hanging out with Sky tonight."

"Yeah, she's cute when she's not trying to hold her breath in protest for one reason or another."

"She's doing that now?" Whitney whispered, her voice pitching slightly higher in surprise.

"Yup." Jax nodded. "Michelle consulted some childcare expert who claims it's normal for her age. So we're working the tantrum steps and watching to see if it escalates. Anyway"—he tapped the belt molding with one hand—"I'll get her out of your hair so you can get on with the rest of your night."

Rest of your night? Andy mulled over the words as Jax opened the back door and unbuckled a still sleeping Sky from her car seat. In her mind, the night was practically over. She hadn't dared to hope for anything beyond the show. Surely Whitney had an early morning tomorrow, and Andy probably had her biggest day of shooting yet—the interview with Jenn.

The door shut with a faint thud and Sky stirred, though Jax's impromptu swaying seemed to do the trick of keeping her asleep. He stared past Andy to Whitney, mumbling, "Thanks. Both of you. I'd ask you how it went, but I'm pretty sure we'll be hearing about it for the next week."

"With good reason," Whitney said, her tone playful. "You missed an A-plus show."

"I'm sure." Jax chuckled, bobbing his head toward Andy. "Don't be a stranger, Vahn."

"Oh, I don't plan on it." In fact, if all her nights ended with Whitney next to her, she was hoping they'd be seeing a lot more of each other very, very soon.

16

Whitney shifted into park, peering up at The Alexander, an imposing beacon of blue reflective glass towering at the center of SoMa. She'd driven by it more times than she could count, but somehow, letting herself be drawn in by its sharp angles and modern aesthetic now came easier than wishing Andy good night and driving away, especially after the comfortable silence of the last ten minutes. The night felt unfinished, like they still hadn't gotten to the part that was just for them, which was absurd, considering the figurative *them* she longed for no longer existed.

"Thanks for the ride," Andy said softly.

Whitney wondered if her stomach would ever not flip when Andy's voice attained that delicate, just-for-you tenor. She willed herself to look at her, study everything from her sage-green moto jacket to the deep cut of the black V-neck she wore underneath, how the line of her neck and sharp edge of her jaw danced between a silhouette and a hazy glow from the LED lights on the dashboard.

"You did give me that spiel about greenhouse gases and carpooling and whatnot," she said with a smile.

"I have deep-seated guilt over my third failed attempt at being vegan," said Andy. "A forced carpool is the least I can do for the environment."

Whitney dropped her head against the headrest, laughing. "The burdens of being a responsible millennial."

"I know. Where the fuck is my participation trophy?"

"Andy Vahn, is that entitlement I hear?"

"Yup. I've decided to really lean into the stereotype."

"Uh-huh. You were probably the kind of five-year-old that refused to accept a trophy you didn't outright win. Actually"—Whitney touched an index finger to her chin, tone laced with amusement—"you were probably the kind of five-year-old who *won* all the trophies."

"Do you want to come up?"

A crack of adrenaline zipped through her at the abruptness of the question, tingling straight down to her toes.

"Just to hang out," Andy clarified. "We could... have a glass of wine or something, keep talking."

After an already emotionally charged day, intensified by an afternoon of watching Andy be adorable with Sky, ending the night with a glass of wine on Andy's couch seemed like the last thing Whitney should be doing, especially when she thought about how she'd woken with Andy's name on her tongue this morning. Still, it was impossible to deny that she wasn't ready for this night to be over.

Her hand moved toward the gear knob as she held Andy's gaze. "Where do I park?"

WHITNEY WOULD NEVER TRADE her picturesque Victorian in the Theatre District for anything, but the sweeping view afforded by the window wall of Andy's twentieth-floor condo held its own grandeur. It boasted a vibrant blend of creativity and commerce, where green open spaces coexisted with sporadically lit skyscrapers beneath the night sky.

"Red or white?" asked Andy.

Whitney shifted on the sectional, directing her attention to where Andy stood across the open floor plan in the kitchen. "Red, please."

In the low, amber light of Andy's apartment, it was impossible to ignore the intimacy of how alone together they were, how the only thing between them was a span of ash-wood floors and unconfessed feelings. She stood, drawn in by the lock of hair nestled at the base of Andy's neck, her exposed arms—her jacket long discarded and thrown across the back of a dining chair—even the temptation of her top being tucked into the front of her jeans but loose at the back. It would be so easy for Whitney's hands to slip beneath the hem and trace the arch of Andy's back.

Andy popped the cork on the wine and drew the glasses closer. "This one's from my favorite winery in New York. Really tiny place in the Hudson River Valley."

"I never would have guessed Andy Vahn would become a wine snob."

"Hardly. I just judge everywhere I go by the food and wine."

"You do realize that does very little to negate you being a snob." Whitney closed the distance between them and paused, debating whether to reach out and trace the sliver of skin along Andy's hips.

Andy turned, a muted gasp stretching between them as cold liquid seeped into Whitney's top. "Fuck." She spun, lowering the glasses to the counter before whirling back to survey the damage, both hands firmly planted on Whitney's waist.

The red stain spreading from her chest downward had to be instant karma, a stark reminder that whatever she'd intended by slowly coming up behind Andy was not friendly enough for the relationship they were trying to build.

Rattled hazel eyes flicked up to Whitney's. "You're going to have to take off your shirt."

Neither were comments like that. Still, Whitney doubled down with, "And bra."

Andy blinked, lips agape. "I'm... sorry?"

"It's really starting to seep in."

"Right." Her eyes fell shut, and a gulp slid down her throat before she locked hands with Whitney and turned. "Here." She herded her through the living room toward the first door in a short hallway and pushed it open.

A light flicked on, and Whitney did a quick pass around the new space—the large walk-in shower, a wide mirror spanning hers-and-hers sinks, charcoal flooring complemented by white walls, and a tan vanity with black accents. "Are you sure this apartment wasn't staged precisely for you?"

"It is kind of perfect, when I manage to forget there's a mystery urn on a shelf in the study." Andy chuckled. "Use whatever you need. I'll grab you a shirt."

Before Whitney could request clarification on the words *mystery urn*, the door swung shut, and she was alone in the bathroom. She moved toward the mirror, fingers busy unbuttoning her shirt, eyes still perusing the space for new and old signs of Andy. The air hinted at tea tree and mint, and a wicker hamper piled with artfully rolled towels stood by the shower. Because of course Andy would work twelve hours a day and *still* maintain her lived-in apartment like a luxe Airbnb.

"Do you want a regular shirt?" Andy yelled from outside the bathroom, startling her. "Or a hoodie, maybe. I don't have a button-up exactly like the one you had on."

Whitney sputtered a laugh, rolling her eyes. "Any shirt is good, Andy!"

"Fine. I brought three." Her answer echoed from just on the other side of the door.

Whitney reached for the handle and pulled it open. "You couldn't have just picked?"

"I could have, but..." Andy stammered to a stop, eyes trailing Whitney's body in a slow descent, darkened with the same reverence of a week ago despite the shirt still draped over Whitney's torso, buttons merely undone to expose her wine-stained bra and abdomen.

Every nerve ending in her body sparked. Knowing she still affected Andy this way was the biggest turn-on of all.

"I didn't, um." Andy drew in a breath, bringing her eyes level with Whitney's as she offered the neatly folded pile of shirts. "I didn't know what you'd want. Take one and leave the others next to yours. I'll get the wine out later."

"Thank you."

"Don't mention it." A brusque nod, then the door was swinging shut again.

Whitney did a quick assessment of the three tops: a plain white crewneck, a sweater soft enough to rival cashmere, and a zip-up hoodie with the words "London Film School" stamped across the chest. As she discarded her own shirt and pulled on the hoodie, she tried not to consider why the brush of cotton against her skin and the earthy-sweet scent of cardamom, linked with the place where

Andy's life without her had begun, gave her even the slightest bit of comfort.

She sauntered back into the living room to the soft tune of a Zola Simone song, two glasses strategically placed on either side of a stainless wine cooler, the lights dimmed to a hue somewhere between pleasing and outright romantic.

Andy sat up straighter on the sofa, setting her phone on the coffee table, gaze clearly drawn to the hoodie Whitney had chosen. A smile ghosted her lips, though it never fully materialized even as her long fingers wrapped around the spine of one glass and she lifted it in offering.

"You know it's okay if you have to work," said Whitney, eying Andy's phone. She settled onto the sofa, close enough that their knees brushed when she pulled one leg beneath her.

Andy picked up her own glass, smiling. "Let me worry about when I have to work."

The wine held notes of blackberry and anise with a smoky undertone—the kind of fruit-forward, dry red Whitney always enjoyed. "How's it been going at Gia?"

"Good. I have plenty of B-roll footage, even a few snips of the staff talking about what it's like to work there." She blinked, brows raised in awe as she angled her body closer to Whitney. "The environment is incredible. I mean, I could never do it. I sweat through a shirt a day just hovering around with my camera, but for them it's nonstop. It's yelling orders and somehow managing to support each other in the process. Your brother's a bit of a joker. Val, too, although she's the sweetest. And Jenn is just..." Andy's shoulders dropped, and she released a slow exhale. "She never loses her cool. I thought it would be harder, you know?"

"How do you mean?"

"I thought she'd hate me being there, in her space, recording all the time. But when she's in that kitchen, I don't think anything else even exists to her. Except maybe Val." Andy stared into her wine, beaming with intrigue and admiration. "Sometimes, Val laughs really loud in the middle of some absurd debate with Landon or Warren. Pineapple on pizza or something."

Whitney rolled her eyes. "Landon will die on that hill, but the correct answer is no."

"Exactly!" Andy chuckled, a stray curl from her pixie cut falling against her right brow. "Sometimes they get a little rowdy, and Jenn kind of glances at them. Everything I knew said she's the type of boss who would be annoyed by that kind of thing, scold them for being too distracted. Except she doesn't, and they're not. The cooking and camaraderie are as easy as breathing to them." She shrugged, tipping her glass for another sip. "I don't think Jenn even notices, but in those moments, she smiles at Val, and it's so soft, Whit. It's so freaking soft I think the only thing she must love more than being in that kitchen is having that laugh right over her shoulder."

Andy shook her head, locking eyes with Whitney. "It's more intimate than I was looking for, but I don't know. It feels important to who she is, somehow."

"Yeah. That makes sense." Whitney had certainly spent more time with Val than Jenn in the months since she'd connected with Avery and Landon, but she knew exactly what Andy meant. She'd seen it, the incomparable, euphoric wonder whenever Jenn observed Val doing something no one else would find particularly remarkable. She'd seen it when her own sister looked at her girlfriend, Ky, or when Dad looked at Norah. She'd even seen it on Landon lately. It was so instinctive, so inherently tied to the hyperawareness of her own body every time Andy's skin so much as brushed hers.

It had been years since Whitney had been able to sit and listen to Andy's excited recount of her day, experience the raw passion oozing from her whenever she gushed about a subject like this. Maybe that was the reason Whitney's resentment over her leaving was a perennial ebb and flow. How could she ever resent Andy doing what she felt she needed to do to have become the woman staring back at her? Passionate, fearless, breathtakingly beautiful.

Maybe she would be gone in a week, having swept through the city like the calmest of storms. Whitney didn't think she'd be able to deny herself moments like this either way.

"Sorry." Andy's expression turned bashful beneath her stare. "Talk to me about you. After your injury I never thought you'd go the gym route, or have anything to do with athletics, really. I thought maybe you'd reach for Broadway."

Whitney leaned back into the sofa. "Still terrible at small talk, huh?"

"Do you not want to talk about it?"

"No. I can talk about it."

Talking about it was the only way she'd gotten past it—over-rotating on a dismount and tearing her ACL. It didn't have to be career-ending, but after surgery and ten months of physio at twenty years old, her Olympic prospects were abysmal. Then again, maybe she hadn't wanted it badly enough; not the way Andy had wanted filmmaking, anyway.

"I'll never stop loving gymnastics," she said. "I still choreograph floor routines in my head, get the urge to do a triple tuck when no one's watching." She scoffed a laugh. "Sometimes I even do it just to remind myself I can. But I think I had to let it go for the same reason I never considered pursuing Broadway. Not that I was even good enough for Broadway."

"Of course you were good enough." Andy reached for her hand.

"Maybe. But I'm not a competitive enough person to have wanted to find out. Plays, being in the gym, they're just things I loved, Andy. Besides, I don't think I could've handled an ounce of popularity. I don't know how you do it."

A crease emerged between Andy's brows, though she smiled through her confusion. "Hardly anyone remembers a documentarian's name, Whit."

"Except maybe ones who dated Livia Lincoln."

"God." Andy winced, shaking her head. "That got blown way out of proportion, which I guess comes with dating a TV actress. But it lasted all of five minutes, and her publicist hated me. Apparently, I wasn't on Livia's level."

"That's ridiculous."

"I'm not broken up about it. In a lot of ways, it feels like I'm exactly where I'm supposed to be." Her thumb traced Whitney's knuckles in a gentle, sweeping motion, and Whitney grounded herself in the moment, trying not to read too much into the words. "What about you? You said things were off with Isabel, but has anyone else felt like, I don't know, the one?"

Not since you, Whitney thought. The words out of her mouth were, "I don't know if I believe there's a *one*. I guess I just want someone to..."

...sit on the couch and drink wine with after a long day. Someone who knew all the songs from her favorite musicals and sang them like no one was listening, like they didn't care if anyone was listening. She was self-aware enough to

recognize that she was describing Andy, that she wanted the exact opposite of what she *should* want.

"I don't know." She shrugged. "If I'm being honest, I don't think I trust myself to know anymore."

"Why?" Andy's free hand settled onto Whitney's knee, her thumb employing the same stroking motion as the one against Whitney's knuckles. Whitney's jeans were doing nothing to ease her sensitivity to the touch.

Her thoughts grew more muddled, blending truths too sincere to confess with words she should be saying, words meant to keep her grounded in the now instead of then. "Because the last person I truly wanted didn't want me back. Not the way I wanted them."

A hand cradled Whitney's cheek, and her eyes fell shut as she fisted Andy's shirt.

"I'm trying really hard not to be presumptuous in thinking that person was me," Andy said.

"Andy..."

"I know you said you don't want to talk about it, but if it was me... I *did* want you, Whitney. Almost as badly as I do now."

"Friends aren't supposed to talk like that."

"Then I call timeout."

"You can't call timeout on being friends. That's not how it works."

"How does it work?" Andy whispered. "What are the rules here, Whit? Because I'm pretty sure friends don't look at each other the way you've been looking at me all night."

"You said you didn't think we should do this again."

"That doesn't mean I don't want to."

"God, Andy. Me too, but—" Whitney really needed to catch her breath before she was full-on hyperventilating.

"Did you touch yourself?"

"What?" Her eyes sprang open.

"That night. After we—after you fucked me on that couch in your office."

"Andy..."

"Tell me."

A shiver darted down Whitney's spine at the memory. She couldn't think of another night she'd gone to bed so frustrated and turned-on that it physically hurt. She just couldn't do it. The second she closed her eyes and trailed her fingers down her stomach, into her underwear, she knew whose face she'd see in her mind, knew the voice she'd hear, and she couldn't. Somehow, it felt like betraying an unspoken vow to never let Andy that close again. "I didn't. I couldn't. I *can't*, Andy."

"Yes, you can. Right here if you want to."

Whitney squirmed beneath her gaze, her arousal making itself known between her thighs. "What are you saying?"

Andy moved onto her knees, and somehow, Whitney's brain decided the only rational response was to lie on her back. Gawk, anticipate, *want*. Andy fingered the zipper of Whitney's hoodie—*her* hoodie—and pulled, slowly exposing Whitney's chest and stomach but never breaking eye contact. "Is this okay?"

Whitney nodded. As if she could do anything but nod.

"What about this?" The button of her jeans snapped open.

"Yes."

Hands emerged on the waist of her pants, signaling Andy's intent to remove them, and Whitney lifted her hips enough to comply, both their shoes long discarded by the front door. Heat crept through her, her chest and stomach fluttery with expectation, with Andy's stare sweeping up her exposed legs to black, French-cut underwear, her tensing abdomen, the curve of her breasts, her hard nipples barely shielded by either half of the hoodie, to land on her face.

"I think I get it," said Andy. She moved closer and settled onto her side, so close her breath echoed in warm pants against Whitney's ear. "I get why you hesitated when I wanted to reciprocate."

"I had training with a client."

"Mm-hm. White Collar. But it was more than that, right? I haven't earned it back. Your trust. So I get it if you needed it to be one-sided, even if you still do. You can have me however you want, but first, I think you should listen to what your body is trying to tell you."

Whitney clenched her thighs together, her attempt at a laugh coming out stuttered and choked. "You expect me to just touch myself while you watch?"

"You say that like it would be the first time."

"That was different."

"It feels the same." Andy licked her lips. "But I won't if you don't want me to, if it's too much."

"You won't what?"

"I won't watch."

Whitney trailed a hand along Andy's neck, through the tapered curls of her hair and pulled her nose to nose, keeping her there, assuaging any doubt that Whitney wanted her anywhere but right on this couch, stealing the air from her lungs, making her skin too hot and her body tremble. As she walked her own fingers to where she desperately needed them, beneath the hem of her underwear, through trimmed curls to her aching clit, she ignored the logic that this was just as intimate as letting Andy touch her. She bit her bottom lip to suppress a moan.

Andy's palm dragged up her ribs to cup her breast.

Her breath caught. "Andy—"

"Sorry." She sounded breathless, teetering on the edge of wrecked.

Whitney caught her hand as she withdrew it, bringing it back to her breast and arching into the touch. Their mouths collided, though she couldn't remember who closed the gap if she tried. Not with the glide of their tongues, and her own fingers circling her clit, the pressure downright delicious as her body reeled closer to the precipice. Too fast. Way too fast.

She jerked her head back, needing to catch her breath, to look Andy in the eyes despite the crushing weight on her chest. "Andy. Andy, I—" She fumbled for a tighter hold, her grip painfully tight, almost as if she was afraid the second her orgasm hit, Andy would disintegrate before her eyes.

"I'm here. I'm right here."

It hit like a shock wave down her spine, ripples of pleasure curling her toes, reducing her to a quivering, tongue-tied mess. Spots flashed behind her closed eyelids. Vaguely, she registered fingers tracing shapes along her stomach and unintelligible words being whispered into the crook of her neck. Her vision swam as her gaze met glimmering hazel eyes and kiss-swollen lips. And she waited. Waited for the embarrassment, panic, fear to set in.

It never did.

Instead, she swept ruffled curls off Andy's forehead, and she thought, if she never felt this way about anyone else again, why shouldn't she let herself have it? At least this time, she knew it was temporary.

Andy pressed a soft kiss to her lips, asking, "Good?"

Whitney shook her head. "Better."

17

Day five of shooting at Gia began exactly like the others. Andy arrived hours before open with only Avery to let her in, the two of them skirting around conversation until someone else arrived. Over the past week, she'd gotten used to the dynamic of their non-relationship. They'd probably never be friends, but Andy held a healthy respect for her nonetheless. Sometimes, like the day they'd first met, or even in those moments when she'd drop in to check if Andy needed anything, a ghost of a smile would cross her features before she turned on her stilettos and strutted back to her office, and a sliver of thought would slink into Andy's mind that maybe Avery respected her too.

It was a functional if not simple relationship that had become almost normal. Except, this morning, Andy hadn't been able to look her in the eyes once.

She'd yet to decide if it was because last night she'd lain next to Whitney, kissing and caressing her while she stroked herself to orgasm, or if it was because of what had happened after. How Whitney's eyes had darkened and she'd commanded, voice strained and sexy, Andy to undress before proceeding to take her piece by piece with her tongue. On the desk in the small study of the apartment. Minutes later on the California king in the master bedroom. This morning when Andy had woken to the press of lips on her shoulder blade. Whitney had been so fucking relentless Andy had taken an extra two minutes in the bathroom just to reaffirm that the tattoo next to her clavicle didn't in fact read *power bottom*.

It was nothing short of a miracle she'd made it to work on her own two legs.

"Did you have fun last night?"

"What?" Andy's head snapped up so fast she went dizzy, losing her grip on the telephoto lens in her hand, then scrambling to catch it before it clattered to the floor. She blew out an audible exhale, relief overwhelming her shock at Avery's question only long enough for her hands to stop shaking. *Smooth, Vahn.* She drew in a breath, aiming for composed when she looked up at Avery again. From what she'd observed, Avery was brilliant at a lot of things. She had exceptional style, was evidently well versed in managing multiple aspects at Gia without ever breaking a sweat, and she was the quintessential sibling and friend. But surely, she wasn't a goddamn mind reader. "Sorry. You were saying?"

Avery's brows inched up in suspicion. "The ice skating show. Did you have a good time?"

"Oh, yeah. It was great. Jax's daughter loved it."

"I bet Whitney did too. She's hopeless when it comes to that kind of thing," said Avery. "Weird she didn't text me about it last night or send at least one picture."

"She was probably just tired. Not that I would know for sure," Andy tacked on quickly. "I'm sure you'll be hearing all about it soon enough."

"You seem a little tired yourself. Did you sleep okay?"

Was it only in her mind, or did that sound like bait? Bait she would absolutely not be taking. She shrugged, telegraphing all the nonchalance her body could muster. "I'm always tired during shoots. It's the longer days. Post-production's worse."

"I imagine it is. Reviewing and organizing all that footage." Avery leaned against the paneled accent wall by the entrance of the room as she crossed both arms under her chest. "My girlfriend's a travel influencer. It's not nearly on the same scale as what you do, but she edits her own videos, and I watch her lose hours at her desk for a two-minute reel."

Andy snickered, inadvertently drawing a smile from Avery, a gesture so mundane it took them both a moment to perceive the crack in the icy exterior Avery had maintained so well. She dipped her head and tapped a heel against the lacquered floor.

Andy shifted her gaze from her tripod to the semi-staged space. The dark oak tabletops were arranged with plate settings and wineglasses, contemporary pendant lights dangling between the exposed rafters of the ceiling. "I should get back to setting up. It's been a while since I've done this without a camera operator and sound recordist."

"Do you need to call them in?" Avery frowned. "Why didn't you say something?"

"Jenn didn't seem crazy about having a full crew here, which is fine," Andy clarified. "Don't worry. It's nothing I haven't done before."

Muted voices traveled from beyond the room, gradually increasing in pitch, and seconds later, Jenn and Val emerged next to Avery.

"Hey, you two." Val glanced between them, her smile

fueled with that easy way of making any space feel lighter. "Shooting the breeze before the big day?"

Jenn groaned, prompting Val to spin in her direction.

"I mean, this completely normal, *insignificant* day."

"I love you, but subtlety has never been your strong suit," Jenn deadpanned.

"Ay, baby." Val leveled both hands on Jenn's shoulders, looking her in the eyes despite the conceivable height difference. "We talked about this. It's not an interview. It's just chatting with a friend. That's all Andy is." Val shot Andy a look, Jenn's expectant stare following. "Right, Andy?"

"Yeah. Of course." Her nod was undoubtedly too enthusiastic. "I'm... friendly."

Avery's raised brow said Andy wasn't at all convincing.

She cleared her throat, stepping away from the tripod and closer to Jenn. "We went over the discussion topics, remember? Nothing makes it in that you're not comfortable with. And it's just the two of us. If anything, I should be the one who's nervous. You're—"

"Please don't say my name with that veil of disbelief." Jenn grimaced. "I'm a chef. Not a celebrity."

"Well, for some people you're both. But"—Andy held up a conciliatory hand—"okay. Jenn and Andy having a talk. Just like Val said."

"Sure." Jenn pursed her lips.

"I know you want to wrap before the rest of the staff is in. I just need about ten minutes to finish setting up. Do you want to hop straight in with the pre-interview now?"

"Yes." A decided nod. "Yes. Let's do that."

"Do you need a coffee? Breakfast?"

"I'd much rather just get this over with," Jenn insisted.

Avery and Val exchanged a look. "So we're going to go,"

Avery said. "But we'll be right downstairs if either of you need anything."

Val tipped onto her toes and pressed a kiss to Jenn's lips, the blatant affection endearing but still so jarring whenever Andy thought about the woman she'd researched. It didn't fit—this image of reserved tranquility and public displays of affection with a subordinate in her own restaurant. "No te preocupes," whispered Val. "Lo vas a hacer genial. I love you." Then both she and Avery headed down the stairs.

Jenn drew in a breath, facing Andy. "Where should we start?"

"Over here would be great." Andy pointed to a four-top toward the center of the room. She'd decided almost on her first walk-through that this room—Private Dining 1, they'd called it—would be perfect for the interview. Great lighting. Minimal ambient sound. Aesthetic appeal. "We can do a few shots sitting, then we'll go down to the kitchen and you can cook something while we talk since that's where you're most relaxed."

"Sitting is good." Jenn nodded. "I spent the way over trying to decide what to do with my hands."

Andy sniggered. "Get comfortable. I'll be ready in a sec."

"Okay. Let's start simple." Andy sat out of frame, a single sheet of paper on her lap, eyes locked with Jenn. "Did you always know you wanted to be a chef?"

"Not always. No."

Andy nodded, waiting.

Jenn's eyes widened with realization, and she shifted in her chair. "I'm supposed to elaborate."

"That would be nice, yeah." Andy laughed.

"It started with my first visit to my nonna, Gia. We hadn't met until I was fourteen when she sent a ticket for me to come spend a few weeks of the summer with her in Florence. I was an only child. It was just me and my mom, and she had to work a lot. Before that first visit, I never met anyone who'd taken as much care, as much pride, in cooking as my nonna did. She made me her sous-chef for every meal until eventually I was the one bringing her recipes for us to try. I suppose you could say that's when I truly *knew* I wanted to cook for a living."

"Gia," said Andy. "Your restaurants are named after your grandmother, then?"

"They are. Nothing else felt right."

"Is she the reason you went to culinary school in Italy?"

"Most of it, yes."

"What was that like? Being young, queer, brown in a foreign country?"

"Remarkably not much different than it is here. I find comfort in structure. Always have. So I planned. I learned Italian, spent enough time with my nonna to convince myself my pronunciation was good enough to not sound *too* foreign. If I stood out for anything, I wanted it to be for my knowledge and talent with food." A dip emerged between her brows. "But someone like me walks into one of the best culinary schools in the world and before you even pick up a pan, half the people look at you like you wandered into the wrong building."

Andy nodded in understanding. Half her career had been spent battling exactly the sentiment that she was somewhere she wasn't meant to be.

"I figure part of the reason was because eighty percent of my class were men," said Jenn. "The other part was probably because I was one of two students of color in our class, which didn't make for an unpleasant experience in itself. It just didn't do much for my sense of belonging."

"Is there anything that made that easier for you?"

Jenn's gaze wandered, and she breathed in, seemingly gathering courage. "My mother. She always used to say we don't exist for other people, that we are under no obligation to make sense to them." She scoffed a laugh. "I think she hammered it into me without me even realizing, but in many ways that has carried me through my whole career. Perhaps it made me a bit single-minded, insular, but keeping those blinders on... all I ever had to think about was where I wanted to be and how hard I had to work to get there. I didn't open my own restaurant at twenty-seven wondering what other people thought of me."

"Twenty-seven?" Research had yielded that information, but it didn't make hearing it from Jenn's lips any less awe-inspiring, especially considering the average restaurant owner was ten years older. "That's ambitious. Some might even say brave."

"My mother would say it's because I like my own systems too much to get stuck in someone else's."

"So you like being your own boss?"

"The polite way of saying I'm a control freak, yes."

A laugh bubbled up in Andy's chest.

"Sorry." Jenn frowned. "Was that too casual?"

"Not at all. You're doing great."

Jenn nodded briskly. "Good."

"Let's keep going." Andy smiled. "I noticed some of your staff have pronouns on their name tags. Tell me more about that."

"Well, I certainly can't take credit. Our youngest front-of-house staff, Joey, suggested it in a team meeting. I signed off on the new name tags the next day. Gia has always been my safe haven. I spent more time here than in my own house the year my mom died. Anything I can do to make my staff feel a little safer here is an automatic yes."

"That's really encouraging. Are you hiring by chance?"

Jenn chuckled. "Not someone with your skill set, no."

"Sounds like I might need to start looking into culinary schools, then."

"Feel free to call me if you ever do."

"Okay, let's cut it here." Andy clicked off the camera, beaming as she got to her feet.

A heavy sigh resonated between them, Jenn fisting and then stretching her fingers in a repeated motion that made her seem far more nervous than she'd looked on camera. "Did you get everything you need?"

"We touched all the initial topics and then some." Andy moved closer to her, turning off the mic that stood a few feet away. "I'll review it and let you know if that second sit-down is needed, but I really requested it as a contingency. I think we're good."

"Wonderful." Jenn's eyes darted toward the watch on her right wrist and Andy found herself reaching for her phone to check the time, if only to ensure they'd stayed on schedule. She'd planned to end before most of the staff came in for their pre-shift meeting. She was relieved to find that they had, though the general silence beyond the walls served as confirmation enough.

"I know I've said it before, but I truly appreciate you allowing me to come in and do all this. Filming. Getting to talk to you. All of it."

"Avery's the one you should be thanking," said Jenn. "She was very convincing on your behalf."

Andy still couldn't figure out why. Why would Avery go to bat for someone she'd explicitly stated she didn't know—and didn't *want* to know, at that?

"I suppose you also remind me of someone, which made this a bit personal for me too."

The base of Andy's neck tingled with curiosity. "Can I ask who that is?"

"Myself," Jenn said matter-of-factly. "A younger version, anyway. Maybe it's your evident ambition or this idea I've formed that you think you have something to prove to the world." She held up her hand, unaware of the tightening vise in Andy's chest. "Forgive me. I know you're not here to be analyzed. I truly don't make a habit of it."

"I wouldn't assume you do." Andy swallowed despite the rising ache in her throat. "I know the interview is over, but um, is that how you felt? Like you had something to prove to the world?"

"I don't think I always knew it, but yes. My father wanted nothing to do with me before I was even born. I had no siblings. I was much too awkward to find friends to validate me." She laughed, but there was no humor in it. "Eventually, I learned it wasn't just my father. People will write you off without knowing a single thing about you. Because you're a person of color. Because you're a woman. Because you identify as anything other than straight or binary."

Blood rushed in Andy's ears.

"But you deserve as much space here as everyone else. You shouldn't have to work twice as hard to convince yourself you've earned it. But if you *do* work twice as hard, make sure it's because you love the thing you do so much you can't imagine being anything but exceptional. But also, remember, it's okay to want other things. To let yourself have them."

Andy couldn't help feeling like Jenn knew a lot more than she was saying, like Jenn knew *her*. How bizarre. Apart from their original meeting, which had mostly been about the logistics of Jenn being in the docuseries, they'd had maybe one five-minute conversation a day in the last week. Nothing as profound as the things they'd talked about today. How could Jenn speak so entirely to feelings Andy had never shared with anyone else? Her desire to prove she *was* good enough. Her simultaneous longing and fear of *other things*.

Her thoughts drifted to yesterday, to the ring she'd seen on Val's necklace, and she braced herself to ask the question she'd been wondering every time she saw Jenn and Val together. "Can I ask you something personal?"

"Isn't this all personal?" Jenn smiled.

"Touché." Andy shuffled her feet. "Is being with Val one of those things? I mean, how does someone like you make the decision to be with someone so far down the chain of command?"

Jenn hummed, considering the question long enough for Andy to doubt whether she'd overstepped or if there had been another, better way for her to have phrased it. But Jenn didn't seem bothered by it. In fact, the glint in her eyes seemed to have brightened. "What are you doing tomorrow night at eight?"

"Um." Andy blinked, caught off guard. "Working."

"Of course." Jenn bobbed her head with an acceptance few people would display having heard Andy planned to spend her Saturday night working.

"Why? I could probably move some things around."

"Well, don't go out of your way. It's very short notice, but if you can make it, I'd like to invite you to a party at my house."

"A party?"

"A... small gathering," she amended. "Friends and family. Very, as you would say, low-key."

A chuckle escaped Andy's lips. She wasn't sure what she'd done to earn an invitation to a party attended by Jenn's notoriously small circle, or what it had to do with the question she'd asked about Val, but she wasn't stupid enough to say no. "Eight o'clock. I'll be there."

Jenn patted her on the shoulder. "Good. I'll text you the address."

18

Whitney tucked a towel along her chest, drying her hair with another as she exited the en suite into her bedroom. Her eyes drifted to the watch on her wrist. She had about half an hour before she had to meet her mom for dinner, but she'd decided to take her time. It wasn't like Mom would be at the restaurant on time. Actually, Whitney wouldn't be surprised to receive a frantic call in twenty minutes that kicked off with an anxiety reel about how Mom had just left work and they should either push their reservation or have a charcuterie board night at home. With the exhaustion winding its way through her limbs, she wouldn't be opposed to the idea.

Still, she couldn't bring herself to regret last night or how her morning had begun with the pleas of *oh my God, Whit, please don't stop* looping in her head. Maybe it was only in her imagination, but Andy had gotten more vocal, and Whitney had liked it a little too much. So much that she'd rolled out of bed the latest she had in years. Between leaving Andy's well after seven and dropping by her own apartment to check on Wes, she'd been more than an hour late for work. It was safe to say he was not impressed by her staying out all night. There was a drying pee stain on her living room carpet to show for it.

An insistent buzzing drew her out of her thoughts, and she moved from her closet to her bed to pick up her phone, instantly warmed at the name linked to the incoming video call. Sliding onto her bed, she tapped the answer button. Andy's face filled the screen—makeup light, hair the perfect balance of coiffed and curly, eyes the brightest shade of meadowy brown.

Excitement slipped into Whitney's words and tone before she settled on something more conservative. "I was just thinking about you."

"Should I take the towel wrapped around you to mean those thoughts were anything but innocent?" Andy beamed.

"I mean, they weren't *all* that innocent, but it's not what you're thinking either. So wipe that grin off your face."

"Hmm." Her tongue swiped across her lips, making Whitney's stomach dip. "I'm not sure I know what you mean. What am I thinking?"

Warmth crept up Whitney's neck. "Stop it."

"Is that a blush?" Lines creased Andy's forehead, though her smile never wavered. "I could almost mistake you for shy if you hadn't tried to bend me into a pretzel last night."

"You weren't complaining then, or this morning for that matter."

"Oh, this is not me complaining. I may not have your flexibility, but everything aches in the absolute best way."

"Sounds like a good problem to have." Whitney crossed her legs to take the edge off. All this talk was making her body remember too much, and the last thing she needed was to be all keyed up half an hour before heading out to meet her mom. "I'm assuming you didn't just call to tease me..."

"Says the person who answered a video call in a towel and nothing else."

Whitney rolled her eyes, laughing. "Stop deflecting."

"Come over tonight."

Her brows shot up. She wasn't sure what she'd been expecting, but those words combined with the level of certainty in Andy's eyes wasn't it.

"Not for sex," Andy rushed out. "Not that it's off the table either. I just... I want to see you, if that's okay."

"I thought you had to work."

"I do. Is it crazy I'm asking anyway? I'll make dinner." Her face scrunched up in the most adorable fashion. "No. I'm a terrible cook, but I'll buy dinner. Mexican, or whatever you're in the mood for. We can eat and just catch up on our days. Then I'll work for a couple of hours, and you can..." She trailed off as if she was literally making it up as the words left her mouth. "I don't know. Watch floor routine videos? Do you still like to do that after a long day?" A wince. "Sorry. I'm rambling, I know. This all sounded like a much better idea in my head."

Whitney's throat thickened. Had she ever seen Andy this flustered?

"Okay, wait." Andy drew in a breath. "Let's rewind. Forget I said any of that. It's Friday night. You probably have plans and me inviting you to just stay at home with me when I can't even properly entertain you is crazy."

Whitney didn't need to be entertained all night. If she was willing to admit it, having Andy close by would be more soothing than any night out. More than that, Andy having to put in a few extra hours after a day of filming felt like a window into a typical day in their life. It almost seemed cruel that Whitney was being offered it now when she couldn't *really* have it.

"You're not saying anything," said Andy. "Did I make it weird? I made it weird."

Whitney shook her head. "You didn't. It's just, I'm getting ready for an early dinner with my mom."

"Right. That makes sense." Andy nodded.

"But I could come by after if you're up to it?"

"Yeah?" Hope flashed in her eyes.

"I mean, I'm not sure what time that'll be. My mom has a new boyfriend, and once she gets talking, it could be a while."

Andy smiled. "Take your time. I'll wait for you."

Conflict stirred in Whitney's chest, clenching it tighter. She didn't know whether Andy was being purposefully ambivalent, coding her words with an intensity that left Whitney so vulnerable to misinterpretation, but for the sake of her sanity, she decided to take everything at face value.

As if he'd heard Whitney planning another night out without him, Wes plodded into the room and plopped down at her feet, his head cocked and snout trained up at her. She switched to the back camera to give Andy a clear view of him. "I think he's still mad I didn't come home last night."

Andy pouted. "We're sorry, buddy. You can come with her tonight."

Wes yipped, prompting Whitney to flip the camera back toward her. "Don't get him excited. He's bizarrely attached to you, and I can't guarantee he'll behave if you're still working when we get there. I'll just ask my mom to take him for the night."

"It's okay." Andy shook her head. "Bring him with you. It'll be nice to see him."

"Are you sure?"

"Yes, I'm sure."

"Okay," Whitney softly acquiesced. "I have to get ready, but, um..."

"Yeah. Say hi to your mom for me." Andy's eyes fell shut. "Or don't. I don't know why I said that."

Probably because back then, it was exactly what Andy would say whenever she knew Whitney would be seeing her mom. Before Whitney could respond, or maybe subconsciously searching for an out, her gaze shifted to the expanse of blue sky in Andy's background. "Wait, where are you?"

"On the roof of Gia. The section not designated for private dining. Avery warned me about coming up here, but it's kind of nice. Calm."

Of course Avery had warned Andy about the roof, although she claimed her aversion to heights wasn't a fear so much as a strong dislike of "being too high up without purposefully designed barriers." Whitney's brain clung to the word *calm* all the same, her curiosity piquing over whether Andy had needed it for some reason. "Is everything okay?"

"Yeah. I had a great talk with Jenn today. The interview, but after too." Andy's expression was riddled with the kind of confusion and contentment brought on by a pleasant but baffling dream. "She actually invited me to a party at her house tomorrow night."

"She did?" Avery's voice echoed in Whitney's head, reiterating how Jenn agreeing to be in the docuseries might lead to Andy orbiting their social circle for weeks. An invite to Jenn's house was proof Andy had practically infiltrated their ranks, but somehow, the idea didn't seem all that bothersome. If anything, Whitney wouldn't be the newbie to their circle anymore—at least temporarily—and she'd have someone she'd known longer than a few months to talk to. "Val texted me about that too. It's kind of weird. They're usually a little less random about their dinner parties. Invites like weeks in advance."

"Hmm." Andy shrugged. "I don't know. I guess we'll see."

"Yeah."

"Text me when you're on your way later?"

"I will." Whitney clicked off the call, though it took her another thirty seconds before she stopped staring at her darkened screen and headed to her closet to get dressed. She settled on a pale purple, puffed-sleeve top and dark jeans with block-heel booties. Simple and sophisticated for the little French bistro Mom had picked for dinner, but casually sexy enough that Andy might do that slow head-to-toe appraisal that drove Whitney crazy. She left Wes with an extra treat, a kiss between his eyes, and a promise to be back soon.

Fifteen minutes later, her thoughts of Andy quelled by a stroll through the ever-lively Theater District in fifty-degree weather, she sat across from her mom with a bottle of Châteauneuf-du-Pape between them.

"I think I'll have the duck confit since dinner's on you tonight." Mischief twinkled in Mom's eyes, though her smile gave away her teasing. Paying being the late person's obligation was a five-year tradition between them. Even so, they never failed to take advantage of that fifteen-minute window most restaurants allowed for holding reservations.

"You beat me here by two minutes," said Whitney. "And only because I decided to walk instead of driving."

"Snooze you lose, honeybee."

Whitney narrowed her gaze. "You're in an exceptionally good mood. Is this that honeymoon phase people are always on about?"

Mom waved the thought away with a flick of her wrist. "Cillian and I are just getting to know each other."

"Otherwise known as dating. You can say the word, Mom." Whitney chuckled.

"Well, he is wonderful, but you've heard enough of that."

"I can always stand to hear more. But only for you."

"You're in a pretty good mood yourself," said Mom, her gaze still glued to the menu. "Maybe I'll go for the salmon."

Whitney scanned her own menu for the salmon on the off chance that she might be interested. *Grilled salmon with red quinoa pilaf and bell pepper coulis.* She hummed to herself, eyes flitting to the pasta dishes. "The fettuccini carbonara looks better."

"I bet you already knew that's what you wanted. I've still never met anyone who's as decisive at restaurants as you are."

"It's my one and only superpower." Whitney laughed.

The server emerged and announced himself, hands gracefully tucked behind his back even as they reeled out their orders. Once Mom had sufficiently prodded him with questions of "How's the" and "Would you recommend," she plied him with a zealous thanks and he disappeared to have their orders put in. Whitney asked her mom about her week and whether she had plans this weekend, which prompted her to monologue about how she didn't have plans but Cillian had surprised her with a lunchtime helicopter ride to Napa two days prior.

"If things keep going well, I may be going to Dublin in July."

Three months away. Enough time to feel out any major red flags.

"You should come," Mom went on, her tone imbued with excitement.

"With you and your boyfriend to Dublin?" Whitney grimaced. "Mom, I love you, but I'm going to have to pass."

"Cillian is not my boyfriend."

"Your... *man companion*. Whatever we're calling him, thank you, but no."

Mom reached for her wine. "Well, you have lots of time to reconsider. Do you want to see a movie later?"

Whitney wrapped her fingers around the spine of her own glass and took a sip, letting the bold flavor marinate on her tongue. Not too sweet, modest acidity. She hadn't told anyone what she and Andy had been doing partly because she wasn't sure how to define it, but also because she didn't want to have to explain feelings she'd yet to sort through herself. Still, she'd never been able to lie to her mom. "I promised Andy I'd come over after dinner."

"Oh?" Mom's brows crept up, though she didn't seem too surprised. "Have the two of you been spending much time together?"

"Not much, but *some* time, yeah." Whitney wilted, uncomfortable with her confession, maybe also her mother's scrutiny. "You know what? I'll just message her that I'll be over later. She should be working, anyway."

"You promised to go over even though she'll be working?"

"Yeah. We're going to hang out after."

"After?" Mom tipped her head to one side. "By the time you're through with dinner it'll be nine. Add a movie and you won't be there until midnight. What exactly do you two plan on doing at that hour?"

Whitney's gaze wandered to the low ceiling of the bistro, the bright yellow walls, servers caught in a dance too harried for the slow instrumental underlying the diners' quiet conversations.

"I see." Mom pursed her lips in acceptance. "Are you being careful?"

"Jesus, Mom." This was what happened when someone grew up with one parent at the forefront of every major conversation in their life. No topic was off-limits. Whitney loved that she could tell her mom anything, but that didn't make it any less awkward when Mom decided she would just *ask* anything. "Yes. I had my annual checkup last week, and she hasn't been—" Whitney cut herself off with a wince. "Everyone's being careful."

"Well, that's comforting, but it's not what I meant, honey."

Whitney frowned.

"I meant are you taking care of you?" Mom tapped the spot over her own heart with two fingers.

The answer should've been an immediate yes, but Whitney wasn't sure she knew how to be careful with her heart when it came to Andy. She'd tried respecting the distance when Andy had left. She'd tried resentment. She'd tried anger. Nothing worked. Andy had always been the one person capable of breaking through her walls even when she'd fortified them with titanium. She'd tried everything except acceptance, so this was where they were. Andy would leave again. It was going to hurt. Whitney had made her peace with that.

"Does she know you were going to propose? Before she left."

The words slammed into the fragile mental box in which Whitney had kept that detail carefully sequestered, taking it out and reliving it only in her darkest moments— moments when she'd tried and failed to make sense of how she'd gotten it so terribly wrong. Twenty-two, fresh out of undergrad, was a delicate age riddled with so much uncertainty, but it didn't matter. Whitney knew she wanted forever with Andy or as close as they could get. They'd wanted all the same things. At least, she'd thought so.

"She doesn't know," said Whitney. "And I don't really think that's relevant to what we're doing."

Their server swept in, announcing each dish of grilled salmon and fettuccini carbonara as he placed a steaming plate in front of Mom, then Whitney. A simultaneous thanks resonated as he turned to leave once more.

Mom picked up her knife and fork. "And what *are* you doing?"

Whitney huffed out her fleeting hopes that the arrival of their dinner would take their conversation in a different direction. "We're just spending time together. Does it have to be more than that?"

"It is more than that. It always was with you two. I knew that the day you brought her home for dinner claiming she was just a friend from school."

In Whitney's defense, she *did* think Andy was just a friend from school. She didn't bother to say that, though. Mom clearly wasn't done speaking, and her own throat felt too tight to even try.

"If you still look at her today the way you did then, you can't pretend you're only spending time together."

"I don't know how not to want her, Mom," Whitney choked out, the cracked tenor of her voice jarring to her own ears. She drew in a calming breath, surveying the room to ensure her outburst hadn't drawn too much attention, then faced her mom again. "Even after she left, even after years of not speaking, she still... I don't know how to stop or turn it off or whatever it is I'm supposed to do."

"Honeybee." Mom reached across the table to squeeze her hand. "Who says you're supposed to stop? Maybe the only thing you have to do is tell the truth. Sometimes people find their way back to each other."

"You and Dad never did." Regret coiled in Whitney's stomach the second the words left her mouth. She wasn't a kid anymore. She understood that not everyone who'd once been together was *meant to be*.

Mom sighed, her expression softening in a way that said the childish longing in Whitney's words hadn't been lost on her. "Your father and I were never meant to be more than your parents. You and Andy…" She shook her head. "I don't think I've ever seen you happier than when you were with her, and I don't know why she left, but don't you think it's time you two talked about it? Things could be different this time."

"Stop." Whitney scrunched her eyes shut, one hand held up as if to physically ward off the words. "Please stop. It's not different, and I'm fine with that, okay? I'm fine, Mom." She released a heavy breath. "Can we please eat our dinner and talk about *anything* else?"

"Of course, honey."

She spooled a generous bite of fettuccini onto her fork, avoiding eye contact in favor of scrutinizing her food. She knew what Mom was trying to do, but she couldn't let herself go there. She couldn't build her hopes up only to have them crushed like last time. She couldn't survive last time again. So she repeated the words like a mantra in her head.

Andy was leaving.
That was okay.
She was okay.

19

Condensation pebbled Andy's glass as she took another sip of champagne, her back nestled to one corner of Jenn's backyard, gaze captivated by everything from the décor to the ten or so people milling about. Down to its bones, it was a simple space—brick walls painted the shade of banana cream, a large date palm and another tree with a much smaller trunk sprouting along the edges of concrete floors. But the fairy lights strung along the descending stairway from the house to artfully wind up the curtained lumber pergola sparkled with grandeur, especially considering the white-cushioned wicker chairs, abundance of champagne, and soft music underlying the buzz of laughter and chatter.

Andy stretched one arm across her midriff, surveying the guests as she wandered closer to the firepit. She was grateful for the invitation, but she still wasn't sure why she was here. What did this 'small gathering,' as Jenn had coined it, have to do with Andy's question about her and Val being together? She didn't know any of these people, though research had equipped her memory to pick out Jenn's ex and their son, one of two teenage boys in a sea of women in their late twenties and thirties.

"Do you have to look so outright uncomfortable?"

She spun as Whitney sidled up to her, grinning against the glass of red halfway to her lips. Andy took a second to look at her, to wonder how she'd missed Whitney's arrival in this space of less than a dozen people. The long-sleeved, black dress she wore dipped toward the curves of her breasts and melded to her waist, perfectly complementing the pair of sandal stilettos on her feet. Sweet traces of jasmine lingered in the air.

Whitney's eyes swept down Andy's body in equal appraisal, leaving her acutely aware of her own gawking. Her black jeans and leather jacket left her feeling more than a little underdressed next to Whitney despite the satin sleeveless top she'd chosen to "dress things up a bit."

A hand wrapped around her forearm, gently withdrawing it from her midriff. "Relax."

"I am. I just... feel a little out of place?" The fact that Whitney's grip had only drifted lower, to a loose hold on Andy's hand, assuaged the feeling the slightest bit. It also came riddled with the temptation for Andy to go a step further, to lean in and brush their lips together, only to remember that, whatever they were doing, public kisses didn't make the cut. Andy was still trying to figure out what did, especially since Whitney's mood had been so difficult to read when she'd shown up after dinner with her mom last night. They'd shared ice cream on the couch and easy kisses that never progressed to sex. Whitney still stayed the night, though, leaving well past midday, after the two of them had shared breakfast and walked Wes together. It wasn't purely platonic, but she got the feeling Whitney wasn't ready to call it anything else.

"Nine months ago, I didn't know any of these people either," said Whitney. "But you're among friends, I promise."

"Yeah. Jenn's friends. *Your* friends."

"Fine." Whitney's red lips quirked in a smile as she squeezed Andy's hand, leaning in to whisper, "Then stick with me, and if you're really, *really* good... I just might take you home tonight."

Goose bumps speckled Andy's skin at the warmth of Whitney's breath against her ear, the teasing lilt to her words. "Okay." Andy stuttered a laugh. "I think we should implement a rule that you can't say anything suggestive to me while we're in public spaces. Especially not with your sister ten feet away."

"Avery?" Whitney jerked back, eyes darkened though amused. "What does Avery have to do with anything?"

Andy refused to give in to the compulsion to glance toward the pergola, where Avery, Jenn's ex, and a tan, silvery-haired white woman shared a sofa and a bottle of Perrier. A cackle of a laugh crackled through otherwise quiet chatter, drawing Andy's attention precisely to the three women, where Avery's studying stare lay in wait. Because, of course, she'd already noticed Andy and Whitney together.

"You're afraid of Avery?"

The incredulity in Whitney's voice drew her back. "Afraid isn't the word I'd choose."

"Oh my God, Avery is incapable of even raising her voice. Wait." The buoyancy in Whitney's expression dissipated with an abruptness that gave Andy whiplash. "Did she say something to you? About us?"

Avery had said a number of things, implied a few more, but nothing Andy felt inclined to report to Whitney. The last thing she needed was to fuel any kind of conflict between Whitney and Avery when they'd only just begun to explore being sisters. It wasn't as if Avery had explicitly asked Andy to stay away from Whitney. It wasn't as if she *could* stay away. Before Andy could fabricate a response that would ease Whitney's concerns, the rhythmic clinking of utensils against glass drew their attention to Jenn and Val standing hand in hand on the landing of the stairs.

"I'm sure you're all wondering why we asked you here at such short notice," said Jenn, garbed in a halter-neck, midnight-blue jumpsuit that made Andy balk, having spent the last week seeing her in nothing but chef's whites and button-down shirts paired with slacks. "The truth is, I've been planning this for months, but your presence here tonight was contingent on one thing." She gazed down at Val, who met the affection in her eyes with a soft smile.

It took that very moment for Andy to piece it together—why the two of them were standing in front of their closest friends, their love for each other on full display among the questions wafting in the crisp March wind.

Val's left hand shot up, glinting with the ring that had been around her neck two days ago. "I said yes!"

Cheers and applause erupted, and Whitney's squeal pierced Andy's eardrums like a dagger. She laughed, pressing an index and middle finger just outside her ear, her other hand clutching more tightly at the spine of her glass as the attendees flocked in Jenn and Val's direction—everyone except Avery, who simply watched from her spot, the smile on her face telling. She was probably the only person who knew beforehand, had probably even helped Jenn and Val arrange this party down to the fairy lights.

Andy stayed by the firepit, an inexplicable joy radiating within her for these people she barely knew but had zero doubts deserved every bit of happiness life had to give. She let herself be entranced by the communal bliss, the shouts of "Congratulations!" and "It's about time!" She was so absorbed by it all that it took her a moment to conceive the shift in her own chest, her prickling eyes and slowed breathing...

The voice in her head whispering, *You could have had it all, too.*

TWENTY MINUTES LATER, Andy found herself seated beneath the pergola, a delectable tray of fried prosciutto tortellini and half a bottle of wine to keep her company. Jenn and Val's announcement seemed to have upped the ante, doubling the excitement of the evening and the vibrant tone of conversations among groups of threes and fours.

It had been a while since Andy had been able to sit and people-watch this way. Nearly every party she'd attended in the last six years were related to her next or current project, addled with so much schmoozing, small talk, and laughing at just the right pitch and moment, that exhaustion would creep into her bones within an hour, making her desperate to leave. An engagement party attended by people she'd known for less than a month should've been equally uncomfortable, but even seated alone, the sound of Whitney's voice across the yard and the incandescent glow of her smile were so beyond soothing, Andy couldn't think of anywhere she'd rather be.

A glimpse of flowy pant legs flashed in her peripheral, and she turned to see Jenn slip away from her own group, dimples permanently on display. Even having followed her around with a camera for days, this was the most social Andy had seen her. It still took her a moment to realize Jenn was headed her way. She hastened her chewing of the tortellino in her mouth, debating how scandalous the half-empty tray might look to someone who hadn't been there to see it already waiting on the outdoor coffee table when she'd sit down.

"May I?" Jenn paused at the foot of the three-cushion loveseat.

Andy stared up at her. Was she... asking for permission to sit in her own backyard?

Jenn's brows crept up.

"Yeah, of course." Andy blinked, shaking her head. She reached for a napkin and quickly swiped it across her mouth. "Sorry. I was going to come congratulate you once everyone else was done."

"Thank you. It's fine." Jenn waved away the implication with a chuckle. "Though seeing you over here alone, it occurs to me we're more alike than I thought."

"Is that a bad thing?" Andy frowned.

"I suppose it isn't."

Her favorite laugh floated across the yard, and her gaze landed on Whitney, still caught in an animated discussion with Val, Avery, and two other women whose names Andy hadn't picked up among the traveling voices. From the tattooed hand the taller Black woman had on the small of Avery's back, Andy guessed it might've been her girlfriend, Kyla. She redirected her gaze to Jenn to find amused eyes already trained on her, though she couldn't decide if it was because Jenn had been staring at her fiancée or because she'd caught Andy's staring too.

"Yesterday, you asked why Valentina," Jenn said. "Why I would break all my self-imposed rules, expose her to the scrutiny of people wondering if our relationship had anything to do with how she got her job, or if I took advantage—"

Andy shook her head, eyes rounding in alarm. "That's not what I meant."

"I know. But it's the reality." Jenn shrugged. "I was concerned about it at first, but for her it didn't matter. She's the bravest person I know, and being with her dares me to be a little braver every day." Jenn breathed a sigh as wistful as the smile tugging at her lips. Her eyes wandered back to where Val stood. "She lights up everything for me, Andy. And I'm forever grateful someone cared enough to tell me I'd be stupid to let her go."

A knot twisted in Andy's belly.

"So this is me telling you to tell Whitney how you feel."

"How do you..." Andy frowned, too startled by Jenn's comment to finish her own thought.

"Besides the fact that you've spent half the night staring at her like she hung the moon?" Jenn laughed. "It's a secret for some reason, but Valentina tells me you're end game."

Andy's chest warmed despite the yearning and regret winding through her. "That's nice, but I don't think Whitney's ready to hear how I feel even if I did manage to find the words. So much has happened between us the last couple of weeks, even the last few days, but there's this, this wall." Andy squeezed her eyes shut. "I can *feel* it. And I don't even blame her. I don't think I would trust me again either after..." A lump caught in her throat. "I don't think I deserve it."

A brief silence stretched between them. Jenn nodded her understanding, leaving Andy to ruminate on her own confession. Would she ever think she deserved Whitney letting her in again?

"I'm going to let you in on another secret." Jenn reached across the sofa to rest a hand on Andy's forearm. "No one knows what she needs from you better than she does. Let her decide whether you're worth it."

Andy let the words sink in. It was simple advice, the kind of logic she would spew at anyone who'd come asking. But it was impossible to escape the undercurrent of fear that accompanied the words, the reason she hadn't admitted she was still in love with Whitney years ago. What if Whitney decided Andy *wasn't* worth it?

"In any case..." Jenn stood, signaling that she'd said all she meant to say. "You shouldn't stay over here alone, no matter how good those tortellini are."

Andy winced at the half-empty tray. "They *are* really good."

"I know. I made them, and I need this tray." Jenn swiped up the silverware. "But I understand perfectly how overwhelming forced socialization can be, so I'll make you an offer to come help me check on the teriyaki meatballs."

"I'll take it." Andy hopped to her feet without delay.

Jenn tilted her head in consideration. "How are you in the kitchen, by the way?"

"Terrible."

"Very well." Jenn pursed her lips. "I'll show you how to carry the tray."

20

The door to Whitney's Victorian slammed with a rattling thud as she pressed Andy against it, the sides of Andy's leather jacket clutched in both fists, nose sliding along her jaw toward her ear. "I've been wanting to do this since the second I saw you tonight."

She wasn't sure if it was knowing Andy would be gone next week or spending hours with all her coupled-up friends while knowing Andy was mere inches away—not truly hers to have or hold—that had her skin on fire with want. It didn't help that Andy had spent half the night watching her, eyes glinting with desire, fascination, with things Whitney was too afraid to see. In the dark of her entryway, Andy's hands hot and low on her hips, the wet slide of her tongue into Whitney's mouth, Whitney didn't have the will to fight what she wanted or words to express it.

A whisper of a laugh skated across her cheek, breathy and stuttered, as Andy cupped her face and pulled away to look at her. "Do I at least get a tour?"

"A tour?"

"You've seen my place more than once. It only seems fair."

"Fair?" Whitney scoffed a humorless laugh. The concept of fair was so lost on her these days. *Nothing* about this was fair. Her gaze swept to Andy's kiss-swollen lips, and she slipped both hands inside her jacket, dragging palms up her sides, over her breasts and peaking nipples.

Andy gasped, catching Whitney by both wrists, her grip just tight enough to leave Whitney throbbing. "Maybe I wasn't clear. You're supposed to be *giving* me a tour, not taking one."

"See..." Whitney dipped her head to press an open-mouthed kiss along the column of Andy's neck, in love with the way her hold grew firmer as she whispered Whitney's name, all throaty and bothered. "Your lips are saying one thing, but your body is saying that thing should probably wait."

Andy swallowed, hard, if the shift beneath Whitney's mouth was anything to go by.

"But since I come from a long family of exceptional multitaskers..." She twisted her wrists free and tugged Andy forward by the collar of her jacket before pushing it off her shoulders. "Living room's on the left. Wes spends most of his time there. He's actually a big fan of the TV. Cartoons, of all things." She tried not to think about how the more traditional aesthetic of her green accent chair and wooden furniture didn't match the cool, modern structure of Andy's apartment back at The Alexander. An unmade throw dangled from the arm of the sofa and no less than three of Wes's innumerable toys lay scattered by the coffee table.

Hands cradled her face, guiding her mouth to Andy's parted lips, to the traces of champagne on her breath. "Where *is* Wes, anyway?"

"My mom's." Whitney panted, fumbling for a grip on Andy's satin top as they stumbled farther into the house. She pulled it over her head in one quick motion and left it in a puddle on the floor, then planted her hands high on Andy's ribs, the skin like warm velvet beneath her touch, straps of Andy's bralette stretched taut over her shoulders, nipples pebbled under the thin fabric.

Andy shuddered. "How many rooms are left?"

"Well, you've literally only seen one," Whitney whispered through a laugh. "So there's the kitchen, guest room, bathroom, the studio, master—"

"That one." Andy bobbed her head, covering Whitney's mouth with her own, only to pull away a second later. "Let's skip to that one. But promise I can see it all after."

"I promise." Whitney took her hand and herded her down a short hallway, past the open bathroom to her closed bedroom door. She opened it and dropped Andy's hand, allowing her a few moments to visually explore the space as she strode over to her bed and took off her heels. She followed Andy's gaze from the framed *Hamilton* poster autographed by Lin Manuel Miranda on one wall, to the pair of running shoes carelessly discarded by the ottoman in front of her chest of drawers, to the disarray of open makeup kits on her vanity.

Andy started toward her. "It feels very... I don't know. *You?*" She chuckled, her darkened eyes still roaming with evident interest. "Everything down to the unmade bed."

Whitney glanced down at the bed in question, fingering the soft fabric of her comforter but never taking her eyes off Andy. "I bet it's driving you crazy."

"It is. But not in the way you think." Andy paused to heel off her boots, then closed the distance until she was standing between Whitney's legs. "When I think of you all tangled up in those sheets, the only thing I want is to be next to you."

The urge to hook her fingers through the loops of Andy's black jeans and trail kisses toward her navel overcame Whitney, and she gave in, eyes trained up to meet the pair staring down at her. Tense muscles met the soft brush of her tongue, and fingers threaded through her hair, tugging ever so slightly. Everything about it—the familiarity of Andy's touch and murmured affirmations—felt so achingly *right*, like they'd had each other this way in fifty different lifetimes and it still wasn't enough. Her pulse raced and sweat prickled along her spine, the heat of her dress more oppressive the longer she kept it on. But there was something in the intensity of Andy's stare, something untainted by the past, that forced Whitney to maintain a deliberate pace despite the heat pooling between her thighs.

She wrestled the jeans down Andy's long legs, revealing simple bikini-cut underwear, but she barely had a second to appreciate the view before Andy dropped to her knees, the force of her stare almost paralyzing. Fingertips teased at the sides of Whitney's dress, clasping the zipper but staying there. "Can I take this off?"

"I think I'll implode if you don't."

The zipper came apart with a swoosh, Andy's gaze burning a trail down the newly exposed skin, lips rounding at the sight as Whitney's dress gave way to a baby-blue lace bra. She lifted her hips, partly out of impatience, but mostly for the look on Andy's face when the dress slipped past her waist to reveal the matching thong. "Fuck." The word came coated with the kind of lost and awestruck that stole the air from Whitney's lungs every single time.

"Come here." She wrapped an arm around Andy's neck, sliding up the bed and pulling Andy down on top of her, moaning at the glide of their tongues and at the hands sliding from her knees, up the insides of her legs, along the crease of her thighs, everywhere except the spot she needed to be touched.

She understood that Andy was probably being considerate, not wanting to go further until she was positive it was what Whitney wanted. The dynamics of their sexual relationship had practically been one-sided since Andy's return. Two nights ago, Whitney had taken her apart in every way imaginable, but the closest Andy had gotten was watching Whitney touch herself. Somehow, she'd convinced herself that way it would hurt less when Andy was gone. But even lies she'd told herself eventually lost their potency. She wanted Andy, wanted all of her so much that the idea of never fully giving herself over to the crook of Andy's fingers, the swirl of her tongue, the way she knew just how hard to fuck Whitney this time and how gently to kiss her the next, was completely unfathomable.

Her throat burned with the mounting force of their kiss, the lack of pause and the thickening air making it harder to breathe but impossible to stop until they both lay loose-limbed and sated. Blunt nails raked across the tender flesh of her ass, and she tossed her head back with a groan, clutching the soft fabric of Andy's bralette. "I need you naked. Now."

Andy yanked it over her head, smiling when Whitney used the sliver of space between them to reach behind her and unhook her own bra, welcoming the brush of Whitney's lips against her shoulders as it fell to the bed. Their mouths collided, their grazing nipples sending a shock to Whitney's clit. A moan reverberated between them. "Andy, I—"

"How do you want me?"

"Under the bed."

"What?" She flinched back, lips slick and skin flushed, so unbearably sexy even with her brows furrowed and eyes wide. "That's a new one."

"No. I need you to look under the bed. There's a—the box. I need you to get the box under the bed."

Realization crept onto her face, the confusion in her eyes shifting to flagrant confidence as she leaned in and whispered, "Well, why didn't you just say so?"

Whitney's breathy chuckle choked off as Andy crawled toward the edge of the bed, balancing on one forearm and reaching the other hand down in search of the box. The position left her ass jutted out at the perfect angle for Whitney to appreciate the arch of her spine and the black bikinis stretched and melded to her curves.

She sat upright with her legs tucked beneath her, and the faint sound of metal on metal drew Whitney's gaze from her body to the harness in one hand and purple dildo in the other. Shifting onto her own knees, Whitney wrapped both arms around Andy from behind, then pressed a kiss to her shoulder blade, her neck. "Only if you want to."

"Trust me..." Andy twisted to face her, smirk hinting at danger and seduction, as if Whitney wasn't already so far gone she'd all but explode the second Andy's fingers so much as grazed her nipples. "I want to."

One hand shoved at her shoulder, and she fell onto her back with a bounce, eyes trained up in waiting. The brush of Andy's mouth against hers left her dazed even with the bruising pace of seconds ago, but Andy didn't miss a beat, shifting lower to trail kisses along the sensitive patch of skin above Whitney's collarbone, between her breasts to her navel. Her eyes flicked up, an index finger hooked beneath the hem of Whitney's thong. "Should I leave this on?"

With Andy's head between her thighs, mouth so close to

her aching sex, it took Whitney a moment to realize she hadn't been clear enough, that Andy's intention was to crawl down the bed and slip Whitney's feet through the straps of the harness. Her fingers circled Andy's wrist, the pulse fluttery and wild beneath her thumb, and she pleaded with her touch, though she knew she'd have to say the words. "Andy, I want *you* to wear it."

For a second, Andy was so still, Whitney was certain she'd have to say the words again. Louder, with more conviction. She would beg if she had to. The slow rise and fall of Andy's chest was the only clue she was even still breathing. Then her lips parted, unsaid words floating in the dense air all around them. "Are you sure?" she finally uttered. "We don't have—what we were doing before is fine. I'm okay with that."

"Andy..." Whitney drew in a deep breath, channeling her resolve through the directness of her stare. "Strap up and *come here*."

With a subtle nod, Andy shuffled toward the edge of the bed and did as she was told, fitting the dildo into the O-ring and attaching it to the harness before sliding the straps over her own legs and adjusting them. Whitney squirmed at the sight, crossing her legs in a failed attempt to ease the mounting tension, especially when Andy reached into the box again and came up with a bottle of lube. Whitney mentally debated telling her that she really didn't think they'd need it—not when the thin fabric of her underwear was doing so little to conceal how wet she was—but before she could say a word, Andy climbed back onto the bed.

Instinct drove Whitney's gaze to the dildo, but Andy tipped her chin up, greeted her with a whispered, "Do you trust me?"

"Completely." She tried not to focus on how it resonated

only half-true in her mind, because she did *trust* Andy. She trusted Andy with her body more than she'd ever trusted anyone, probably more than she ever would trust anyone. Her heart? Well, she didn't think that was what Andy meant either way.

"Then let me do this right."

"I don't..." Whitney shook her head, brows drawn in confusion. "What do you mean?"

"I need to kiss you," said Andy.

"You have been kissing me."

"*Everywhere*. I need to kiss you everywhere. I need to slide my fingers inside you and feel the way your entire body tightens when you're right on the edge of coming. I need you to trust me to fuck you exactly how you taught me."

Whitney's body thrummed with anticipation. If anything, they'd taught each other—shy explorations turned feverish with experience. She opened her mouth to speak, but the brush of fingers coiling around her ankles unleashed a moan instead.

"Is that a yes?"

"Yes. Yes to all of it. Just *please*." She understood why this was a conversation they needed to have—that Andy needed to have—but she'd had enough talking and waiting, of the slow, winding trek that left her right on the edge of desperate. She longed for the fervent whirlwind of *then*, moments when they'd been so familiar with each other's wants and limits. She longed for the Andy who just *knew*.

One hand parted her legs as Andy settled between them and swiped her tongue over Whitney's nipple, the warmth of her mouth and the toy trapped between their bodies inflaming Whitney's desire. Her hips jerked, seeking friction, and she bit down on her bottom lip at the hand sweeping up the inside of her thigh, the faint pressure of knuckles stroking her over her underwear before slipping beneath the wet fabric. "*Oh* my God," she gasped.

"Fuck, you're dripping."

Whitney writhed beneath her, thighs quaking at the nimble fingers making tight circles on her clit, teeth teasing her nipple into a hardened bud. "Andy, I'm going to come if you keep doing tha—" The word choked off with a whimper as the pressure on her clit shifted, fingers painting her vulva with a carnal, needless reminder of just how turned-on she was. Now she was certain Andy was teasing.

"Three?" Andy rasped, eyes expectant, daring as she licked a trail to Whitney's hips.

Whitney's chest heaved. "Three what?"

"The number of times I've made you come in a row before you're so sensitive you're begging me to stop."

Whitney tossed her head back in a breathless laugh before propping up on both elbows, slowly licking her lips at the recollections flipping through her head, the view of Andy *finally* tugging her panties down her hips. The record was four, actually, but Whitney liked letting Andy wonder, even welcomed the idea of her competitive streak rearing its head if she thought Whitney needed reminding. "I forgot how power-trippy you get when I let you top me."

"I just like to be thorough." She pushed Whitney's legs farther apart, licking a long stripe from her center to her clit, moaning against her.

Whitney's back arched, one hand clutching at the comforter beneath her as the other burrowed in the curls of Andy's pixie cut, desperate for anything to ground herself, though she tried not to tug too hard. Andy braced her forearm against Whitney's lower abdomen, pushing one of Whitney's legs up and onto her shoulder before flattening her tongue and lapping at her gently. Something mumbled, incoherent even to Whitney, clawed its way from the back of her throat on the hinges of a ragged exhale. Two fingers slowly slid inside her, rubbing against that one spot that made her toes curl.

In the quiet after midnight, the zoom of cars beyond the walls so faint, so otherworldly, all Whitney could perceive were heavy pants and the explicit sound of Andy's fingers finding the perfect rhythm inside her. She was so close. She was so fucking close, all she needed was—

Andy sucked her clit into her mouth, and she toppled over the edge with a strangled moan, pleading and shuddering as teeth dragged across the sensitive skin of her thigh. "You're so good. You're so fucking good." Her eyes scrunched shut, aftershocks pulsing through her, her body screaming for more even as Andy kissed a trail back to her mouth.

When Andy slipped off to the side, hands palming at her breasts, murmuring bitten-off declarations against the shell of her ear, it took a second for the haze in Whitney's mind to clear, for her to realize Andy was only just getting started. A hand slid between their bodies, tracing the curve of her ass, then nudging her forward. "Lie on your side."

A gasp echoed as the toy rubbed against her swollen sex, coating it in her arousal. "Baby." She reached one arm behind her, searching for purchase—a grip on the back of Andy's neck, in her hair, anything to ground her.

"I've got you." A faint pop, then squirt signaled the lube being opened, and a second later, Andy's hand was between them again, stroking up and down the toy. It wasn't as if Whitney could see with her back to Andy's chest, but the image her mind conjured had her strung so tight she was ripping at the seams. For all Andy's unwavering confidence,

Whitney didn't miss the way her hand shook before steadying when she positioned the tip of the dildo at her entrance and eased inside. "Is that okay?"

She pushed past the lump lodged in her throat, her nod frantic, voice brittle. "Yes. Don't—don't stop."

Despite the urgency in Whitney's tone, Andy sank the toy deeper with excruciating leisure, filling her inch by inch until her ass was flush against Andy's hips and they both went still. She shivered at the openmouthed kiss pressed to her shoulder, her neck, the hinge of her jaw, her eyes rolling back as she adjusted to the sharp bite of pain underlying pleasure. "Baby, talk to me," Andy whispered, hips rocking ever so slightly.

"*Fuck me.*" To Whitney's credit, she had every intention of being more articulate, but the rhythmic thrust made it impossible to do anything but gasp and groan and grab at the fingers brushing past her stomach to circle her clit—the pressure so sharp, so delicious, Whitney knew she was seconds from coming all over again. She'd never given much thought to the way her body worked, the way her first orgasm mounted and crested for what felt like ages, Andy so skilled at keeping her right on the edge before sending her crashing. She never gave much thought to how every orgasm after the first zipped through her body at a blinding pace, rolling into each other like one earthshattering storm. She definitely hadn't given much thought to what came after tonight—how every kiss, every touch and whisper seared Andy's name further into her chest. There was no *after* Andy. Not for her.

"Whit..." Andy ground her hips deeper, harder, seemingly seeking friction, the tremor in her hands matching the one in her voice and the hot puffs of air against Whitney's neck. For the first time since Andy had rolled her into this position and slipped inside her, Whitney wished they were face to face, that she was on top or bent over, anything that would afford her a better angle to give as good as she was getting. "Baby, I think—" Andy's voice cracked with tell-tale signs. "I think I'm going to come."

"I know." Whitney thrust back as Andy rocked into her, twisting enough to bring their mouths together, raking her nails over Andy's ass, clutching and clawing, in a desperate attempt to keep her close. "I know. Me too."

She shuddered, moaning into Whitney's mouth and driving deeper. The edges of Whitney's vision blurred. Her body tensed as she crunched forward and a cry wrenched from the back of her throat, waves of uninhibited pleasure surging through her. Teeth sank into her shoulder, Andy muffling her own cry, the burst of pain intensifying the throbbing at Whitney's center despite the fact that Andy had ceased all movement.

For a moment, they both lay spent before she slipped the toy out of herself and rolled over to cup Andy's jaw. She kissed her slow and soft, tracing patterns along the glistening column of her neck, between her breasts, across her forearm.

When Andy pulled away, glimpses of amber ringing her pupils, the glimmer in her eyes was so reminiscent of how she used to look at Whitney in moments like this, right before the words *I'm so in love with you* rolled off her lips. A visible gulp moved down her throat. "Whitney, I—"

"Don't say it," she whispered across Andy's lips. She couldn't explain why, but the shift in Andy's tone stirred a deep sense of foreboding in her stomach, like whatever Andy was about to say would shatter the moment to pieces. "Can we just be here? I just want to kiss you and feel you and know that you're here for a little bit longer."

Confusion crossed Andy's features—the furrow of her brows, the almost imperceptible downward tug of her lips—but instead of asking what Whitney meant, she simply nodded, touching two fingers to Whitney's bottom lip before leaning in with a whispered, "I'm with you."

21

Andy hadn't slept a wink. Not since Whitney had curled against her and snuggled into her neck, fingertips exploring the dips and curves of Andy's belly until she drifted off to sleep. There was a part of her that was too afraid to move, let alone close her eyes, but the last hour had bolstered her memories of Whitney's face—the smooth plane of her jaw, the purse of her heart-shaped lips, even the steady rhythm of her breathing as she slept.

There were cracks in the wall between them now, but was this *it*? The signal Andy hadn't known she'd been waiting for? She needed some semblance of *okay* that confessing everything brimming within her wouldn't send Whitney running so far Andy would never reach her again. If she even believed a word Andy said.

Was that why Whitney had stopped her earlier? Had she sensed that Andy was on the verge of telling her how impossibly sorry she was?

She wanted to tell Whitney that she'd have to be back and forth between SoMa and LA for post-production and to discuss what her moving back would mean for Vahn

Productions, but she never wanted to leave the way she once had ever again. She wanted to say she loved her, she loved her, *she loved her*. She'd never stopped loving her and never would, even if it took years to regain her trust. She also had to consider the possibility that maybe Whitney wasn't ready to hear any of it and never would be. Maybe tonight, the last few weeks, were merely the dying embers of a flame that had once sparked so fierce and bright that neither of them stood a chance of escape without permanent scars.

Jenn's voice echoed in Andy's head. "Let her decide."

There was comfort in the uncertainty of what they'd been doing the last two weeks, comfort in letting it play out however long Whitney wanted. But Andy didn't want uncertainty. Maybe there was even some part of her that found it unbearable never saying the words out loud.

Warm breath skated across her bare chest as Whitney sleepily dragged the inside of her foot up Andy's calf. An endearing mewl escaped her lips and her eyes fluttered open in the dimness, only a faint, silvery glow beyond the curtains lighting the space. "How are you awake right now?" she murmured.

Andy's chest clenched as she thumbed a lock of thick, black hair out of Whitney's face. "I could tell you the truth, but you probably wouldn't believe me."

Whitney rolled onto her stomach, folding her forearms across Andy's chest, then resting her chin atop her hands, eyes gleaming as if she hadn't been fast asleep thirty seconds ago. "Try me."

"Being here, having you next to me like this, it's better than dreaming. I don't want to miss a second of it."

Whitney's gaze shifted downward, but she didn't pull away. The moment dragged, leaving Andy to wonder whether she'd said too much even barely having said anything at all. When their eyes locked again, Whitney's lips quirked in a sleepy grin, though her words said maybe she'd been aiming for flirtation. "So, what I'm hearing is..." She shifted to brush her lips against Andy's. "I didn't wear you out enough."

"Oh, you wore me out plenty." She leaned into the pressure of Whitney's mouth, fingers tangling into her hair to maintain the languid glide of their lips, but not passionate enough to signal she needed anything more than slow kisses and quiet talks in the moonlit hours. "You were talking in your sleep."

"Was I?" Whitney flinched, eyes wide with a hint of alarm. "What did I say?"

"Nothing I could clearly make out. Just whimpers."

"I don't think I've done that since I was a teenager." She shook her head in disbelief. "Some doctor my mom took me to claimed it could be stress-related."

"I remember." Andy nodded. She remembered everything.

Whitney's eyes fell shut, and she exhaled a soft laugh. "Sometimes, there's a part of this, of you, that feels so different that I forget the last six years was a blip and we've actually known each other forever. At least long enough for you to know embarrassing stuff like how I talk in my sleep."

Andy's mind snagged on *different*. She wanted to ask what about her or them felt changed, whether it was good or just another thing stacked against them, but it didn't feel like the time when that wasn't even the point of Whitney's comment. "Talking in your sleep isn't embarrassing. And it *did* start at a really stressful time for you."

"You mean finding out I'm my dad's secret love child the same week I realized I'm in love with my best friend wasn't supposed to be easy?"

Hope fluttered in Andy's belly, wild and boundless. A breath bottled in her chest.

Whitney scoffed as if the words "I'm in love with my best friend" hadn't catapulted Andy into a state of temporary paralysis through the sole absence of *was*. She had said *I'm*, not *I was*, hadn't she? Or had Andy well and truly gotten to the grasping-at-straws stage—conflating their past with a blurred reality. Her attempt to swallow grated like sandpaper in her throat, and she squeezed her eyes shut, forcing those thoughts down in favor of keeping the conversation on track. "You haven't talked about him much. Your dad."

"Not much to talk about. I mean, he's still the same person you knew back then. Frustratingly charming. Annoyingly lovable. We try to catch up at least once a week, even if it's just a ten-minute call."

"That's good." The distant look in Whitney's stare had Andy rethinking her reply. "That is good, right?"

"Yeah. I think maybe it's been a little weird between us since he and Norah seem to be giving things another shot. He hasn't told me yet, because he never actually wants to talk about anything difficult unless he's backed into it, but I saw them together that night Landon had us all over for dinner to meet his girlfriend." She grimaced, raking a hand through the messy waves of her hair. "It's whatever. My mom moved on a long time ago, so I don't think about it too much. Besides"—her tongue darted between her lips, the frustration that had reared its head seconds ago dissipating with a sigh—"what kind of person would I be if I didn't want my brother and sister to see their parents happy?"

"I don't think you don't want that," Andy said softly. "I think finding out about Avery and Landon the way you did hurt you. I think you knew something was wrong even before you did find out because he was always in your life, but he was never really *there*. Not with the constancy you wanted him to be. And I think all of your parents keeping it a secret as long as they did made it worse." She paused, trying and failing to gauge Whitney's expression. "I don't mean to rehash the details because I know you're the one who actually lived it. But after you spent that week at my house, so mad you swore you'd never talk to him again, it was like when you did go home you figured you had to put all that sadness away just so things wouldn't have to change. Like you needed to give him a reason to stay so you could still have at least a part of him, even if his 'real' family was out there somewhere."

Silence hovered between them, forcing Andy to dissect her own response word for word, everything down to her use of *real*. She'd never thought of Avery and Landon being more real to their father because he'd been married to their mom when Whitney found out they existed. It was just the way Whitney used to refer to them in the aftermath, when she'd been so vulnerable and torn Andy was the only person she'd truly let see her. Was it selfish trying to appeal to that again? Had she sent the completely wrong message?

"Maybe you're right." Whitney rolled her lips inward as she sat up straighter, and Andy sensed the shift in her demeanor even before the words came out. "Or maybe you don't know me as well as you think you do."

Andy sighed. "I didn't mean to overstep. You're right. I don't know anything about it. Not anymore. Just... don't."

"Don't what, Andy?" Whitney slid off the bed, all but stomping across the room to her closet. Andy stood to follow her, but she reemerged seconds later with a T-shirt over her head.

"*Don't* push me away. I don't want to do the push-and-pull thing anymore. Can we just, I don't know, rewind a minute?"

"No. Because life isn't one of your films, Andy. People don't get to rewind. And I didn't *push* you away." Her face hardened, voice dropping when she said, "You left."

"I did leave. I got scared and I ran, and I know I hurt you in ways I could never make up for—"

"Hurt me?" Lines drew in her forehead. "Andy, you *broke* me." Her voice splintered on the word, and Andy reached for her hand only for her to yank it away.

So this was it then. The conversation they'd been avoiding for weeks. The one Andy had been dreading before she'd even set foot back in San Francisco.

"I wanted *everything* with you. *For* you. And you literally woke up one day and decided your dreams no longer included me."

Nausea swirled in Andy's stomach, her lungs constricting tighter by the second. "That's not what happened."

"You left. And *I* had to pick up the pieces of myself. Even the sad, desperate pieces that wanted to chase you to fucking London. So you don't get to come back and pretend you know me better than I know myself."

"I was scared, Whitney!" Her chin trembled, but she hated the conviction in her tone, like those four words were even close to being enough.

"Of what?" Whitney clenched her jaw, the sleep-addled beauty of minutes ago entirely overcome by pain and fury. "The distance you blamed everything on? All that bullshit mumbo jumbo about time differences and not wanting me to wait for you—"

"No." Andy shook her head.

"Then what? Tell me what I did to make you so afraid of me."

"We hadn't even graduated, Whit!"

"What?" Her expression blanked, her gaze clouding, and for a second something shifted in her expression that made Andy wonder if Whitney knew exactly what she meant.

Andy knew she'd have to say it either way. They'd never get past this if she couldn't. "We hadn't even graduated, and you bought a *ring*."

It came out whispered and hesitant, but Whitney withdrew a step, almost as if the force of the words was too much for the space between them. "You—you can't know that." Her voice quaked, disbelief wound into every syllable, tears welling in her gleaming dark eyes. "*How* would you know about that?"

"The first weekend after finals when we—when I was at your apartment. You were in the bathroom, and I was looking for that shirt, the one I got with Kasey at The Cranberries concert. You said it was in the wash, that I should look for the spare, and I—" A breath hitched in her chest, her throat closing in on itself. "I didn't know what the fucking spare was or where to find it and the box was *right there*. Tucked away at the back of your drawer. I didn't—I didn't *mean* to see it, or for things to spiral the way they did. I just... panicked."

"No." Whitney shook her head, back turned as she dragged both hands through her hair, mumbling to Andy or to herself, Andy couldn't be sure. "We were together for weeks after that day. Weeks before—" She rounded on her, bringing them face to face again. "You completely shut down! I drove myself crazy wondering what I did wrong. Why didn't you just talk to me?"

"I tried! I ran a million scenarios in my head, and every single one said any answer but yes would *ruin* us. Because then... then you would think I didn't want you back. Not the way you wanted me. And I did want everything with you, Whitney. I still want everything, but back then, I didn't know if we..." She trailed off. She'd always had trouble putting it into words. Maybe that was why she hadn't told a single person all these years. Not even Kasey. "I had just gotten into LFS, and you had barely recovered from your injury."

"I would have come to London," said Whitney. "I would have gone anywhere with you if you had just asked."

"Don't you think I know that?" Andy shot back. "I still knew what my dreams were, and you weren't sure anymore. You would have lost yourself chasing everything *I* wanted, and I would have let you. Then what? If I didn't wake up hating myself for it one day, you would."

Whitney scoffed, then sucked her bottom lip between her teeth. "Do you list psychology and prognosticating on your resume as job experience, or do you just slot them in under hobbies?"

"That's not fair."

"No. You know what isn't fair, Andy? This 'I dumped you to save you' bit. But we're all grown-up now, so why don't we admit what it was really about?" Her nostrils flared, anger at the forefront all over again. "You are terrified of being anything but extraordinary. You've always been. A has-been college athlete for a wife doesn't do much to help you make your mark on the world, does it? Not the way someone like Livia Lincoln would."

"Whitney—"

"Admit it! I would have held you back. That's what you were really afraid of."

"You really don't get it, do you?" Andy shook her head.

"Every time I've walked into a room and felt like I didn't belong, it has been *your* voice in my head telling me I do. I see your face in strangers on the street no matter what city I'm in, and every time I wrap a project, I fantasize about what it would be like to go home to you. I fall asleep to memories of your laugh and the taste of your lips, and I've woken every morning of the last six years wishing I'd been brave enough to fucking stay." She took a step closer, tears in a freefall down her cheeks, still dressed in nothing but her underwear, more exposed and terrified than she'd ever been, begging to be seen by the only person she'd ever trusted to see her this broken. "If I am anything close to extraordinary, it's because *you* made me believe I could be. Every time you lay in the dark and listened to me ramble about some idea I'd daydreamed in math class. Every time you squeezed my hand and smiled at me like I was even close to deserving you."

A sob escaped Whitney's lips and her body shook, but Andy held her ground, knowing any attempts to comfort her would only be rejected.

"I love you. There isn't a single day since we were fifteen that I haven't loved you, even if I didn't know how to define it then. And I know I don't deserve to say any of this to you. I know we can't go back to the way it was, but if there's a chance you feel even a fraction of what I do, then I can't go on letting you think I could ever belong to anyone but you. That I don't want everything. The ring, the marriage, Wes, a whole soccer team of kids, and budget musicals on ice."

"Andy—"

"I even want this. I want the work of earning your trust back. I want to spend every day of the rest of my life showing you how much—"

"Stop!" Whitney flattened a shaky hand against Andy's

stomach and squeezed her eyes shut. Her face scrunched up as she wrestled with her emotions. "Just... *stop*."

"Whitney—"

"No, Andy. I can't—this isn't—*I can't*. I need you to go."

Their gazes held—Andy's pleading, Whitney's pure resolve—tears on both their faces. So this was what Andy had been afraid of all along. That she'd say it all, lay all her cards and cowardly feelings on the table, and it still wouldn't be enough. The word tattooed on her shoulder didn't make her brave, and a world of sorries couldn't undo the damage she'd done. Yet a part of her clung to scattered memories of them. She hadn't imagined the last few weeks, hadn't imagined the way Whitney looked at her even with roses for someone else clutched in her grip, hadn't imagined the intensity of her kiss and touch, or how sometimes—rare instants when the shield slipped—flickers of vulnerability would emerge only to retreat within seconds. How many flickers had Andy seen just tonight?

I just want to kiss you and feel you and know you're here for a little bit longer. Those were the words Whitney had said mere hours ago.

"Okay." Andy nodded, taking a slow step back before going in search of her clothes. Whitney's eyes trailed her all around the room, the silence haunted by muffled sniffles and stuttered breaths. It took a trek back to the living room to retrieve her shirt and jacket, but when she was completely dressed, standing on the doorstep swathed in cold air beneath the pre-dawn sky, she allowed herself to look at Whitney one last time. "I *am* here, Whit, and I know you may never be ready to take another chance on me, but I'll be waiting if you ever are."

22

The hazy glow of sunrise beaming through gauzy curtains found Whitney on the floor in the entryway, back pressed to her front door. She'd lost track of how long she'd been sitting there, how long it'd been since she'd watched Andy disappear down the sidewalk and into the gloom. Maybe she shouldn't have asked her to leave. It was the middle of the fucking night. Maybe she should've driven her home herself, or at least insisted Andy text once she got there, if only to ensure she was okay.

Whitney scoffed, dropping her head back against the door with a mild thud. Who was she kidding? Nothing was okay.

Andy knew. She'd known all along—about the ring, Whitney's impending proposal, the depth of emotion it signaled. She'd known exactly how Whitney felt, and she'd still left. Somehow, even having convinced herself she was okay with Andy leaving to begin with, with her return being only temporary, it all went back to that. Was Whitney really supposed to believe that in some warped way of thinking Andy had done it to protect her?

A trio of raps echoed on hardwood, so muted by the rush of her thoughts she didn't even startle. Her eyes drifted to the decorative clock mounted on the adjacent wall. *7:37 a.m.* Too early for Mom to be back with Wes. Too early for anyone to be knocking on her door on a Sunday morning, and too late for any other day, considering she'd already be at the gym. She didn't make a habit of going in on Sundays, but suddenly she couldn't think of anywhere she'd rather be than in an empty studio dancing like no one was watching, barefoot and sweaty, primed to leave it all on the floor.

Another series of knocks rang out, punctuated by the chime of the doorbell.

Whitney let her eyes drift shut. If there was a fire somewhere, she'd be no help to anyone. Not like this.

"Whit?"

Her eyes sprang open, recognition and confusion inching her brows together.

"Open up! It's Ave."

"Ave, now isn't—" Her voice cracked, tears welling in her eyes all over again. She drew in a ragged breath, scrounging for every ounce of composure her body would yield. "It's really not a good time."

"Whit, please open the door."

"We have banana bread breakfast cookies from Cakes and Stuff!"

"Val?" Her chest clenched, her thoughts spiraling further by the second.

Avery showing up without so much as a call or text before nine on a Sunday was one thing, but Val too? The morning after her own engagement party? One hand drifted toward Whitney's thigh in search of her phone, only to be met by the touch of her skin and fraying hem of the T-shirt she'd tugged on as a paltry shield against Andy's eyes.

Somehow, she'd still felt so cut open, so exposed, bothering to put it on seemed like wasted effort.

It occurred to her with startling clarity that she wouldn't know if Avery or Val had texted. She hadn't held her phone since she and Andy had left the party together last night. She hadn't even thought of it with everything she needed right within reach.

She pushed herself to her feet but took a moment to rest her forehead against the door and summon even a ghost of her best self, the version she always tried to be for her sister, her friends, even her parents. Her eyes burned, but she dried her cheeks. Her chest still felt seconds from caving in on itself, but she fortified it with a deep inhale before taking the handle of the door in her grip and swinging it open. "Hey," she chirped. "Is everything okay?"

Avery and Val stared back at her. Avery wore a cashmere sweater and lounge pants, hair dangling on either side of concerned eyes, her face bare, though she never left the house without makeup. Dressed in a simple hoodie, shorts, and her favorite Chucks, Val carried a paper bag in one hand.

Whitney's throat tightened. The sad, knowing look in the two pairs of eyes staring back at her was a dead giveaway, but they couldn't know what had happened last night. She tugged at the hem of her shirt, fidgeting, sparing a glance down at herself and wishing she'd had the foresight to take a glimpse in the mirror before she'd opened the door. Was it something on her face? Did she look as disheveled and broken as she felt? Even that wouldn't explain why they were here. "Will someone please tell me what's going on?"

"Come here." Avery stepped forward, arms set to wrap Whitney in a hug she was too frazzled to rebuff. It still took a moment—Avery holding her, stroking her hair—before the dam shattered and she was sobbing, clinging to her sister like this hug, her very presence, was the only thing keeping Whitney from disintegrating on the very spot Andy had said words she'd been waiting years to hear. She'd never been able to say it out loud, never been able to think it without feeling pitiable for *still* wanting someone who had left her behind.

She wasn't sure how long they'd stood there before Avery shifted, guiding her farther into the house. It wasn't until the backs of her knees hit the sofa that she realized they were in the living room. "Sorry." She pulled away, swiping at her own cheeks as she glanced up at the bronze molding along her ceiling. "I'm fine, I swear. It's just... hugs." It was nothing she could explain, but she was almost certain to fall apart whenever someone hugged her while she was trying to keep it together.

"Yeah. I get it." Val squeezed her arm.

Whitney fell back against the sofa, glancing between them. "Did I space on a breakfast date, or did one of you forget to mention you're telepathic?"

Avery and Val shared a look, a silent exchange lost on Whitney until Avery pursed her lips and nodded. Val reached into her pocket and came out with her phone, thumb swiping across the screen before she handed it to Whitney.

Her vision tunneled to the screen reflecting an open Instagram window. A message.

Andy Vahn (4:42 a.m.)

We don't know each other nearly well enough for this to make sense, but can you and Avery bring Whitney breakfast in a couple of hours? Banana bread breakfast cookies. I don't know if she still likes those. Take whatever you feel she'd like.

What I'm asking isn't lost on me. I'll apologize to Jenn. I just...

Please, Val.

I'll owe you one.

Whitney's eyes welled, but she refused to let the tears fall. She shoved the phone back in Val's direction. "I can't believe she asked you to do this. Your engagement party was barely twelve hours ago. You should be in bed with the person you're marrying. And you—" She huffed a breath as she locked eyes with her sister. "Doesn't Ky leave for Bangkok in, like, three days?"

"Yes." Concerned brown eyes—a mirror of her own—stared back at her. "That's three more days I get to spend with her before she leaves, then she'll be back."

"And I have a lifetime to be in bed with Jenn," Val added. "Trust me, you letting me be here is doing us both a favor. She's convinced she gave Andy bad advice or something, and whatever happened is partly her fault."

"What?" Whitney's brows snapped together. "Of course it isn't her fault."

Andy had mentioned having at least one momentous conversation with Jenn outside of work. Whitney even remembered seeing them together last night, secluded beneath the pergola. She'd warmed and chuckled at the two most socially awkward women at the party finding each other. She still felt like she'd missed a whole lot.

"Since when is Andy even going to Jenn for advice?"

"Jenn claims it was mostly unsolicited." Val rolled her eyes. "Clearly, I've turned her into a romantic."

"Why don't you tell us what happened?" Everything from the glimmer in Avery's eyes to the concern overlaying the anger in her tone said she already had an idea of what had happened, but if Whitney had learned anything about her sister in the last nine months, it was that poise and timing were everything to her.

Whitney sighed. "I know you don't think we should've been spending time together to begin with, especially after what you said that night at Lan's about—" Her stomach hardened. "About being friends with someone I'm still in love with."

"Whit..." Avery's hand landed on hers. "This isn't about what I think, and you don't have anything to explain to me. I'm just asking."

"Fine. We've been hanging out. I mean, more than that night we took Sky to the ice skating show."

"I assumed as much," said Avery. "Is 'hanging out' code for having sex?"

"Ave!" Val scolded.

"What? I texted you both for strap-on advice. How are we suddenly being coy?"

"Okay, but it wasn't just sex," Whitney blurted. Her eyes fell shut, and she drew in a breath, voice dropping as she went on. "It was supposed to be. One time. Get it out of our systems and done."

"Whit..."

"I know. It was stupid, I know, but it was fine. *I* was fine. I knew what it was. Even with the memories, and the added emotional chaos of her being incredible with Wes and Sky and apparently all of you, I knew what it was. I was fine, Ave. And then last night she just..." Whitney shrugged, a tear rolling down her cheek. "She decided to change the rules again."

"What do you mean?"

"It was perfect." Her mind flipped through it all. The moment she'd seen Andy at the party, standing by the firepit in a satin top, leather jacket, and impossibly tight jeans, only a glass of champagne to keep her company until Whitney inevitably approached. The two of them stumbling into the entryway well after midnight. The forgotten tour Andy had made her promise to resume later. The raw need and yearning in every kiss, touch, whisper of her name. Waking up in Andy's arms mere hours ago. "It was so incredibly perfect," Whitney murmured. "Then I was talking in my sleep, and she started saying all these things about Dad."

"You were talking about Dad in your sleep?" Avery frowned.

"No. I mean, I don't know what I was saying, but it brought up some old stuff about when I started doing that and about him and your mom getting back together, and why I felt I couldn't stay mad at him because..." She squeezed her eyes shut. "It doesn't even matter. She was right, and it made me so mad that she knows me so well. She *still* knows me so well. And she says she loves me, but that didn't stop her from leaving, even after finding the ring."

"Ring?" Val's jaw dropped. Her eyes darted to Avery's. "Did we know there was a ring?"

"*No one* was supposed to know except my mom, but Andy did, and the way she tells it, that's the reason she left. That, and my injury and some bullshit about me losing myself chasing her dreams instead of mine. But if she loves me the way she says, why didn't she stay? Why not help me understand? Why wait six years to come back and tell me she wants it all? Why would she do that?" The way her voice cracked on the words, the desperation in them, the way her eyes moved between her sister and her friend as if they held all the answers made Whitney feel about fifteen years younger.

Signs of tears welled in Avery's eyes as she offered a helpless headshake. "I don't know, Whit."

"You said the way she tells it," said Val. "How does she tell it?"

Avery shot Val a look. "Is that the question we should really be asking?"

"I know you're mad, but *look* at her."

Whitney didn't completely understand the exchange. It was moments like this that she remembered how new her relationship with both of them still was, even if sometimes it felt like she'd known them forever. Even in the stretching silence, she recognized the resolve when Avery visibly swallowed, then asked, "How *does* Andy tell it?"

Whitney shifted on the sofa to lay her head on Avery's lap. She drew in a breath, unsure where to begin, but the second she opened her mouth, it all rolled off her tongue in one breathless exhale. Everything from her and Andy's dreams as teenagers to Whitney losing hers to injury but wanting to have at least part of it—the part where she got to be with Andy. She would've figured out the rest. *They* would've figured it out, had Andy given them the chance.

When she finally got it all out, neither Avery nor Val said a word. So she waited.

And waited.

And waited...

"Is one of you going to say something?"

The fingers combing through Whitney's hair stilled as Avery sighed, wavering before she said, "There's a part of me that hates her for doing that to you. If I hadn't spent the last week skirting awkward conversations with her, reluctantly catching glimpses of the person you told me about months ago, then I'd be telling you to run in the opposite direction. Maybe it's what I should be telling you anyway.

But I saw the way she looked at you last night, the way she couldn't stop looking at you. If I'm being honest, I knew there was something about her the day you showed up at my apartment in her shirt because wearing it helped you feel a little braver about spending the day with two people you barely knew." Her gaze flicked skyward. "Everything in me has wanted to protect you from this moment since the second you told me she was back, but I knew I couldn't. Not entirely. That night at Lan's, you told me you remembered what it was like to be in love with her, and you didn't feel that anymore. Is that still how you feel? That you're not in love with her?"

Whitney allowed the words to seep in, to lay roots in her mind. She knew the answer. Deep down, she'd known it that night too. But there had still been so much between them then—so much sadness, anger, resentment. There was also Isabelle and the quietly fading hope that it could work out between them. Whitney was so far past that now. "I don't think I ever stopped. I think I've always been a little in love with her even when I was raring to forget she even existed. And I think somewhere, I don't even know when, I gave up on hoping I'd ever feel like this about anyone else."

Sadness lurked on the wings of Avery's smile. "Then it sounds like you have your answer."

"But how do I trust her again?"

"Maybe you don't." Avery shrugged. "Not all at once. Maybe trusting someone is exactly like falling in love. You fall one smile, one kiss, one breath at a time. As quickly or as slowly as feels right for *you*. And if she meant everything she said last night, then she *will* be there when you're ready, Whit."

"Ave's right," said Val, reaching for Whitney's hand. "So take your time. Figure out what you need. More than trusting her, you need to be able to trust yourself. To trust that she's the right person for you."

Was Andy the right person? There were things Whitney knew beyond a doubt, things the aching in her chest reaffirmed without fail. She *was* in love with Andy. Being with her was like listening to raindrops from the warmth of her own bed, the euphoric chill Whitney got from seeing one of her favorite musicals live. It was like forehead kisses and heartfelt hugs and car karaoke with her best friends. Being with Andy was all of Whitney's favorite feelings bound up in a single person. She'd never questioned whether Andy could make her happy. Loving her was easy. It was losing her that was hard.

Maybe Avery and Val were right. If Andy meant what she'd said last night, she would be there once the emotional anarchy wreaking havoc in Whitney's brain had calmed. But it had been years since Andy had left, and the hurt hadn't faded.

Whitney wasn't sure it ever would, and if she couldn't get over her fear of losing Andy again, did they even stand a chance?

23

*A*prils in San Francisco had always been Andy's favorite. Maybe it was the infinitesimal shift to warmer temperatures, though fickle fog rolling in off the bay could always change that. Rainy days fell off one by one. If she listened, looked closely enough, the shift in the air was almost palpable. She'd never been sure if it had anything to do with the influx of eager tourists or because the change in weather left the locals jauntier between the Union Street spring parade and, her personal favorite, the International Film Festival. She hadn't counted on being home for it this year, hadn't counted on being seated on a park bench with nostalgia coiling in her stomach as she ignored her most trusted work colleague in favor of watching dogs and their humans interact.

"So you're really not coming back to LA?"

Andy dropped her gaze to the phone in her hand to find Riva staring back, their eyes squinted, expression dubious, though they'd had this conversation at least three times since Andy had announced her intentions to stay in SoMa.

"I'm coming back, Riv," said Andy. "I was literally in

Porter Ranch last week for the Senator Cortez shoot. I just won't *live* in LA anymore."

"Right. But I still don't understand how you, Andy Vahn, workaholic extraordinaire, plan to run your own company from a city six hours away."

The laugh bubbling in Andy's chest was a rare burst of joy given the last month. Between the Cortez shoot and diving straight into compiling interview transcripts and editing—the endless video calls with Riva and the rest of their team working on sound design, narration, music—the docuseries had kept Andy this side of sane. She never said it enough, she knew that, but she was grateful for Riva, that the transition she'd have to make due to the move would be that much easier with someone she trusted still in LA.

"I plan to do it with your help," she said. "Hopefully, I mean."

Slick, dark brows inched up Riva's forehead. "Did Andy Vahn just ask for help?"

Andy rolled her eyes. "I'm serious, Riv."

"I can tell. This just…" They winced, accentuating faint laugh lines in their deep brown complexion. "I don't know. Feels a little 'retired at twenty-nine.' It's a big step, Andy."

"I know. But this isn't me quitting. Not even close." She couldn't if she'd wanted to. "I just have to do this."

Riva leaned forward, the angle leaving them closer to the camera as realization crept onto their face. "The woman in the yellow dress."

Andy's chest clenched, an image lighting up in her head like a billboard. It was the same picture she'd seen of Whitney, Avery, and Jenn at a wedding last year, the one where Whitney glowed in that honey-colored dress, her skin and smile equally radiant.

"The contact you didn't want to use to get to Coleman. It's her," said Riva.

Andy could've denied it. Two months ago, she would've evaded Riva's comment with an expert redirect to something work-related. They hardly ever veered into *personal* territory, but the words that slipped out when Andy opened her mouth were, "It's always been her."

There were other reasons to stay—her parents, Kasey, the fact that South of Market still felt more like home than anywhere she'd lived in the last six years. This place, with park benches she'd shared with the love of her life and a temperamental terrier, where she drove by 7-Eleven parking lots that still made her heart race, was where she belonged. The last month had been hell. Not knowing what Whitney was thinking, how she felt, what she needed. Andy would stay, anyway. She'd stay and wait and *hope*.

Riva's lips quirked into a smile. "Good for you, Vahn."

"I should be back there in a couple of weeks, but you should come up sometime. We'll grab a drink or something."

"Jesus. First, I catch you park-dwelling in the middle of the afternoon, and now you're inviting me to a non-work-related outing. Who even are you?"

"Shut up." Andy chuckled. "I need your notes on episode three by tomorrow."

"Already in your inbox." Riva grinned, entirely too proud of themselves.

"Perfect. Thanks, Riv."

"Don't mention it." They clicked off the call with a wink, leaving Andy with a fading smile.

She stared out at the stretch of green ahead, her eyes drawn to a couple reclined with a book each, their golden retriever sound asleep between them. She'd consciously devoted an hour a day to sitting here, watching people go by, an audiobook or obscure movie soundtrack streaming over her earphones, barked exchanges acting as background noise. A part of her knew she also came here to feel closer to Whitney. The two times they'd been here together looped in her head. The morning after their first time in Whitney's office at the gym. A week later, after a night of cherished touches and couch time that never progressed to sex, though she hadn't been sure what Whitney had been thinking that night either.

Her head, chest, *everything* ached at the thought of never being that close to Whitney again, but maybe it was supposed to. She'd spent so long trying to block it all out, she clung to the yearning now, cradled it in her chest like a fragile reminder of what it must have felt like for Whitney back then.

The buzz of her phone on her lap jerked her attention to the incoming call on her screen. Unlike Riva's impromptu check-in earlier, this one Andy had been expecting. She swiped her thumb across the screen and Kasey's "Are we still on for dinner at your parents later?" crackled through her earphones by way of greeting.

Andy scoffed. "How are you asking me when you and Mom basically planned this thing, then mentioned it to me after?"

Andy wasn't all that surprised. Kasey running into Mom at the supermarket and leaving with a dinner party on the books was almost reminiscent of their teenage years. Back then, there had been nights when Kasey, having tried Andy's cell without an answer, would call the landline at home and end up in a twenty-minute conversation with Mom.

A huff echoed from Kasey's end of the line. "I'm going to start by saying consent is hot as fuck, but Tía Gracie promised to teach me her curry chicken recipe, so I'm not taking no for an answer, Andy. I need a yes."

"Yes, Kase. We're still on," Andy deadpanned.

"Good. Because I know you, and I can't have you getting any ideas about staying holed up in your office, listening to sad love songs and daydreaming about Whit calling you back. Not tonight."

Andy grimaced. She liked sad love songs as a matter of principle. If her current Cutler-Zucker-Swift playlist happened to speak to her heart's fragility, she could live with that coincidence. She knew Kase never minced words, but still. "I think that one left a bruise."

"Well, that's what you get for waiting six years to show up and tell her how you feel, Casper."

Andy threw up a hand in exasperation. "How are you still not out of ghosting metaphors?"

"They just come to me. I don't ask questions."

Her mind conjured a vivid depiction of the shrug that came with that response, but she latched onto the mention of Whitney. It was instinctive. Compulsive. "How is she?" Andy closed her eyes, rushing out the rest before Kasey could respond. "I know I promised to not put you in the middle. That's not what I'm trying to do. I just need to know she's okay."

Silence. A heavy sigh. Then Kasey said, "She's stronger than you think."

Andy had zero doubts about that. Whitney was the most resilient person she knew, always baring her heart for all the world to see. Temptation lingered on Andy's tongue. More questions. So many questions. Had Whitney talked to Kasey about the night Andy had confessed her feelings? Did she miss Andy too? Had there been any mention of her at all?

But she didn't ask. She knew all she needed to. At least for now.

"I know she is," Andy mumbled. "Meet around seven?"

"That works. I'll uber to your place so we can head over together."

"Sounds good."

"Hey…" Kasey waited until Andy hummed her acknowledgment. "I know we're already pretending you didn't ask, but I'm going to say this anyway. I know you're hurting. You put it all out there, and it hasn't exactly gone how you hoped. But you left her with a lot of feelings to work through, And. She needs to do that her own way. If it's right, she'll come to you when she's ready."

A knot twisted in Andy's belly, her throat taut with tension, eyes stinging. Maybe Kasey couldn't say one way or another when Whitney would be ready to talk or what she'd say if she ever was. Somehow, the words still resonated like they were exactly what Andy needed to hear—concern and validation of her feelings delivered the only way Kasey knew how, with a heavy dose of truth.

"Love you hard, Kase."

"I know, but if you felt inclined to prove it by bringing the good wine tonight, I wouldn't be mad at that."

Andy laughed. "So noted." As she hung up and slid her phone into her pocket, she allowed herself one more sweeping look at the dogs and their owners, those scurrying after a ball and lying on the grass alike. She let herself believe she'd be back here again with Wes swiping his favorite treat from her palm and Whitney smiling at them both, her eyes alight with fondness as much as feigned annoyance.

One month.

It'd been a month since Whitney's smile had made

Andy's pulse stutter and race. She'd count the days until she got to see it again. She'd hope and dream and *stay*.

Dinner with her parents was exactly as promised. Mom hobbled around the kitchen, her feet swollen from a ten-hour shift at the hospital, directing Andy and Kasey to chop this, taste that, complaining without fail that the chicken needed more of some spice or another. Dad hovered between the living room and kitchen, relentless in his jabs at Andy's subpar cooking abilities amid hot takes on the sporting world according to ESPN. Kasey wasn't much of a cook or sports buff herself, but she was more than happy to encourage him.

Andy didn't bother to mention that her growing text thread with Jenn was probably an indicator that her cooking tips would soon be coming from a world-class chef, because well, she was more interested in Jenn's friendship than her celebrity. Besides, as bothersome as her dad and best friend could be, she understood that teasing was their love language. It all felt so overwhelmingly homely and right, like a basic instinct she'd denied herself for far too long. By the time they'd sat in front of the TV with glasses of milk and too-large slices of potato pudding for dessert, she had to excuse herself under the guise of an incoming call.

Outside, she sat on the steps of her parents' well-cared-for Edwardian and zipped up her jacket against the bite in the air. Light, flowing traffic hummed in the distance—rush hour long gone—and with only a pair of unfamiliar neighbors streaming in and out of their own homes, she surrendered to the reason she'd stepped out to begin with. Phone in hand, she swiped her way to the note of unsent messages to Whitney and began typing.

I think Kase missed my parents almost as much as I did. Or maybe being with them is just a filler for Mr. and Mrs. Santiago living out their retirement with all those cruises. She never gets to see them as much anymore, but I guess you already know that. I'm still glad she feels at home here after all this time, though.

I would give anything to have you on that couch with us. I miss you so much I can't even catch my breath sometimes. I miss the calm of your head on my lap and the winding journey of thoughts when you tell me about your day. I miss how you squeeze my arm, laughing until you cry when something's too funny, and the way your eyes soften right before you kiss me.

Her eyes fell shut at the uproar of laughter coming from within the house. Mom and Dad never gave her grief for working too much, even all those years she'd cited being too busy to visit, but Kasey knew better. It was only a matter of time before she came looking for Andy. She narrowed her gaze to the note again.

Dad's agreed to drive less. I think all those hours are destroying his back, anyway. And Mom... well, I'm working on it. I should probably get back in. They want to watch Conditional *for the third time. It's supposedly my best work, but it's never not weird having the people closest to me watch my films with me in the room.*

You never did tell me if you cried. I did. At least once a day during filming. Kind of made me think how lucky we were having parents who never thought having a kid on the street was better than having one that's queer. But if I start ranting about this I'll never shut up. Give Wes a head scratch for me.

I love you.

She slipped the phone back into her pocket, then retreated to the warmth of the place she used to call home.

It wasn't until midnight that she'd slammed her car door shut and entered the parking lot's elevator to her building. Her parents had never exactly been able to say they were proud of her, but she clung to the longer hug Mom had given her with credits rolling up the screen, how Mom had stepped back, eyes shimmering and direct before she squeezed Andy's shoulder and moved to hug Kasey too. Dad's mumbled, "Good work," hadn't been missed either. Maybe the potato pudding was still Andy's favorite part of the night, but those were thirty seconds she'd carry with her forever.

She'd yet to experience how difficult the transition would be, working here instead of LA, but however it worked out, she wanted to factor in more time with them. Biweekly visits or calls. Dinner once a month? More cooking lessons with Mom and Kasey?

As the illuminated numbers on the elevator panel signaled its ascent, she skimmed through her emails, knowing she was too wired to sleep any time soon. Post-production always turned out to be more intensive than filming. The number of messages that needed her attention had already climbed to thirty-three since she'd cleared them earlier today, but she went directly to Riva's, skimming through the notes as she exited the elevator and blindly followed the path to her condo.

"Walking and texting is a delicate art."

Her head snapped up and she stopped in her tracks, eyes confirming what her brain had already discerned. Whitney stood by her door, hair shrouding her face in thick, dark waves Andy would give anything to run her fingers through. She was dressed in running shoes, leggings, and a hoodie, the same London Film School hoodie Andy had given her more than a month ago, having spilled wine on her shirt. The same night Whitney had stayed, that they'd—

Whitney glanced down at herself, following Andy's gaze. "I was actually returning it, but this hallway gets surprisingly cold after the first ten minutes of being here."

The first ten? How long had she been waiting? Why hadn't she called? More than that, what did it mean that she was apparently here to return the hoodie instead of latching on to it the way she'd clung to Andy's The Cranberries T-shirt when they were teenagers?

"It's late, I know."

Not that late. Not for them. Somehow, they always found each other in the midnight hours, even if it was only to lie awake and talk all night.

Whitney took a step forward. "You're not saying anything."

Andy blinked, her heart in a death sprint toward something she'd yet to understand. "Sorry. I'm just... I didn't expect you to be here."

"I would've called but Kase mentioned dinner with your parents, and I didn't want to interrupt."

Was this what Kasey meant earlier when she said Whitney would come to Andy when she was ready? Did she know that would be today?

"Can I come in?" Whitney's brows crept up.

Andy jolted forward, hands fumbling through the pockets of her bomber jacket for her key. She brushed past Whitney, through the haze of petitgrain and jasmine radiating from her skin and hair, and she opened the door in a daze before stepping back to wave Whitney inside.

"Thanks." Whitney spanned the short entryway in slow steps as Andy shut the door behind them. A scoff echoed.

She rounded on Andy, her full, soft lips quirked at one corner. "Are you sure you even live here? There's not even a cushion out of place."

"I like cleaning. Cleaning helps me think."

"Said no one ever."

Andy knew Whitney was teasing, but everything from her casual demeanor and beauty to the fact that she was standing here—in Andy's apartment—a month after Andy's confession was so beyond baffling, her brain couldn't focus on a single thing else. "Are you okay? Can I get you some water, a drink? Do you need anything?"

"I'm good, Andy." Her smile widened before fading as she turned and crossed the living room to the window wall. "I, um..."

Andy dug her boots into the floorboards, willing herself to wait until Whitney found the words she seemed to be searching for. But there were thirty days of unsent messages in Andy's phone clawing their way up her throat, and suddenly she couldn't help feeling like she'd choke on every last one if she didn't open her mouth and say something. "I didn't mean to ambush you."

Whitney cocked her head to one side, her face riddled with patient disbelief when she turned to Andy. With the silhouetted skyscrapers at her back, she glowed like everything Andy longed for—this city, with her family and best friend never more than fifteen minutes out of reach, and the one person who never failed to leave her breathless. "You found me on your doorstep at midnight and you're worried *you* ambushed *me*?"

"No." Andy dared a step, then stopped, fisting both hands in quiet frustration. "I mean, that night. The night we —that I—I didn't mean to put all that on you. I just didn't know how to push it down anymore. I get it if that's not what you needed from me. I'm... Fuck, I'm so, so sorry, Whit."

"I was there, too, Andy. I felt it. I felt it the moment Wes led me to you on the sidewalk on Valentine's Day. I felt it that night in my office, especially in the days after. The slower kisses, how we sat on that very couch"—her eyes darted toward it, then back—"with my head on your shoulder and me wiping ice cream from your lips, pretending it was nothing. Like I have any control over the way my chest rips open whenever you're near. Or how having you near just isn't enough until I can touch you and *feel* that it's true. I was there. And pretending this wasn't fucking inevitable was just—" She raked a hand through her hair, eyes closed as she drew in a breath.

Andy didn't move. She needed to be clear on what Whitney was saying, clear on the inevitable.

Whitney walked toward the sofa and slid onto it, shaking her head. "When you left, there was a whole week I thought I'd never fully function again. And maybe you're right." She shrugged. "Maybe I threw too much of myself into us back then. Maybe we were way too young to know. But you should've trusted us."

"I know." Andy nodded.

"You should've trusted *me*."

"I know."

"You didn't have to stay. A part of me gets why you needed to go, but you could've told me. I would've waited for you."

"I know." Andy surrendered to the urge to close the gap between them, but instead of joining Whitney on the couch, she kneeled between her legs and looked her in the eyes. "Leaving you was the biggest mistake of my life. Saying that doesn't fix it, I know. I'm not saying it to push you. I know you need time. I know you're not ready, that you may never be. But you deserve to hear me say it at least this once. I should've stayed."

Hands cradled Andy's face, thumbs stroking her tear-dampened cheeks and coaxing her eyes shut. The brush of lips against hers made her breath catch.

"You always did need me to spell it out," Whitney whispered. "Even when I was sixteen and terrified, pulling you under my blanket just to work up the nerve to finally quiet my curiosity to know how you taste."

A thumb traced Andy's bottom lip. Her heart hammered, her stomach a swarm of dips and flutters.

"Andy, *you* are my inevitable."

"Whit." Andy fought the urge to close her eyes. That way, she'd convinced herself, she'd know she hadn't come home hours ago, fallen into bed and into her wildest dreams.

Whitney's lips stretched into a smile, though Andy felt more than saw it. "I always knew that. I just never wanted to admit it because having you means opening myself to the possibility of losing you again, and just the thought of it makes everything feel a little less bearable. But I guess that's what loving someone is, living with the fear that they may be gone someday. I get that you were scared. I get that there are times when you will be again, but I need you to be able to trust me with that. Fears and dreams and all."

"I do. I did. I just—" Andy's throat tightened, cutting off the words, but apparently Whitney had more to say.

"I don't know what would've happened if I'd asked you to marry me and you weren't ready. I don't know where we'd be if I'd chased your dreams instead of mine. But I know I don't want to live there anymore, stuck as someone I used to be, waiting for someone you were in one of your darkest moments. I want the person you are now—the woman who stumbled into my gym searching for her *home*, who ran to me in spite of everything else, who always picks up when I call and knows me like no one else." She paused, fingers drifting to the back of Andy's neck and into tapered curls. "I'm not saying it's going to be easy."

Andy shook her head, holding Whitney closer. "I don't want easy. I've never wanted easy. I just want you. I've only *ever* wanted you, Whit, and I promise you'll never have to question that again."

"I love you, in case that wasn't clear."

"I might've picked up on that somewhere before the fears and dreams part of your monologue." Andy braced both hands on the sofa, using the momentum to lean in and press her lips to Whitney's.

Whitney laughed, pulling Andy on top of her as they tumbled backward in a tangle of limbs. "Is that mocking I hear?"

"Never, but I may need you to say the whole thing again. Just to make sure I got it all." She leaned into the kiss, dwelling in the soft glide of Whitney's lips and the warmth of her hands on Andy's hip, in her hair, until they both needed to catch their breath.

"How's post been going? Do you have a final cut of Jenn's episode?"

"Not yet. But we're working on it."

"Good, because I know it might be a little soon for labels, but I feel like my girlfriend perks should include a first look at all your future projects."

Andy's entire being warmed at the very mention of the word *girlfriend*. She didn't know how serious Whitney was. She was ready for all the labels, to jump through every hoop, to have and hold this woman forever, but she knew there was also so much to learn about the person Whitney had become, and Andy didn't want to miss a second of it by going too fast. "Careful. Keep talking like that and you just might be stuck with me."

"I can think of worse things," Whitney whispered.

Andy laughed, brushing the tips of their noses together. "I can't think of anything better than being here with you."

EPILOGUE

Whitney wrapped both hands around her steaming cup of chamomile tea as she snuggled into the window nook, Wes curled up at her feet, snoring softly. A trio of jack-o'-lanterns and two faux skeletons adorned the front porch, and giant spiderwebs spanned the wooden railing of the steps down to the curb. She still wasn't used to seeing Andy's matte black sedan parked behind her own midsize silver SUV on their hill street, or to how they'd managed to strike the perfect balance of *home*, not just in each other, but in their restored twentieth-century neo-Victorian. Andy's attachment to its open, contemporary design and white sofas had only been made more snug by Whitney's choice of colorful throw pillows, blond wood furniture, and potted plants. October rays painted it all in a soft, golden hue streaming through bay windows, and it always, always, smelled of sea salt and sandalwood, even with Halloween party décor strewn all over the living room.

A faint brush of fingers swept across her neck. She startled, eyes darting toward her tea to confirm she hadn't spilled it before she turned to find Andy sliding in behind her. Wes perked up, his tiny, black eyes narrowed at them as if in scolding for disturbing his nap, but Andy reached out to scratch between his ears, mumbling a placating, "Sorry, bud," and he nestled against Whitney's feet without further protest.

"I'm starting to think you creeping around here barefoot has more to do with you being so damn sneaky than your compulsive cleaning habits," said Whitney.

Andy looped her arms around Whitney's waist and squeezed as Whitney relaxed into her arms. "I wasn't trying to be sneaky. I just like knowing this is as easy as walking to the next room now."

"You know there were simpler ways of achieving that than asking me to buy a house with you."

"If you consider the fact that you and Wes were practically living at my place already, then yes, that was simpler," Andy admitted. "But I know a condo twenty floors up isn't where you want to spend the rest of your life, and inviting myself to live with you seemed a little on the presumptuous side."

"Only a little?"

"Just a smidge." She smiled against Whitney's cheek. "Besides, this house... It isn't mine or yours. It's something we did together."

It had taken weeks of discussing whether they could even afford a house in one of the most expensive and competitive real estate markets in the country. If Whitney never heard the term "price-to-rent ratio" again, it would be too soon. Never mind the mortgage approval process and the countless meetings with Andy's real estate agent that Dad had tried to subvert by insisting his agent was better. The actual house hunting had turned out to be an exciting exploration of what both she and Andy had been looking for in a home, though. She'd been so intrigued by the idea of Andy's commitment to lay down roots here that the hard parts had faded into the background.

"It isn't mine or yours," Whitney repeated. "It's ours."

"Exactly."

"I still think it might be a lot bigger than we need."

Andy hummed, pressing a kiss to Whitney's neck, warming her body with an embrace and the promise of something more daring. "I don't think it's so big. All those toys your mom keeps getting Wes practically take up half of one bedroom. And I can think of one way to make use of the other one." Her fingers slipped beneath Whitney's sweater to stroke her abdomen, lips trailing upward toward the lobe of her ear.

Whitney chuckled, her breath coming out stuttered as a knot coiled in her stomach. "Are you trying to make a baby right now?"

Andy laughed, subtle and melodic. "Well, the science isn't on our side, but that doesn't mean we shouldn't get to enjoy the journey."

Whitney's brows snapped together, though the rest of her body went still. She lowered her mug to the wooden bench and shifted to face Andy. "Are you serious?"

"As serious as you want me to be."

"Baby, we just bought a house." Her voice echoed disbelief despite the quiet flutter of hope in her chest.

"We did just buy a house," said Andy.

"And you're still adjusting from working in LA to being here."

"I mean, I feel pretty adjusted."

Whitney held her gaze, searching for any trace of doubt in the hazel eyes gleaming back at her. Her mind flashed back to the night she'd shown up at Andy's apartment and waited for forty-three minutes, how she'd held Andy's tear-streaked face and admitted everything she'd been trying to push down for years, everything she'd been afraid to still want with the only person she'd ever dreamed of sharing them with. She remembered telling Andy that starting over wouldn't be easy. Only it had been, even when Andy had to fly down to LA because some aspects of running her own production company just couldn't be fulfilled remotely. They'd made a weekend of it more often than not. Marriage still hadn't come up as a topic of discussion beyond Andy's periodic teasing that they just might beat Jenn and Val to the aisle, but Whitney was fine with that. She was content to just *be* with Andy, knowing Andy wanted that too. Yet moments like this, when Andy suggested having a baby without a flicker of reluctance in her tone or eye contact, it was overwhelmingly clear that maybe this time she *was* ready for it all. Maybe there was even a part of her that thought Whitney was the one who needed more time. Time to forgive. To forget.

She wove her arms around Andy's neck and straddled her, leaving no space for doubt between them. "You're serious about this."

"Everything, remember?" Andy traced indistinguishable shapes along her waist. "The ring, the marriage, Wes. A whole soccer team of kids and budget musicals on ice. I want all of it, Whit."

Whitney's heart hammered in her chest. "I want it all too."

"I know. Just maybe sometimes I need to test the waters to know at what pace."

She chuckled, leaning in to brush her lips against Andy's. "Still claiming you're not sneaky?"

Andy smiled into the kiss, one hand trailing Whitney's spine beneath her shirt, stirring goose bumps all over her skin as Andy tilted her head to deepen the kiss.

Whitney jerked back, hands on Andy's face, every nerve in her body alive with want, love, and sparks of unquestionable joy. "We *are* kidding about the soccer team, though, right?"

"Oh, totally." Andy nodded, already pulling Whitney back in. "Maybe just enough for doubles tennis." She lurched to her feet, prompting a squeal from Whitney as she tightened her legs around Andy's waist. Wes barked his displeasure before hopping down from the window nook and scurrying off somewhere he likely wouldn't be disturbed. Whitney and Andy exchanged a look, both erupting into laughter at how much of an adorable grump their dog was, but it lasted all of five seconds before Andy started walking them toward the bedroom, her mouth soft on Whitney's, grip tight, intentions clear.

"Babe, we have guests—mmm—" Whitney gave up on mumbling through the kiss, losing herself in the sensation of her own blunt nails dragging through the trimmed curls of Andy's hair. The hint of citrus on Andy's lips and glide of her tongue intensified the throbbing between Whitney's thighs, especially when Andy stumbled into their bedroom and dropped her onto the bed. Andy ripped her own tank top over her head and let it fall to the floor as Whitney propped herself up on both elbows, gawking at the sight of her—the *brave* tattoo etched next to her clavicle, the toned arms, and smooth, soft plane of her stomach leading to lounge shorts gracing legs that went on forever.

Whitney hooked two fingers into the waistband of the shorts and yanked Andy forward until they were kissing and Andy had a fist full of Whitney's hair, the pressure gentle but precise. This was the Andy she longed for all those nights ago, the one who *knew* Whitney's every boundary and need. She shifted her hips forward, seeking friction despite the ticking clock in her head. Andy's lips disappeared with a catch of breath, her teeth dragging down the column of Whitney's neck and sending a shiver through her.

"What time are they supposed to get here again?"

Whitney swallowed, struggling to keep her eyes open. "In an hour. An hour and a half if we're lucky."

Andy pulled Whitney's shirt over her head and dropped it on the bed next to them. "Sounds like plenty of time."

"It would be—" A bitten-off whimper severed Whitney's concentration as fingers tweaked her nipples, her own hands grappling for a grip on Andy's wine-colored bra. "We still need to shower and do costume makeup."

"Right." For a second, Andy's lips and hands went still, and she looked to be reconsidering whether they really did have time. Then her eyes darkened, gleaming with sex and danger as she moved back and off the bed. She smoothed her hands up Whitney's legs, settling at the juncture of hips and thighs before tugging Whitney to the edge of the bed with surprising force.

Whitney gasped, a coil twisting tighter in her belly, making her that much more aware of how acutely turned-on she was. She braced herself for Andy's fingers wrapping around one leg and flipping her onto her stomach. Hands wrestled her capris and underwear down her thighs, and the devilish grin that graced Andy's lips almost suggested she'd read Whitney's mind. Not that they even had time for the teasing drag of Andy's fingers and whispered dirty talk that would ensue in *that* position.

"Quick." Andy nodded, kneeling just in front of the bed and lifting one of Whitney's legs onto her shoulder, the half-discarded capris dangling from the other. "I'll start with my tongue then."

Whitney's answering laugh choked off at the first swipe up to her clit.

ARTIFICIAL STEAM FLOATED from the bubbling cauldron of lemon-lime soda, red dye, and lemonade as Whitney scooped up a refill and poured it into her glass. She swiped a cheesy spider from a snack tray and popped it into her mouth, still in awe over how Landon had gotten food built to mimic something that crawled to taste so damn good. The Halloween nachos Jenn and Val had brought over were still her favorite—not that she'd ever mention that to her brother. Somehow, even having been to almost a dozen dinner parties at either of their homes, it had taken planning her own get-together and having them all offer to bring at least one dish for her to realize the true perks of having three chefs in her inner circle.

Jax sidled up next to her, a ghoulish glass embellished with streaks of fake blood halfway to his mouth. He drained the last sip of amber liquid, then smacked his lips lightly, using his glass to point across the room. "Those two look more friendly every time I see them together."

Whitney followed his gaze to Andy, Avery, and Ky seated on the smaller of the two sofas in the living room, though technically, Avery had claimed Ky's lap in lieu of an empty chair. Andy gestured with her hands, waving one in a circular motion in front of the other as Avery and Ky erupted into a fit of laughter. It was strange, seeing three otherwise composed people so rowdy in conversation, but there were few things that warmed Whitney up like seeing her sister and girlfriend get along. Ave's Elle Woods costume was a bit on the nose, but Andy made an absurdly hot Storm, and the faux bee clinging to Ky's cheek was almost tempting enough to make Whitney break her own "no horror series" rule.

She smiled, taking a sip from her own glass as she redirected her attention to Jax. "They were always going to get along. Ave's just... protective."

Jax scoffed. "That's because she didn't know you two back then."

"What do you mean?"

"You know why I didn't even flinch when you told me you invited Andy to the ice skating show with Sky that night?"

Whitney furrowed her brows, considering the question, though she sensed it may have been rhetorical. Now that she thought about it, Jax was probably the only one who hadn't been wary of Andy's return. Even Kasey had been more concerned, and Jax was the one who'd actually seen Whitney through the aftermath of her and Andy's breakup.

"The only people who could ever keep you and Andy apart are you and Andy," he said. "Plus, I guess there was a part of me that always thought maybe she was the one you were waiting for. That same part always thought she'd come back. It was the only thing that made sense."

Whitney didn't know what it meant that Jax thought she'd been waiting for Andy all this time. If she had, she'd never been conscious of it. In fact, there were times, especially in those first months after, when she'd been desperate to move on. Not once had it occurred to her that they'd be here again—back together, better than before—but maybe it was like Jax had said. Nothing else made sense. Nothing else felt right. Not when two people fit as perfectly as they did.

"And you staring at her all dreamy-eyed, leaving me to have this conversation by myself just proves my point."

A laugh bubbled up in Whitney's chest as she looked up at him. "Sorry." She winced, a realization darting through her mind. "Wait! How was Mads's first trick-or-treat?"

Jax rolled his eyes. "He slept the whole walk around the neighborhood. Sky is happy with her candy haul, though. Thanks for the Mirabel costume. It was a big hit."

"Was there ever a chance it wouldn't be?" Whitney grinned.

"You're such a dork." He tossed out a playful elbow, then reached for an open bottle of whiskey to refill his glass. "I'm going to get back to kicking Kasey's ass in horror movie trivia. You should go over. I think someone's waiting for you."

Whitney looked back at the sofa to find Andy's eyes already trained her way, their group now expanded by a confused-looking Jenn in a Medusa costume and Val, a hilarious parody of a deviled egg, seated on the arm of the chair, listening intently.

As Jax went off in the opposite direction, Whitney held her spot by the snack table, taking it all in for a few more seconds—the brother and sister she'd spent years craving a connection with and the found family she never knew she needed, all together in a home she'd built with the love she thought she'd lost years ago. It was so surreal, but she couldn't wait for countless days like this, days that started with her in Andy's arms and came to a close with laughter, music, and silly costumes. She was so ready for everything they'd always wanted, including filling their empty rooms just like they'd been talking about earlier. Maybe not with a soccer team, but just enough for doubles tennis.

When Andy beckoned her closer with a wave of her hand, Whitney finally surrendered to the urge to go over, feeling inexplicably weightless as she accepted Andy's outstretched hand and fell into her lap.

Arms circled her waist as Andy leaned closer, tone laced with concern when she whispered, "Everything okay?"

"Yeah." Whitney nodded, smiling against Andy's cheek. "Everything is exactly as it should be."

THANK YOU

Thank you for reading *TAKE TWO*!

If you enjoyed Whitney and Andy's second chance at love, please consider leaving a review by clicking the links below!
Amazon
Goodreads

For updates on upcoming projects, sneak peeks and giveaways, subscribe to my newsletter or follow me on Twitter, Instagram or Facebook.

Never miss a sale or a new book release!
FOLLOW ME ON BOOKBUB

Please remember to take breaks and be kind to yourselves.

— STEPH

KEEP READING

If you enjoyed *TAKE TWO*, and you want to know more about Jenn and Val's origin story, keep reading for the first two chapters of *Chef's Kiss*, the first novel in the Gia, San Francisco Romance series.

CHEF'S KISS

PREVIEW

CHAPTER 1

*R*ichmond, San Francisco, was a gorgeous place to die.

Valentina's heart raced, her lungs burning, feet quick against the paved trail as she upped her sprint through Golden Gate Park. The sun beamed across the sparsely cloudy sky, casting a glow over the evergreen shrubs and goldfields, and faint traces of lavender wafted in the air—always lavender, despite the medley of wildflowers scattered about the park. J Balvin echoed from her earphones at a reckless volume, drowning out the burble of the lake and chirp of birds she'd failed at identifying.

A pair of men darted by her in a blur of leopard print shorts. *Seriously?* The taller glanced back, shooting her a wink and a crooked smirk. If Val wasn't on her final mile and seconds from passing out, her competitive streak might've won out. But the Tai Chi group on the north lawn seemed that much more tempting.

Why had she decided to take up running again?

The words "stress relief" ricocheted in her mind in a voice that sounded suspiciously like Zoe's. Zoe, who was undoubtedly still asleep back at the apartment. A lifetime of friendship and Val still hadn't tapped into Zoe's level of Zen. Then again, it had been Val's idea to move an entire time zone and burn through her savings in one of the most expensive cities in the country, with its beautiful weather and varied terrain and art, and culture—*her* culture. And food. God, the food. Maybe moving was completely worth it even if she was verging on broke, and her dream was dead. She could almost hear her father's voice now, accent twice as heavy as the lilt in his tone. "You're a great chef, cariño, but your true calling is drama." Her lips curled up at the thought as she slowed her pace beneath the shade of a large oak tree and doubled over to grip her knees, catching her breath.

The beat of her music cut off, replaced by the insistent chime and buzzing of her phone. She cast a glance where it had been strapped to her left bicep, the screen lit up with an unidentified number. With as many job applications as she and Zoe had filled out lately, she did not have the luxury of letting her phone ring unanswered. Even if she would pick up sounding like a pack a day smoker. Then again, she couldn't remember ever getting a job offer on the weekend. "Hello?"

"Valentina Rosas de Leon?" The woman's tone carried the buoyancy of someone who spoke to people for a living, or at the very least, enjoyed it.

Val could relate—sort of—but the use of her full name meant one of two things. Offer or rejection. She forced down a gulp, trying to keep her tone even. "This is Valentina."

"Hi. I'm Avery, calling from Gia, San Francisco."

The pace of Val's heart picked up.

"Congratulations! You are this year's recipient of our

coveted staging post hosted by our very own Jenn Coleman."

Val blinked, her brows drawing closer, chest tightening. She mulled over the words in her mind, actually trying to pick out traces of Zoe's voice in the woman's tone. The staging spot for Gia had been announced. Three weeks ago. If ranting about it as recently as last night was any indication, Val had not made peace with losing something she'd dreamed of all through culinary school. But she wasn't delusional. And this was a prank too far. Even for Zoe. "Zo, if this is you—"

"This is Avery," the woman cut in gently, an audible smile in her voice.

Val paused, mumbling, "Avery," as if saying the name herself would somehow erase her confusion.

"Yes. From Gia. San Fran-cisco." She separated the syllables the way one did for a small child, and Val crossed her arms over her chest.

If this person was actually calling from Gia, she had very nearly ruined any prospect of making a positive first impression. But Avery was still on the phone, reiterating how Val had been picked for the staging position, and this made about as much sense as one ply toilet paper. She slid a hand across her sweat-dampened forehead, into her hair and down her ponytail. "I'm sorry. How is this happening?"

"What do you mean?"

"I mean, didn't the spot already go to that guy from Auguste Escoffier?" Tall, blonde, skipped too many leg days, looked like he could barely tell when oil was hot. Okay. Definitely not over it.

"Right," Avery chirped. "Unfortunately, he's no longer able to participate. Unforeseen circumstances and all that. But you, Valentina, come highly recommended by all your instructors at the Institute, and we would be so happy to have you if you're still open to joining us."

"Uh—Um. Yes. Of course." Was that even a real question?

Avery chuckled. "We understand this is unexpected and your plans for the summer may have changed. Would you be able to give us your answer in a day or two?"

How could she gracefully tell this woman that working at Gia was the plan of her life? "Yes." She shook her head. "I mean, thank you. I...don't need to think it over."

"Okay. I'm seeing here that you're in New York, but just so we're clear, you do know the summer staging role is for San Francisco, not Manhattan?"

"Yes. That won't be a problem. I actually moved recently."

"To San Francisco?" The question resounded with a skepticism that made Val balk.

"Yes?" Her answer was more than a little bashful.

"Wow. You are impressively prepared for this call."

Val could think of a few other ways to phrase moving to another state for a job she hadn't been offered, but there was nothing tying her to New York anymore. Besides, after a perfectly acceptable period of sulking, she'd convinced herself it was still possible. Okay, her parents and Zoe had convinced her. And sure, she'd have to do it the hard way—by waiting for an opening that met her qualifications, hoping her application caught their attention, then somehow impressing Jenn Coleman enough to be offered a spot in her kitchen. But here she was, running through a gorgeous park in San Francisco on the hinges of an audacious if ambitious plan, with Avery from Gia offering her the equivalent of an internship. Her favor with the universe was fickle as fuck, but days like this definitely made up for it.

"Well, we were slated to begin on the sixth, and while we are prepared to allow you an extra week, something tells me you're ready for that, too."

A laugh bubbled up in Val's chest, her breathing finally back to some semblance of normal. "The 6th works just fine."

"Be here at 10 a.m. I'll get you settled with some paperwork and give you a tour."

"Sounds perfect. Thank you, Avery."

"Looking forward to meeting you, Valentina."

The call ended with a beep and her thumb moved to cut off the booming resumption of "Loco Contigo" over her earphones. Her lips stretched in a smile as she replayed the conversation in her mind, wondering, *did that really just happen*? Across the lawn, the Tai Chi instructor had begun an awkward combination of bent knees and slow flailing arms that left him looking constipated, and Val's smile turned to a full-on laugh. When at least one participant in the front row—an older woman with striking silvery hair—shot her a disapproving glare, she turned toward the burbling lake and readied herself for a run back home. Zoe was never going to believe this.

Val jogged up to the door of their building and keyed in the entrance code. It still amazed her that they'd managed to land an apartment in a recently constructed building that had all the new wave amenities of Virtual Doorman and Google Fiber Webpass, but no parking for her charmingly aged Prius. It made for its fair share of wrangling for nearby spots on the street, and each night, a routine glance out the window of their second-floor apartment before she could sleep, but what was the alternative? Trading the first meaningful thing she'd actually been able to buy herself for a bicycle she'd definitely wind up pushing up more hills than she cared to count?

Not. Fun.

Inside, she crossed the empty lobby, taking the stairs up to their apartment. Her body buzzed with excitement, and for the first time in the week since she'd started running again, she didn't feel on the verge of passing out at the door. As she unclasped her necklace to get to the key she wore as a pendant, she tried to remember if the lump beneath the blanket on Zoe's bed had looked big enough for two people to have been underneath when she'd left earlier this morning. Perks of sharing a place that had been advertised as a two bedroom, but actually turned out to be one with a second bed off to the far end of the living room. If Val had anticipated getting an eye full of some guy's remarkably manscaped junk a week into moving in, she would've thrown the deciding round of Rock, Paper, Scissors that had landed her the actual bedroom. It was her fault, really. She knew Zoe. Loved Zoe.

Zoe loved sex.

Sex with strangers? Even better.

Val pushed open the door with measured caution, one hand clasped tightly over her eyes. "I have news I'd prefer to share with everyone's clothes on."

Zoe's soft, infectious laugh filled the room. "Don't we have a standing promise to at least text if we have someone over?"

"Like you've never forgotten that promise." Val dropped her hand, grateful to find Zoe alone in a tank top and shorts as she straightened the corners of her comforter. She stood to her full height—a dignified five feet three with curves for days—and swept ruffled blonde curls out of her face.

"Okay, Val. Be a snarky bitch." She rolled her eyes—greyish blue orbs that always shone a little too brightly against her pale ivory skin. "So, I forgot once. Twice."

Val shot her a look.

"Maybe three times, but you're the one who brought home a screamer last week."

One of Val's brows inched up and she cocked her head to the right. "Fair." Of course, she had no way of knowing the woman would turn out to be so... expressive, but she did feel bad Zoe hadn't been able to sleep half the night. Especially since she'd had her first shift as a junior pastry chef at Cakes and Stuff the next day. A grin spread across Val's face at the memory of her call earlier, and she bent to start undoing her laces.

"Tell me you're not having flashbacks right now."

"What? No." She laughed, crossing their modest open floor plan to Zoe's "bedroom". "I got a staging offer."

"Really?" Zoe's eyes widened. "Where?"

"Gia."

Lines drew in her forehead. "How?"

"I don't even know, Zo." Val fell into the loveseat with no grace and too much drama, her smile never leaving her face. Could a person feel high on good news? Her memory's comparison to the few times she'd had pot brownies said yes. Absolutely. "The woman who called said the guy from Auguste had to drop out. I actually thought it was you for a second."

Zoe tsked, frowning. "I know my prank skills at the institute were A1, but I also know how badly you wanted that spot. I would never."

"I know." Val nodded. "I guess it just seemed so unbelievable." Somewhere, deep in her subconscious, there was a part of her that was disappointed to not have been the first pick—to have been offered the spot only because someone else could no longer take advantage—but she couldn't bring herself to dwell on it. It's not like she'd pass on the opportunity out of pride. She was a lot of things. Stupid wasn't one of them.

She gave Zoe a quick rundown of the details, knowing she'd have to go over them again when she called her parents. The look on their faces would be worth it though. Maybe they'd returned to Mexico having never quite attained the American dream, but she knew how much it meant to them to see her succeed. Even if it had taken an MBA she'd barely used and leaving a job with a comfortable salary to start all over at culinary school, then become essentially an intern at twenty-eight years old.

Zoe chuckled, shaking her head as she plopped down next to Val on the sofa. "Leave it to you to land exactly the job you wanted. I swear, I don't know if it's magic or sheer willpower."

"Probably both. Besides, it's not *exactly* the job I want."

"Right. Because your real plan is to walk into Gia, learn everything you can from Jenn Coleman and mutiny your way to head chef."

Val tossed her head back in a laugh. "I can't believe I'm two days away from standing in a kitchen with a living, breathing legend."

"A *gorgeous* living, breathing legend," Zoe enhanced.

Val shrugged, her gaze fixed on the lines of the ceiling. "Minor detail."

"Minor detail?"

"Mhm."

"I don't know, V." Amusement laced Zoe's exhale. "You

may swing both ways, but women like her are definitely your kryptonite."

Val sat upright and narrowed her eyes at Zoe's baby blues. "You have zero evidence to back that up."

Zoe's brows rose. "Our Intro to Gastronomy instructor?"

"Healthy admiration."

"You were ten minutes early everyday all semester."

"*And* an enthusiastic interest in my education."

"Sure."

"Even if you were right," Val acquiesced. Barely. "She was my instructor. I wouldn't have actually done anything about it. You know how badly I wanted Gia. Trust me." She stood to head to the bathroom for a shower. "I am not jeopardizing my chances of actually working there someday just because Jenn Coleman happens to have a nice face. Besides…" She glanced over her shoulder, actually thinking back to the screamer this time. Stevie, was it? "This city is full of beautiful people. I'm sure I'll do just fine."

CHAPTER 2

*G*ia, San Francisco, sat on the corner of Harrison Street, marked by a polished hanging wooden sign with the name in glorious swooping font. In the beaming glow of midmorning, it stood out like a beacon of hope—an aspiration come to fruition, built on blood, sweat, tears, and Jenn Coleman's genius take on Italian meets Mexican cuisine.

Val tightened her grip on the steering wheel of her third-hand Prius, angling her head to peer out the window at the building. Not that she had time for it. In fact, the digital clock on her dashboard screamed that she *really* didn't have time for it, but there was something enthralling if not intimidating about seeing the building up close; it's taupe horizontal siding and casement windows were the picture of simplistic. Maybe it was physically being there—this wasn't a rabbit hole Google search brought on by another fit of daydreaming. This was her opportunity to prove that finishing top of her class at the Culinary Institute of America was not a fluke, to charm these people with her talent and grace—okay, probably not grace per se, she was kind of clumsy sometimes—

Shit. Ten minutes before your first shift is not the time to be working through your imposter syndrome, Val.

A scarier thought entered her mind and she glanced down at her white button down. Had she put on deodorant? She tilted her head and chanced a sniff, almost immediately met by a subtle whiff of shea. Of course, she had.

Her phone buzzed in the holder fixed to her dashboard and the screen lit up with a text from her mom. Then another.

Mami (9:53 a.m.)
Buena suerte, mi vida.
Your father is planning a celebration for your first day.
Any reason to throw a party.

Val's grin exploded to a hearty laugh at the eye roll tacked onto the end of the message. When had her mom gotten so versed in emojis? Still, the presence of her, through a simple series of text, filled Val like the calmest of deep breaths, reminding her that belief in herself stemmed from an infallible support system, even with thousands of miles between them now. She gave herself a steadying look in the rearview mirror and made a mental note to reply to her mother later, when she had more time for the string of questions that would certainly ensue.

She grabbed her bag and exited her car onto the inclined sidewalk—not the steepest she'd encountered in the city so far—and crossed the few feet to Gia's main entrance. The scent of cheese and garlic hit the second she opened the door, and her eyes roamed the modest entryway. Ashwood floors, exposed beams and hanging lights. A simple layout of polished tables and chairs that read as modern rustic through daylight, but at night could easily pass as more elegant. Romantic, even. Although, the image her mind had recalled of the dim lighting and candle-lined wall ledges probably had everything to do with that. Unlike the well-stocked bar, the bread rack stood bare, and she found herself wondering if bakers were kneading away in the dough room right that second.

"Valentina?"

Her head snapped up at the sound of her name, the tap of heels more apparent at the sight of the woman approaching. She led with a smile that graced every inch of her delicate Asian features, dark hair caught in a ponytail that swung in her wake. "Avery?"

"Yes. Right on time." Her perfectly arched brows shifted in a way Val took to be approval.

"I'm just happy to be here."

"We're happy to have you." She gestured toward a four top then moved to slide one of the chairs back. "Sit, please."

Val took a settling gulp, sitting in the opposite chair. A sit down in the dining room two minutes after walking in wasn't what she'd been expecting. Nerves crept through her like tendrils on a vine. Interviews were a necessary evil. But were they? Wasn't the point of a stage that she wouldn't have to go through the nightmare of a personality test that usually went with a resume?

"Relax." Avery chuckled. "This isn't an interview. The stage is already yours. You're still required to do all your best work in the kitchen."

Val breathed a hopefully casual laugh. "HR and a mind reader."

"No. My brother just happens to be a chef, too. Aren't you all a bit anti-interview by default?"

"I feel like that's a trick question and I need to find a more diplomatic answer than yes."

Avery raised both hands. "No tricks here, I promise. But —" She glanced down at the gold classification folder in front of her and skipped over page one of, well, a lot. "There are a few things we need to go over before getting you into your whites. As you probably know, our staging process is more intricate and longer than most in the States, rounding out at four to six weeks. By the fourth, you'll know where you stand, if there's a chance of joining us on a more permanent basis, or trying elsewhere. Either way, a brief stint at a Michelin starred restaurant is usually enough to at least get our former stages in the door almost anywhere."

Didn't Val know it. But she didn't want just any starred restaurant. She wanted this one. She tempered the urge to blurt out as much, reaching for the small notepad and pen in her bag, listening intently as Avery went over salary, which, legal or not, didn't always come with a stage. Not that she minded either way. She'd budgeted this move down to the penny, and she had a six-sheet Excel doc to show for it. Pie charts included. Besides, she was confident that with enough drive and charisma—neither of which she'd ever been lacking—she could land a twelve-hour stage anywhere. Six weeks of hard work—zero delusions about that—for a chance at her dream seemed like a no brainer.

When Avery stood, announcing it was time for a tour, Val grabbed her notepad and followed with restrained zeal. At least, she hoped she'd managed a little restraint. Coming off as the eager, young intern was not the game plan. More of a seasoned newbie, one who'd seen enough of the world to know what she was about now. And, well, she'd seen New York, and Mexico City, which was close enough.

"I *will* let one of the kitchen staff take you through the actual tour of the kitchen since they are so much better at knowing where everything is, but in addition to the main dining room, we do have two private dining areas and a dough room. Guest bathrooms are on the first floor—we'll get to those in a bit—and the staff restroom is just off the break room in the back. There are two offices. One I share with Mel, our head chef, and Jenn's. Those are last on the trip. Questions?"

"How much time does she spend in there?" Val bobbed her head toward the kitchen. "Ms. Coleman, I mean."

Avery laughed, starting up a brief but winding flight of stairs, the spikes of her point toe pumps taunting in a way that made Val appreciate the pair of Chelsea boots on her own feet. "Code for how much opportunity will you have to learn from her?" Avery maintained her pace up the stairs without a glance back. "The answer to your question is a lot. We can't get her out of the kitchen, really. And don't call her Ms. Coleman. She hates it."

"Gossiping about me to our newest, Ave?"

Something tightened in Val's chest—exhilaration and panic bursting at its grip—and she paused a few steps beneath where Avery had gotten to the landing. Was that who she thought it was? Of course, it was. She could pick out the husk in Jenn Coleman's voice in a fifty-person choir. All those interviews. The one Iron Chef appearance Val had watched a questionable number of times. It was inspirational, engrossing. It was...

Jenn. Coleman.

She stepped into view, her hair swept up in a loose bun, skin soft and brown in the glow of morning light all around them, and Val was grateful she'd had the good sense to not utter Jenn's name out loud like a starstruck fan. *Jenn.* Something about it bounced around Val's mind with a distinct newness, which was weird because Val had probably mentioned her by name a few too many times in the last year alone. Had freckles always dusted her nose and cheeks like that?

"Is it even gossip if it's true?" Avery's retort punched a bit of sober into Val.

"I suppose not." Jenn leaned into the wrought iron of the small upstairs balcony, dazzling hazel eyes fixed on Val. "Welcome, Valentina."

Val's stomach flipped. Jenn Coleman knew her name, and she was officially what Zoe would lovingly term a basic bitch. "Hi, Miss—I mean, Jenn." She managed a smile. Barely. "I can't thank you enough for offering me this opportunity."

The closed lip smile Jenn returned seemed forced, awkward at best, though it gave away faint signs of a pair of dimples in her cheeks. She started toward the landing of the stairs, and Val resumed her ascent, bracing herself for a terse handshake and minimal eye contact. This didn't seem like part of the plan—running into their boss midtour. She anticipated quick and painless. She anticipated Jenn disappearing after, finishing her tour with Avery then changing into her whites and getting set up in the kitchen. Twelve hours on her feet would be hard, but she'd anticipated that too, even splurged on a pair of dreadful Birkenstock Londons. She did *not* anticipate tripping on the final step, or the embarrassing squeal that had wrenched its way from the back of her throat.

The pair of hands on her—one on her arm, the other firm on her waist—registered before the fact that she'd closed her eyes. She opened them to a delicate three chain necklace nestled against warm brown skin, gold circular pendant between the open top buttons of a simple black button down. *Shit*. Her gaze snapped up to Jenn's—a kaleidoscope of forests and fire staring back at her—and every rationale said her chest would give under the violent race of her heart. But she *had* almost crashed to the floor in front of her boss on day one. Would the fall have killed her? Unlikely. The embarrassment? Jury's still out.

"Oh my gosh. Are you okay?"

Val shrunk back at the alarm in Avery's voice. "Jesus. I'm so sorry. I'm clumsy on my feet, but great with my hands, I swear."

Jenn's brows crept up and her eyes widened ever so slightly.

"I mean—" Val cleared her throat. This was what she'd brought to the table—terrible coordination and a ruthless case of foot in mouth. *Nice, Valentina.*

"We understand." Jenn straightened, posture nearly as rigid as the lines of her lips. Clearly, Val was not making a good impression. And yet, she couldn't help thinking from her vantage point—close enough for the scent of shea and chamomile to dominate the permanence of spices and cheese in the air—pictures, videos... They really didn't do Jenn justice. She took a step back then moved to walk around where Val now stood safely on the landing. "I'll let you get back to your tour, Ave. Valentina."

Val didn't know what to make of the way Jenn had said her name. All politely dismissive. She willed her head not to turn when Jenn's shoulder brushed hers, to follow with her eyes as Jenn disappeared down the stairs.

Avery's eyes lit up with mischief and a grin spread on her face. "Way to make an impression."

Maybe it was the teasing quality of her tone, or her earlier assertion that nothing leading up to Val's duties in the kitchen had any bearing on her staging at Gia, but she felt comfortable enough to shut her eyes and breathe a laugh. Even having just experienced the third most embarrassing moment in her life. "She hates me."

"No." Avery chuckled. "She can come off as being a little stoic, but Jenn doesn't hate anyone. Once you get in the kitchen and get to know her a little better, you'll see."

Suddenly, the concept of facing Jenn in the kitchen seemed more daunting than anything. How would Val erase the ineptitude of what had just happened? Had Jenn noticed that Val, however briefly and completely unconsciously, had stared at her chest? Did she now think Val was some kind of sleaze? *Ugh*. And the hands. Why the fuck would she say the thing about the hands?

"Come on," Avery beckoned. "I'll take you through private dining and I can't give you names, but I can tell you stories about worse first encounters with our other stages. Starting with the guy who mumbled 'I love you,' on his first handshake with Jenn then proceeded to fake a fainting spell."

Val's jaw dropped, disbelief and amusement all twisted into her expression. The tension in her body began to lift. The last five minutes were still stuck on loop in her head, but she appreciated what Avery was trying to do. When the time came, she'd just have to leave it all in the kitchen—let her skill and the talent she'd spent the last four years honing speak for themselves—and hope that it was enough.

Want to keep reading Chef's Kiss?

ALSO BY STEPHANIE SHEA

Whispering Oaks: a wlw romantic suspense

Liquid Courage

Collide: a Flippin' Fantastic romance

Avalanche: a queer romance novelette

Apt 103: a queer romance short story

The Gia, San Francisco Romance Series:

Chef's Kiss

Missed Connection

Take Two

ABOUT THE AUTHOR

Stephanie Shea is a self-proclaimed introvert, who spent her days in corporate daydreaming of becoming a full-time novelist.

Her favorite things include binging TV shows, creating worlds where no character is too queer, broken or sensitive, and snacks. Lots of snacks.

Someday, she hopes to curb her road rage and get past her anxiety over social media and author bios.

stephaniesheawrites.com

Printed in Great Britain
by Amazon